Murder
at the
Bailey

Murder at the Bailey

HENRY MILNER

\B^b\
Biteback Publishing

First published in Great Britain in 2021 by
Biteback Publishing Ltd, London
Copyright © Henry Milner, 2021

ISBN 978-1-78590-704-3

10 9 8 7 6 5 4 3 2 1

A CIP catalogue record for this book is available from the British Library.

Set in Adobe Caslon Pro

Printed and bound in Great Britain by
CPI Group (UK) Ltd, Croydon CR0 4YY

To Magalys
Valentines can't buy her

'No friend ever served me, and no enemy ever wronged me,
whom I have not repaid in full.'

LUCIUS CORNELIUS SULLA
(ROMAN GENERAL AND DICTATOR, 138–78 BC)

'I know exactly where to draw the line
– the trouble is I don't draw it often enough.'

BIG JAKE DAVENPORT
(LONDON UNDERWORLD'S *NUMERO UNO*, 1951–)

Chapter 1

A Timely Passing

_____

No one paid him the slightest heed. Why would they? Just another shortish, podgy, middle-aged barrister in wig and gown, holding his brief in one hand and a half-smoked cigarette in the other, looking like he'd popped out of the Old Bailey for a quiet smoke in the morning break, and glancing from time to time towards the main door of the building, as if he was waiting for someone.

He was.

*   *   *

'Put up Robert Maynard,' called out the clerk in Court 7 to the dock officer.

Judge Buchanan QC, sitting high up on his throne, grimaced at the expression 'put up'. _Put up, indeed._ He wanted to _put him down_ – and for a long time. The judge stared across the court at the man entering the dock some 30ft away. He was almost as broad as he was tall, with an enormous, shaved head and a thick neck. Striped, flashy brown suit and a bright yellow tie. A pair of mean eyes set deep into a tight face with loose layers of fat that hung downwards from his chin. *You wouldn't want him moving in as your next-door neighbour*, thought the judge.

Prosecuting counsel stood up. 'My Lord, as you are aware, this is the third hearing in this case, and I'm sorry to report that we have not progressed. The unhappy situation remains that our chief witness, Mr William Churchman, refuses to testify. He has been brought to court today by your order, and the senior officer has spoken to him yet again, but he stands firm. He is adamant and will not change his mind.'

'Has it been made clear to him that he will be in contempt of court if he persists with this refusal?'

'Repeatedly, my Lord.'

'And the potential consequences, including prison?'

'Yes, my Lord.'

'Has it been explained to him that the court can offer all sorts of protection for witnesses? He could give evidence from behind a screen, and police protection can be put in place afterwards – all quite common nowadays, unfortunately.'

'In some detail, my Lord.'

'And what did he have to say about that?'

'Quite a lot, my Lord. He told the senior officer, and I quote – "I'd feel safer in a Siberian labour camp."'

The judge grimaced for a second time. 'Well, that certainly has the ring of finality about it. I think I'll have him in court after we *dispose* of Mr Maynard. I may yet grant his wish of incarceration, although I'm afraid it will have to be on British shores. Is there evidence of any threats?'

Prosecution counsel carefully considered his response. 'There's

2

the opinions of the senior officer and the rest of his team, for what they're worth, but nothing that we can use in a court of law. In all the circumstances, and with the greatest of reluctance, the Crown is left with no option but to offer no evidence and ask the court to enter verdicts of not guilty on the two counts of blackmail and threats to kill. Put simply, without Mr Churchman's live evidence, we have no case.'

'Quite right too. Outrageous allegations,' mumbled Robert Maynard from the dock, whilst winking at his peroxide-blonde wife and his son in the public gallery. 'Not a word of truth in them.'

'A good deal more than one word, I would venture to suggest, Mr Maynard,' commented the judge wryly. After an uncomfortable silence, proceedings were brought to an end. 'Very well. Mr Maynard, you're free to go – let us all pray you never return.'

'Amen,' came from the nodding head of Maynard as he fled from the dock.

'Amen, indeed,' echoed the judge.

*   *   *

'Here he comes.' Maynard's wife and son were standing outside the main door of the Bailey as he walked out, arms aloft.

The podgy barrister made his move. Pulling off the pink ribbon from his brief, he grabbed a Webley revolver hidden within and, taking three steps forward, fired at point-blank range at the ample stomach of his target. The barrister then removed his wig before firing again, this time at the heart of his defenceless victim, slumped and bleeding at his feet.

'You!' croaked Maynard, eyes wide open, mouth agape – a flash of recognition passing across his face. It was to be the last word he would ever utter.

There were high-pitched, terrified screams from Maynard's wife which, together with the gunfire, caused a small crowd to gather. The barrister made no attempt to escape. Instead, he placed the gun in his jacket pocket and removed a packet of cigarettes. With a shaking hand, he lit one and pulled deeply, his eyes darting between the faces of the horrified onlookers.

It was only the second cigarette he'd smoked in over twenty years.

Chapter 2

Enter Big Jake

———————

1951

It poured in London the night he was born. The heavens opened up with thunder and lightning to welcome him. The nurses reassured his mum this was a good omen, and that her son would make his mark in life. He was a huge baby, 10lbs 4oz. His mum had been worried as he hardly cried on birth, but the nurses comforted her that this was another good sign and that he would grow up to be big and strong.

'But will he be kind and gentle?' she asked.

'With a mother as soft as you – what else could he be?' was the reply.

*   *   *

On a sunny spring afternoon in London there are few more pleasant pastures to take a leisurely stroll than Kenwood and Hampstead Heath.

Jack Davenport – known to friend and foe alike as Big Jake – had been a frequenter there for years, invariably with Ernie (his right-hand man) and his G Men (Greaves and Gilzean), two Labradors named after his Spurs heroes. This week was no exception. A Friday afternoon amble, a drink or two at the Wells Tavern, where his dogs could roam around at will, annoying all and sundry, before a lazy short drive to Camden, where he bought his weekly food supplies. Well, not exactly bought – *procured*. Jake rarely *bought* anything retail. The word was anathema to him. The very mention of it aggravated his eczema. The truth was he had an inside man in the food department at Harrods who, on the quiet, was running a local branch from his one-bedroom flat off Camden High Street. Meat, wine, Belgian chocolates – you name it, Jake got it trade minus 50 per cent. After all, he lived in a world where VAT was still a nasty rumour. Jake was a veritable cash man, and these days the only banks he visited were in Geneva.

It had not always been so. In a fifteen-year run between the ages of twenty and thirty-five, he had visited banks on a regular basis, kitted out with a balaclava on his head and a gun in his hand. Anyway, no one was hurt badly or, rather, no one was killed. The banks never really felt the loss, and not everybody can go to university and become a doctor or a lawyer. Jake's university was the streets of London, where he graduated with a double first in illegality.

Mind you, Jake had his own unique sense of morality too. He knew right from wrong or, put more accurately, wrong from very wrong. Oh yes, Jake knew exactly where to draw the line. The trouble was he didn't draw it often enough. Still, no drugs, no blackmail, no loan sharking and no pimping. On the other hand, no tax either. Actually, that would be doing him a disservice. He owned a minimarket on a street corner near Tower Bridge from which he threw the taxman a bone or two each year to keep him off his broad back.

And he wasn't without an education. Oh no, Big Jake wasn't your typical villain – far from it. He was comparatively well-read, an avid viewer of the documentary channel on TV and a subscriber to the *Daily Telegraph*. It had the best crime reports, and it was essential for Jake to know at any given time who was going in and who was coming out. And just to show all around that he was no registered moron (as he constantly referred to most of his team), he had kept a thick book of famous quotes on his bedside table for years, from which he stole regularly as the occasion demanded.

Now in his sixties, he was considered *numero uno* amongst the cognoscenti. His business had moved with the times and he now called himself an *entrepreneur*. He bought and sold properties in the names of others, and stolen jewellery in no name at all. He had everything a successful villain could desire: broad shoulders, a big house, a Bentley, a close family, a loyal wife who saw only what he wanted her to see and, of course, a virtually tax-free business. More importantly to him, he believed he had the respect of others (although many called it fear). He prided himself that he could walk into any pub within a mile radius of his home in Primrose Hill and never have to pay for a drink. He was popular as well. Ask any poor family in his manor who it was who came round at Christmas with a turkey and a bottle of stolen whisky, and they would answer in unison, 'Big Jake'.

A modern-day Robin Hood was how he liked to be known. If he could choose his own epitaph, it would read: 'Stole from the rich and gave to the poor (after taking a modest cut).'

Jack Davenport was, by any standards, a huge man. He was 6ft 3in., over 20 stone, plus VAT, with a 52in. chest and a giant gait, which any of his crew and the entire Flying Squad could pick out at 200 paces in a blizzard. He was the proud owner of a thick crop of dark, curly hair, with just a hint of grey to register his experience in life.

On these walks on the heath, Ernie would give Jake a weekly update on his finances. He was Jake's official/unofficial accountant – a poor cousin to the Italian *consigliere*. No documents were ever produced during their stroll and both left their mobile phones in their cars before the walk started. This was strictly de rigueur. Ernie kept all the facts and figures in his head. Had he tuned himself into more lawful pursuits in his youth, he could undoubtedly have qualified as an actuary. Ask Ernie what 8 per cent of £275,000 was and he would answer you in a jiffy. Conversely, percentages were not Jake's forte. He didn't do sharing, and the only figure he really understood was 100 per cent. There was a written record of business conducted each week, but this was kept by Ernie at a location known only to the two of them. Naturally, Jake needed to know where in case Ernie was unlucky enough to be hit by a passing bus or a stray bullet.

Jake and Ernie had been friends for over thirty years. Their paths had first crossed in the late 1970s when they found themselves sitting next to each other at the roulette table in the Playboy Club in Mayfair. They were both laundering their ill-gotten gains from thick wads of cash on entry to a thin cheque on their departure, and they soon discovered they had a good deal in common other than gambling – crime! The pair quickly entered into an unholy alliance, with Jake as the boss and Ernie his trusted lieutenant. Jake found the work and Ernie the team to carry it out.

On this particular walk, Jake was deep in nostalgia. 'Ernie, do you remember that quarter of a million we had to leave behind on that botched City job years ago? When that blind idiot, Bungalow Bill, roared into a cul-de-sac and we had to scarper on foot with the Old Bill in hot pursuit? It's a wonder I didn't have a heart attack. It was the last job that I went tooled up on. After that bloody disaster, I sold my stock and moved on.'

'What stock might that have been, Jake?'

'My gun and balaclava, of course – what else? Do you remember that I had to call a meet because I had a regular stiff neck from looking around the whole time, wondering which one of us was a wrong'un?'

'How could I forget it?' said Ernie, before starting to mimic Jake's voice. 'Lads, there is a grass in our team – and I had a good look in the mirror this morning whilst I was shaving and it ain't me!'

'We never found out who it was, did we? Wasn't you by any chance, was it?' Jake glared at Ernie. 'Only joking, only joking.' These days Jake kept himself in the background. True, he still financed a deal here and there, and he may not have been strict-ly kosher, but he knew where the crease was, and he kept his right foot firmly on the inside. You'd find no drug dealers at his door. Maybe a bit of unofficial pawnbroking here and there, and the contents of some errant lorries, but no longer anything beyond the pale. 'Anyway, Ernie,' Jake continued, 'I'm thinking of hanging up my boots. I mean, how much money does a man need? I've had a real good run. I don't want to wind up being the richest man in Wandsworth Prison, do I?'

'Yes, there's always a vacancy for that position, Jake. But look at the upside. You'd be sharing a tiny cell with no more than one or two other losers with free board and lodging – and think what it would do for your figure.'

Jake gazed down despondently at his indiscernible waistline. 'I'll make the jokes around here, Ernie – you stick to bookkeeping. Talking of jokes, I heard a great one from an old mate of mine, who I bumped into outside the Scrubs waiting to see Albert on his twenty stretch. Want to hear it?' Ernie rolled his eyes and sighed. He'd been listening to Jake's jokes for decades.

'No, not really. You've probably told it to me already.'

'No, this one's fresh to the market. OK, it goes like this: So, two old mafiosos, Luigi and Alfonso, meet up for a reunion dinner. They haven't seen each other for about fifteen years. "How's your wife, Luigi?" asks Alfonso. Luigi replies, "Actually she's not so good – in fact, she's dead." "Dead!" exclaims Alfonso. "Such a beautiful woman, dead! What did she die from, if you don't mind my asking?" Luigi replies calmly, "She died from an incurable disease." "What incurable disease?" enquires Alfonso. "Herpes," says Luigi with a straight face. "But Luigi," protests Alfonso, "herpes isn't an incurable disease." Luigi answers, "It is when you give it to Luigi!"'

Jake started chuckling. Ernie didn't – he'd already heard it. 'What do you like about that joke, Jake?'

'Well, it's so delicate – just like me.'

They strolled on at a snail's pace with Ernie bringing Jake up to date on the week's nefarious activities. This always took a while. Forty minutes later, they were nearing the end of their trek and both were relishing the prospect of a couple of beers at the Wells.

As always on a late Friday afternoon, the Wells was beginning to come to life, and being outside of his manor, despite the fact he was a regular, Jake was actually going to have to pay in hard cash. 'Two pints of lager, Bessie,' he ordered, as they strode up to the bar. The TV was on in the background but no one seemed to be watching. Jake waited impatiently at the bar and glanced at the screen. The headline running across the bottom of the screen shocked even him.

'MAN SHOT DEAD OUTSIDE THE OLD BAILEY'

Sky's ubiquitous Martin Brunt was giving a report from right outside the very court, just a few yards away from where the killing had taken place, which had now been barricaded off and was guarded by two police officers.

It seems that the victim, Robert Maynard, against whom charges of threats to kill and blackmail had just been dropped in court, was leaving the building and being greeted by his wife and son, when he was approached by a middle-aged man disguised in a barrister's wig and gown. Two shots were fired at close range. Apparently, the suspect made no effort to escape and was arrested at the scene. At present, there is no information as to whether the killing was related to the charges Mr Maynard was facing, although it appears Mr Maynard was well known in criminal circles.

'I've gone to heaven,' said Jake, slapping one hand down hard on the bar whilst punching the air with the other. 'Mercenary Bob, topped at the Bailey and all. That's a perfect storm, if ever there was one. My prayers have been answered.' Then, after a rare moment of reflection, 'This Sunday I'm going to church with my missus – and that's for sure.'

Jake volleyed new instructions at the barmaid. 'Bessie, bugger those two lagers, bring us your best bottle of bubbly.' For such an order the pair didn't have to wait long.

'Well, Ernie my boy,' announced Jake, whilst giving Ernie a friendly shoulder barge as the two of them clinked glasses. 'It seems that our old friend Bob has been a trifle careless and caught an incurable disease himself in the form of a bullet or two. Cheers! Here's to you, Bob.'

They both drank long and deep.

Chapter 3

Bored!

—

Adrian Stanford was just taking his seat with his wife for an early supper at Le Vesuvio on the seafront in Cannes, with nothing on his mind but an unimpeachable sole meunière, when the call came through from his office manager. He and his wife, Sally, had flown out the day before. They had stared up together at the departure board at Heathrow and tossed a coin. Sally had chosen Cannes, Adrian Rome. Adrian had won the toss, for what it was worth. A marital pyrrhic victory.

* * *

Two days earlier, late on a bleak Wednesday spring afternoon, Adrian had been slumped in his regal red leather chair, feet up on his desk, hands behind his head, with his collar open and his tie pulled halfway down, staring vacantly out of his Wigmore Street office window at a brooding grey sky. A bottle of Chivas Regal and a half-empty glass stood in close attendance.

'Bored, that's what I am – bored rigid,' he sighed.

His long-suffering secretary, Joanne, stood nearby with a pile of letters to sign. 'Stop behaving like a spoilt child, Adrian, and stop complaining so much. You're doing very well.' Joanne took no prisoners. Why should she? In her second job as Adrian's in-house therapist, she had listened to his constant moaning for more than twenty years. Win or lose, he would find something to grumble about – usually the barristers he instructed. For example, 'That was the worst mitigation I've ever heard and, believe me, I've heard a few bad ones in my time – no heart.' Or, 'For what he's charging you'd have thought he could afford to fork out for a coffee at the break.' Or, 'Couldn't hear a word he said – the old mumbler – nor could the jury… probably for the best.'

'Oh yes, I'm doing very well indeed,' Adrian responded. 'One dull fraud case after another. Piles of papers everywhere and you won't find a fingerprint of mine on any of them. What's happened to real crime? Daring bank robberies, underworld killings – all gone for ever. I tell you, Joanne, it may sound arrogant, but I wasn't put on this earth to study receivers' reports.'

'No? Why were you put here, then? Remind me.'

Joanne needed no such reminder, but Adrian grabbed the opportunity to let off some more steam. 'To sit back in an armchair, listen to a client's woes, give my opinion on their prospects and advise on tactics, of course. If I never see another balance sheet it'll be too soon. Worse still, virtually every client is a first-time offender who hasn't a clue about crime or the court system. I feel like a university lecturer when they first come in. They don't know the Old Bailey from St Paul's Cathedral. What I need is a case to get my teeth into. But what have I got? Mortgage frauds, confiscation hearings and a few miserable drugs cases.

And, whilst I'm at it, what's happened to the alibi defence? These days it sounds like something out of a chess manual. You know, Joanne, what's killed the crime game? It's those bloody mobile phones, DNA and CCTV cameras everywhere. A man can't even put his dustbin out without being snapped.'

'Go and buy another vintage car, that should keep you happy for a couple of days. Or why don't you get away for a few days? You won't be missed.'

Adrian gave Joanne a look as if she had just invented an instant solution to his boredom. 'Not a bad idea, not a bad idea at all. I think I will.' Then he picked up the phone and dialled home. 'Sally, pack a couple of bags for us – we're going away for a few days, first thing tomorrow morning. Yes, I know it's Nora's fiftieth birthday tomorrow, that's the best reason of all to get away. Where are we going? Haven't the foggiest. When we get to Heathrow we'll stare up at the board and toss a coin. Yes, yes, OK, the usual rules – heads you win, tails I lose.'

Buoyed by the call and downing the remainder of his whisky in one gulp, Adrian turned his attention once again to his in-house therapist. 'You know what, Joanne? I'm feeling better already.'

* * *

Now, two days later, in France, the telephone call from Adrian's office manager on an early Friday evening could only mean that a new case had come in or a report of a bounced cheque – usually the latter.

Adrian was in high spirits. The sea air was working wonders.

'OK, Jeremy, whet my appetite. Who's been arrested – a Texan oil tycoon or Carlos the Jackal?' asked Adrian whilst his eyes carefully scanned the restaurant's ample menu.

'Neither, unfortunately. But listen to this – guess who's been murdered?'

'I just can't wait to hear,' said Adrian, stifling a yawn and eyeing the size of the sole meunière being served up at the next table.

Jeremy couldn't wait to tell him. 'Bob Maynard – the one and only. Yes, Mercenary Bob – shot dead outside the Bailey. It's all over the news, and the killer's asked for us to act.'

Finally, Adrian's ears pricked up. After putting down the menu, he walked outside to avoid the hubbub from the other diners. 'Outside the Bailey? Well, that's a first. Thank God he was never a client of mine or I'd be out of a case.'

'Well, you've got a case now, Adrian. He's being held at Charing Cross Police Station. The police tell me they'll be ready for his interview at 7 tonight. What do you want me to do?'

Adrian weighed up his options. 'Who is this hero? He's due a Duke of Edinburgh award at least, possibly a knighthood and, who knows, maybe even a statue outside the Old Bailey at the scene of the crime.'

'Apparently he's middle-aged and his name's David Dennis. I've made a few calls and no one's heard of him – he's a complete unknown. The police won't tell me any more except that they've got the shooting on CCTV and a confession at the scene.'

'Who's in charge of the case?' Adrian enquired.

'A Detective Chief Superintendent Stokes.'

Adrian started chuckling. 'The Iron-Rod himself, eh?' Adrian glanced at his watch. 'Well, it's 6.30 here now and I can't get to Charing Cross in an hour and a half, or even tonight. They'll just have to wait for me until tomorrow morning before they start interviewing.'

Jeremy was sceptical. 'Adrian, this is a top underworld killing. The police will never put off the interview just to suit you.'

'Will they not? We'll see. Give me the police station number. Stokes and I know each other very well. I'm sure he'll be thrilled to hear from me on a Friday night. We're old friends or, rather, old enemies.'

Then Adrian walked back inside to his table, pausing only to glance at the trays of tarte Tatin on display in the window. 'Sally,' he said, with a boyish glint in his eye, 'things are looking up. What's that fancy wine you like with your fish here – Puligny-Montrachet? Yes, let's have a bottle.'

Adrian's state of boredom was already a distant memory.

Chapter 4

Enter the Iron-Rod

'Say that again, Neil.' Detective Chief Superintendent Rodney 'Iron-Rod' Stokes couldn't believe what he was hearing on the phone from his detective inspector. 'Outside the doors of the Bailey? In broad daylight? You're kidding me!'

Early Friday afternoon had found Stokes attending a conference, deciding with prosecuting lawyers whether there was enough evidence to charge a merchant banker with murder. His wife had been missing for more than a year from the family home and minute traces of her blood had been found on the floorboards under their new carpet, which was exactly the same pattern as the old one.

Then the call had come in.

'What did the hero say on arrest?' Stokes enquired.

'"I did it and I don't regret it" were his only words. But you'll like this part, Rodney. When they got him to the police station, he pulled out a piece of paper from his pocket and guess which lawyer's name and telephone number he had written on it?'

Stokes started scratching his chin, thinking about all the solicitors he despised – it was a long list. He started at the top.

'Don't tell me, Stanford?'

'Right in one.'

He scratched a bit harder. 'That's all I need – bloody Adrian Stanford,' he moaned, as he dug desperately into his pocket for a couple of calming tablets.

Iron-Rod Stokes had earned his nickname when he'd been a detective inspector in the Flying Squad years earlier. He'd wanted to be a cop ever since the mid-1970s, when, together with his father, he would watch, week in, week out, episodes of *The Sweeney* on TV. Too late his eyes had been opened to the cruel reality that the CID did not spend their entire working lives in pubs or in bed with villains' wives.

PC Plod on the beat since leaving school, detective sergeant at the age of twenty-eight and inspector seven years later. He was a straight-talking policeman with no airs or graces. Woe betide any junior officer who crossed him. They would find themselves seconded at speed to a dog-training course or, even worse, a desk job in the complaints department at Scotland Yard. Iron-Rod might not be the first person you would want to accompany you on a world cruise, but you knew exactly where you stood with him. He was simply not the delicate sort. If a thought entered his head, it lost no time exiting through his mouth. By the age of thirty-five, the Met Police had recognised he was a potential high-flyer and had sent him to Bristol University to study English. A Flying Squad officer who could both read and write had become a high priority for the force.

But now he was long in the tooth and short on patience. He was nearing retirement and yearned for summers spent camping and fishing in the Ardennes with his wife and daughter, far away from his mother-in-law and the murder squads. He was also hoping for an easy last nine months, going through the motions, before he turned in his badge. But no, the commissioner himself had decided that he was the man to oversee the Old Bailey shooting. Like it or not, he was stuck with the case – and Stanford as well.

On arrival at Charing Cross Police Station, Stokes went straight to the cells to size up his new customer. There he found Dennis sitting on a hard bed with a pillow bent in two as a backrest. Several well-worn paperbacks left by previous patrons lay stacked by his side.

As soon as Stokes entered the cell, Dennis had the good manners to stand up and shake hands. Not the typical sort of reception he'd experienced from men arrested for murder. Dennis wasn't at all what Stokes had expected. Thick dark-brown hair swept back, clean-shaven, about 5ft 6in. tall, overweight with a nervous but polite manner, as if he were resigned to his fate. *No hitman here, that's for sure*, thought Stokes.

'My name's Chief Superintendent Stokes and I'm in charge of this inquiry.'

'Fair enough,' replied Dennis.

'And let me tell you from the outset, Mr Dennis,' went on Stokes, 'everything's going to be done by the book – no quiet-corridor off-the-record chats. So, you can forget what you might've seen on TV.'

'No verbals either then? Good,' replied Dennis.

Stokes did a double-take. 'You're behind the times, Mr Dennis. That went out of fashion in the mid-1980s – straight after the Brink's-Mat fiascos.'

Stokes told Dennis that his interview was going to start at 7 p.m. that night and that the firm he'd asked for, Stanfords, had been contacted and was going to be representing him. 'May I ask who recommended Mr Stanford to you?' asked the inquisitive Stokes, trying to give the impression that he was just making conversation.

'As you've just said, officer – no quiet-corridor off-the-record chats, if you don't mind.'

He's shrewder than he looks, thought Stokes.

Later, Stokes was in the police canteen with the officers who had been to the scene, going over the basic facts, when the tannoy announced, 'Call for Detective Chief Superintendent Stokes.' He took the call in what the police euphemistically refer to as the *custody suite*.

'Mr Stokes?' said the voice at the other end.

'Who's this?' Stokes knew only too well who it was thanks to his previous encounter with Adrian Stanford years before. Only Stanford persistently refused to call him by his full title just to irritate him.

'Ah, Mr Stokes,' the caller continued unrepentantly. 'Adrian Stanford here. Our firm's been asked to act in the Maynard murder or, should I say, "mercy killing".'

'Yes, I know. How can I help you, Mr Stanford?' replied Stokes, as if he was addressing a complete stranger.

'Well, I'm in France at the moment, hoping to take in some of the Cannes Film Festival. But as things stand, I'm intending to fly back to London tonight, and I can be with you for my client's interview as early as you like tomorrow morning. Shall we say 9 o'clock?' Stanford was already treating his request as a done deal.

Stokes was having none of it, particularly because he wasn't prepared to oblige Stanford. 'Mr Stanford, your client's interview will start at 7 o'clock tonight, as planned. This is a very serious murder inquiry and I have no intention of putting it off overnight for your personal convenience.'

'Well, what's the problem?' Stanford asked. 'As I understand it, the killing was done in broad daylight and captured on CCTV. You'll have hours tomorrow to question him. Anyway, you've already got a confession.'

Though Stokes couldn't deny Stanford's logic, he was damned if he was going to give him an inch. 'Mr Stanford, I've just seen your client in the cells and I've told him, come hell or high water, his interview will start at 7 tonight. So, unless you're as superhuman as some of your clients no doubt think, I suggest you instruct someone else to attend tonight. I repeat, the interview starts at 7 tonight – with or without you.'

The interview did indeed go ahead at 7 p.m. that night, but not without Stanford having his say first. After speaking to Stokes, he rang the station again and spoke to the custody officer, who removed the prisoner from the cells to speak to his lawyer on the phone.

'Mr Dennis, I'm Adrian Stanford. At the moment, I'm in France, but I intend to travel back to London tonight and to be at the police station before 9 o'clock tomorrow. Is there a police officer listening in?'

'I don't think so, Mr Stanford,' replied Dennis calmly. 'They've left me alone for this call.'

'Good, now, here's the score. Your first interview's at 7 o'clock tonight. Of course, I can't get back by then. I could arrange for one of my assistants to stand in, but frankly, with an allegation as serious as this, it's essential I deal with everything myself from the outset. Do you follow?'

'What would you like me to do, Mr Stanford?'

Stanford liked the sound of his new client already. 'Look, I can't stop them trying to interview you tonight. But I would strongly urge you to tell them you have spoken to me and that I'll be at the station early tomorrow and that you've been advised by me not to answer any questions at all until I've seen you, and that you intend to take that advice. The police will then give you a whole spiel that if you don't answer it can be held against you later, and offer to get you some kid duty solicitor to stand in. Don't fall for it. I want to hear your account in private, face-to-face, before we start the interview.'

'Not a problem, Mr Stanford. I'll see you in the morning then.'

'On second thoughts, I'll be at the station by 7.30 tomorrow, at the latest. That'll stop the police moaning later that time was wasted by my tactics.'

At 7 p.m. that night, the tapes were switched on and Dennis was cautioned and offered free legal advice that was politely declined. Forty minutes of questioning followed, but to no avail. Dennis gave a standard reply to each question.

'My solicitor of choice, Mr Stanford, will be here very early tomorrow morning and, on his advice, I won't be answering any questions until I've seen him.'

At 7.40 p.m. the interview was reluctantly abandoned. Dennis was returned to his cell for the night and offered a cheese sandwich and a slice of apple cake with stone-cold custard. He ate the lot – he was starving. Nothing had passed his lips since a bowl of Rice Krispies that morning before he left for his day's work.

The interviewing officers reported the frustrating news back to Stokes. How he hated Stanford, but how Dennis, an unknown entity, had got hold of him of all lawyers remained a mystery.

* * *

That very night, Stokes held a briefing with his murder squad, consisting of eight officers, in the incident room at Charing Cross Police Station. From the outset, Stokes was very much in charge.

'Right, men, I can see from your expressions that you're asking yourself what all the fuss is about. After all, the man's confessed at the scene, hasn't he? And he's done the country a right old favour. Well, you can get that attitude right out of your heads, for starters. I'm retiring in nine months and I don't intend to end my career with some enormous cock-up. No man walks on my watch if I can help it. And he's got Stanford as his brief to boot. He won't be instructing some two-bob QC either. Stanford's buggered me about with the interviews – calling all the shots from France – and the fact is none of us have a clue why this johnny-come-lately has put two bullets into our beloved Mercenary Bob. I tell you, this case has really got me twitching.'

Stokes surveyed the motley crew who stood around the table in front of him. *The usual mix*, he thought to himself – *three who know what they're doing and the rest who couldn't hit sand if they fell off a camel.* 'Split yourself into two teams. I want half of you at Maynard's home for a thorough search and the other half at Dennis's flat. Photograph everything and take any piece of paper you find. I want every single document from Maynard's home, as well as Dennis's. I don't care if it's an overdue council tax notice – seize it! We've already prepared a request for telephone printouts of all numbers – Dennis's home telephone, his mobile, his wife's mobile. Mercenary Bob's far too shrewd to have his own mobile, so that's bound to be a dead-end. But we're getting a printout of his home calls, for what they're worth – which will doubtless be zilch.

'The press are already crawling all over this case, which brings me to another point. No one's to speak to them. Nothing on the record, nothing off the record. No boozy pub chats, no gossiping with your wives or anybody else's wife.' This drew the first and only smiles at the meeting.

'You boys are in for a long night.' There were deep sighs all round. 'Well, off you go then. We'll meet again tomorrow at 7.30 a.m. sharp for an update. And let's all pray that Stanford's plane gets fogbound.' The officers stood to leave. 'And, by the way, I'm going to be doing the interviewing myself tomorrow. Yes, I know these days it's unusual for a senior officer to get himself involved in interviews, but when a man is shot dead in cold blood, bang outside the Bailey, it's time for me to get out of my rocking chair and right back into the action. I'm taking nothing for granted.'

Dennis was not the only one due for a restless night – he had Stokes for company.

* * *

Having finished his meal by 8.30 p.m., Dennis faced the depressing prospect of eleven lonely hours in a cell before his lawyer arrived. He decided to put it to good use. He banged on the cell door. Five minutes later, the custody officer rolled up.

'Yes, Dennis, what's the problem?'

'I wonder if I could have a pen and some paper, please?' answered Dennis, polite as ever.

The custody officer gave Dennis a long stare. He had to satisfy himself that Dennis wasn't a suicide risk before he gave him a pen. 'Pen and paper! What do you want that for? Writing your memoirs already?'

'Sort of.'

'Well, it's bound to be a bestseller,' replied the officer, with a self-indulgent chuckle. 'I'll see what I can find.' The custody officer trotted off down the corridor, returning a few minutes later with some sheets of paper and an old chewed-up biro.

'Not exactly Smythson's, is it?' joked Dennis. The custody officer stared at him blankly. Apparently Bond Street wasn't on his patch.

'This is the best I can do for you,' he said as he passed over the pen and paper. 'Better keep to the point or you'll run out of paper.'

'I intend to.'

The grill was slammed down and Dennis was left alone save for a drunk in the next cell, who was serving up a rather melodic rendering of 'When Irish Eyes are Smiling' with 'I Belong to Glasgow' as an encore.

There was no table in the cell, so Dennis improvised by pulling the damp mattress from the steel-framed bed onto the floor and sitting on it. Using the bed as a table, he leaned back for a few seconds, staring out the tiny double-locked windows high up in the wall for inspiration for an appropriate title. In bold print he wrote, 'Me and Mercenary Bob Maynard'. He began his tale in the smallest script that he could manage. After all, it was going to be a long and sad story. Whether it would have a happy ending was quite another matter.

Chapter 5

The Grudge Match

———————————

U nlike Dennis and Stokes, Adrian Stanford slept like a
baby. Leaving his wife and her credit card running wild
and loose at the Martinez Hotel in Cannes, he caught the last
plane back from Nice to Heathrow and was fast asleep in his
own bed in Belsize Park by 1 a.m. Why should he worry? He
always gave his best and, to him, a new murder case was no
more than meat and drink. The next morning, he rose at 5.30,
drank two espressos and watched Sky News until 6. It was still
covering the Maynard killing, although it told him nothing new.

As the only child born to a working-class family in Willes-
den, north London, Adrian had attended the local grammar
school up until the age of sixteen, excelling in sport and little
else. After getting a handful of O-levels, he wanted to leave
school, which the headmaster thought was an excellent idea.
His parents thought otherwise and forced him to stay on at
school for another two years. To everyone's surprise, he turned
out to be a late developer and managed to secure a place at the
University of Sussex to read economics. On graduating, he had
no idea what he was going to do. So, at twenty-one, with some

money he'd saved from a market stall he ran on Saturdays on Portobello Road, selling old pens and lighters, he set off on a six-month European tour with two school friends. He spent too much time in Paris, where he fell hopelessly in love with a dancer from the Folies Bergère, until he discovered that she in turn was spending too much time with an elderly Italian lothario. Stanford had the testosterone, but the Italian had the Testarossa – no contest!

Back again in London at twenty-two, he was thinking of getting a job as a sports reporter when, out of the blue, he received a letter to attend jury service in a court near Elephant and Castle. The first trial involved a wheeler-dealer found in possession of ten Burberry raincoats, which seemed to have mysteriously walked themselves out of Selfridges. The defendant looked the part, what with a floral handkerchief in his jacket pocket and a pack of thinly disguised lies for a defence. He was duly convicted.

The second case was far more to Stanford's liking. A beautiful Russian croupier was accused of systematic theft from a top London casino. £10,000 worth of chips, which she claimed were tips, were found in her handbag. Her defence was woefully weak. But there were twelve good men on the jury and her cheeks held the blush of a ripe Californian peach. When her tears started to flow in the witness box as she told the court in her delicious Russian accent how she had fled from Moscow at the age of seventeen, having been raped by her stepfather, the game was up for the prosecution. After a twenty-minute retirement, she was acquitted. Even the judge smiled.

This got young Adrian to thinking about a career in the law.

29

It didn't look that difficult and was bound to be a lot of fun – especially the jury trials, which seemed to depend more on looks and first impressions than on hard evidence. His parents were thrilled with his new-found ambition, and so it was that he converted to law. Eventually, at twenty-four, he became articled to a criminal law specialist in the West End. His boss was already in his late sixties, and the pay as a trainee was appalling. But he knew the eventual rewards would make it all worthwhile. Anyway, he loved the life and the challenges a new case would bring.

When he finally qualified at twenty-six, Stanford was already building a reputation in the less-salubrious parts of south London. He was a good judge of character, his boss was on the verge of retiring and, in effect, Adrian was running the show. By the age of twenty-nine, he bought the business for a pittance, changed the name to Stanfords and never looked back.

He married on the same day as the firm's name was changed. He had met his wife, Sally, when he had missed his flight back to London after an extradition case in Belgium. She too had missed the flight and they'd locked eyes at the check-in desk. She had been modelling in Brussels. Their mutual annoyance and her striking good looks led to Adrian suggesting a late supper. The romance blossomed, and all because his taxi had been late for the trip to the airport and her chauffeur's car had conked out en route. As he said in his wedding speech, 'Fate is the cards you're dealt; destiny is the way you play them,' before adding that, in Sally, he'd been dealt the Queen of Hearts, which was met with huge applause.

Now, Adrian was in his late forties and generally considered to be at the top of his game. He never arrived at the office later than 8.30 a.m., worked solidly all day but rarely took any files home. When clients told him he was expensive, he replied that hopefully they'd be free to tell him so again after their case was over. He pulled no punches, and always instructed the best counsel his clients could afford.

At home in the evenings and weekends, he switched off. In August, you would never find him in London. He was unflashy, but he had a good life. His main hobby was vintage cars, on which he wasted far too much money, and tennis, on which he wasted too much time. He was generally impatient, particularly when it came to bureaucracy. He knew the police considered him too cocky, but hopefully gracious in defeat. The so-called underworld treated him with respect, but he kept his distance, never socialising with his clients.

Stanford had first crossed swords with Iron-Rod Stokes about twelve years previously, when Stokes had been an inspector in the Flying Squad. Mickey Moss, a regular client of Stanford's, had been targeted by the Squad for weeks. The grapevine had spread the rumour that he was much in demand as a getaway driver with the nickname 'Stirling the Wheelman' – Rotherhithe's answer to Steve McQueen.

The Squad had watched his every move day and night: whether he was in his flat near Tower Bridge, easing about town in a black Mercedes coupé or hanging around with a selection of local talent at Le Pont de la Tour on the river. One day, they saw him paying rather too much attention to a bank in Bromley, whilst sitting in a stolen Jag with false plates. A Securicor van came and went peacefully, with Stirling looking on intently through his rear-view mirror. A week later, the Jag was there again, but this time, when the guards had finished their collection and were exiting the bank, two of the three men in the car were up and out, leaving the driver in situ with the engine purring. They had balaclavas covering their faces and pistols in their gloved hands. With their swag secured, the chase was on. But the driver of the Jag was a real pro and possibly colour blind as well. The car roared through three sets of red lights on the wrong side of the road with £100,000 rocking to and fro on the back seat, leaving four police cars in its wake.

Stirling's home lay empty for two weeks, but on his return, suitcase in hand, he was nabbed and taken in for questioning. Stanford got a call and attended the police station for his client's interview. Stokes was in charge. Stirling flatly refused to come out of his cell for the interview, so Stokes went in and sat himself on a chair with Stanford sitting on the bed next to his client − a cosy affair. Not a word could Stokes get out of Stirling's mouth, so he tried a novel approach.

'Fancy a cup of tea, Mr Moss?' he asked. No answer from Stirling, who was sitting with just his underpants on. 'One sugar or two?' enquired Stokes jovially. No answer. 'OK, just twiddle your big toe once for one sugar and twice for two.' Stirling twiddled his big toe twice. 'That's much better, Mr Moss,' said Stokes. 'Now we've almost got a conversation going.'

Stirling was charged with the robbery and at his first court hearing Stanford applied for bail. The magistrate listened carefully to Stanford's account that his client had been on a boat to Spain, sharing a room with a one-armed man on the day of the robbery. It sounded like something out of the 1960s' *The Fugitive*.

Stokes told the court that he had actually seen Stirling a week before the robbery sitting in the same stolen vehicle that was used on the day. He said he saw a man of similar build the following week when the robbery was taking place in the driver's seat of the car, although only from the back.

'Stand up, Mr Moss,' said the magistrate. 'I have listened carefully to everything your lawyer has said on your behalf, but…'

On hearing the word 'but', Stirling started walking out of the dock towards the cells.

'Come back, Mr Moss, I haven't finished,' called out the magistrate in exasperation.

'Bollocks,' came the reply from Stirling, as he passed through the door towards the cells, accompanied by high-pitched laughter from young girls in the gallery who were on a school outing – what an education!

Half an hour later, Stirling was brought back into court to face contempt proceedings for swearing. Stanford claimed his client was actually in the corridor when the word was overheard rather than in the court – not his best point. 'Furthermore, sir,' said Stanford, 'when you told my client "I have listened to everything your lawyer has said on your behalf, but…" he knew his application for bail had failed. To use a cricketing analogy, he knew he was out – clean bowled. He didn't need to wait for the umpire's finger to go up before he started walking.'

The magistrate was amused but unconvinced. 'Very gentlemanly of your client, Mr Stanford – seven days for contempt of court.'

'Is that consecutive or concurrent?' shouted out his client from the dock.

But three days later, having appealed to a higher court, Stirling was out on bail. He had served the requisite half of the seven days for contempt. 'Worth every minute,' he told Stanford. 'I haven't had such a good laugh for years.'

Six months later, this time on trial before a jury, he did a second walkout from the dock after the first question in cross-examination.

'Now, Mr Moss, how did you pay for your £30,000 Mercedes?' asked the prosecuting counsel.

'None of your bloody business. I owned it before the robbery, so what's it got to do with this case?' He had a point. Once again, he marched down to the cells, refusing to return to court, and the trial continued without him. Suffice to say that yet another miscarriage of justice blotted the legal landscape – his acquittal!

Stokes was fuming and blamed Stanford for Stirling's court antics. He told him so in no uncertain terms straight after the verdict.

'I'll get you next time, Mr Stanford. Mark my words.'

'Promises, promises, nothing but promises,' retorted Stanford. A response unlikely to curry favour at a solicitor's disciplinary tribunal hearing.

Now en route to Charing Cross Police Station on a bright spring Saturday morning, in his vintage grey Jensen C-V8, Stanford would be in good time to arrive, as promised, at about 7.30 a.m., ready for his eagerly awaited return match with Stokes. He was considering all tactics available at this early stage. Should his new client play ball and say anything in interview? This couldn't be decided until he'd seen him and established the reasoning as to how a middle-aged man with no criminal record had the nerve to slaughter London's most infamous criminal in public. One fact he did know for sure was that it was going to be a remarkably high-profile case.

He arrived a little earlier than anticipated at 7.20 a.m. The police station was already busy with plain-clothes officers coming and going, all looking as if they had something important to do, but taking their time about doing it. These days, it was difficult to tell a CID officer from a criminal, as you rarely saw an officer below the rank of detective chief inspector in a suit. Most wore jeans and trainers. *How standards have slipped*, Stanford thought.

He presented himself at the reception. It was unattended – par for the course. Eventually, a young uniformed officer with a cardboard coffee cup in hand strolled in and asked Adrian his business. 'My name's Stanford and I've come to see David Dennis.'

The officer sized Stanford up. Tall, clean-shaven, dark-brown freshly washed hair, expensive navy-blue suit, light-grey shirt, understated silk tie, a slim black Moroccan leather briefcase in hand. He looked the part.

'Yes, Detective Chief Superintendent Stokes told me to expect you early. I'll buzz the custody officer and tell him you've arrived.' Stanford was left to wait at the entrance to the station, together with an irate mother and her son, who looked like he'd been at the receiving end of a brawl the previous night. He waited for fifteen minutes. This delay was nothing unusual and almost standard practice in his experience. He was sure the police kept solicitors waiting on purpose. *The away match*, he called it.

Finally, another officer arrived and he was taken into the custody suite. Stokes was waiting for him. 'Good morning, Mr Stanford. It seems we're going to be doing battle with each other again. We're ready for interview as soon as you are, but first here's the disclosure sheet.'

Stokes handed it over with a flourish as if it was a signed confession.

Disclosure:

- On Friday 23 May at approximately 11.45 a.m. outside the Central Criminal Court, David Dennis was arrested on suspicion of the murder of Robert Maynard.
- On his arrest, and after having been cautioned at the scene, Dennis replied, 'I did it and I don't regret it.'
- The suspect was dressed as a barrister. A Webley revolver was found in his pocket, with two used chambers.
- There is eye-evidence from witnesses that it was Dennis who fired the two shots which killed Robert Maynard.
- On arrival at Charing Cross Police Station, the suspect produced to the custody sergeant a piece of paper with the name and telephone number of the solicitors whom he wished to instruct.
- The police have gathered all CCTV footage in the area, which will be made available to the defence as soon as practicable on a consolidated disc.

Stanford studied the document quickly but carefully.

'And the motive?' he asked, looking Stokes in the eye.

'Good question, Mr Stanford. Perhaps if you'd allowed your client to answer our questions last night, we could tell you. As it is, we haven't got a clue.'

'Right,' replied Stanford. 'I'd like to see the custody record.' This he was given and, in essence, it told him that his client had eaten supper, asked for a pen and paper and that every half-hour the jailer had peered into the grate to make sure he hadn't hanged himself (which would have been some feat, since the police had removed his shoelaces and taken his belt). The record showed he was busy writing late into the night, but by 3 a.m. he was found to be sound asleep.

'I'm sure you'll want to see your client for a while before we start interviewing. And by the way, I'm going to be conducting the interview myself today.'

'Indeed,' replied Stanford with a raised eyebrow. 'If that's the case, I'd better ask him how many sugars he takes in his tea.'

Stokes rose to the bait. 'Just let us know when you're ready, Mr Stanford. We'll be waiting – sugar and all!'

* * *

'Are you Mr Stanford?' asked Dennis as he was led into the interview room. Stanford nodded. 'I thought you'd be older.'

Stanford took this as a compliment. 'It must be the easy life. How have the police been treating you since you arrived here?'

'Not too bad, I suppose, bearing in mind the circumstances. I could have done with a softer mattress and a brandy or two. But other than that, no real complaints.'

'I can't say I care much for your new clothes,' joked Stanford, sizing up Dennis's paper outfit that had been provided after his own clothes had been taken away for forensic testing. 'Anyway,' continued Stanford, getting down to business, 'all I know to date are the basic facts, but I see from the custody record that you've been up half the night writing out something or other.'

'Yes, I've written out the whole gruesome story for you.'

'Good, if that's the case, I'd like to read it – it's probably the best place to start.'

They both took a seat and Dennis handed over a bundle of lined pages, with every nook and cranny covered in tiny spidery writing.

'I'm sorry for the cramped writing, I was afraid I'd run out of paper. Actually, as you can see, I had to finish off my story on some toilet paper. The custody officer is a bit of a stingy fellow.'

'Probably a relation of Stokes,' joked Stanford.

He started to read Dennis's handiwork, but the tiny writing made it almost impossible. 'We'll be here all day if we do it this way. You read it to me – slow and steady please.' He handed the pages back to his client, who, with a quivering voice, began to read aloud.

Stanford sat in silence, listening to Dennis's tragic account. Even with his vast experience, he was truly amazed at what he was hearing. He made the occasional note but rarely looked at his client directly so as to avoid embarrassing him.

'Right, is there anything else written there that you haven't read out to me?' he asked when Dennis had finished reading.

'No, not a word – and it's all absolutely true.'

'Good. Now, here's my advice as to how we should play the

police interview. It's your decision, of course, and old Stokes will be hopping mad, but I think it's our best option. Now, listen carefully to what I have in mind and tell me if you agree.'

He did.

Chapter 6

Bullets

———

'Open the bloody windows. It stinks in here like a third-class whorehouse in here – not that I'd know, of course!'

Whilst Stanford was busy with his new client, Stokes was holding a second briefing with his murder squad in the incident room above. The searches had gone on way into the early hours. The eight officers looked exhausted and as if they were in urgent need of a shower. The incident room was unimpressive. About 20ft by 16ft with three desks and six chairs scattered about. The walls were dirty and empty, save for a map of London and a large blackboard, which had the names of the officers and their mobile telephone numbers, a list of potential witnesses, including Bob the Merc's widow and son and the pathologist, and a list of exhibits, including the gun and photographs of the scene of the killing, scribbled on it with white chalk. No need for a considered list of suspects – there was only one.

'What are you looking so pleased about, Potter? What did you find in Dennis's flat? What have you got there in that exhibits bag that's got you so excited – porn films?' Stokes was in fine form.

'No sir, bullets, thirty-four of them in their original box. They were there on his kitchen table for all to see. I've checked with the forensics boys and they've just told me they match the ones that killed Maynard.'

Stokes was mystified. 'I can't get to grips with this case. Why leave a box of bullets lying around in the kitchen? It can't simply be a mistake – even for a beginner. What's that piece of paper you've got in a bag there, Jackson? I can see from your face you can't wait to tell me.'

'It's a receipt, guv, for Dennis's barrister's kit. Bought from Ede & Ravenscroft in Chancery Lane for £837.50, two days before the shooting. I found it in Dennis's bedside table. I'm going round to the shop this afternoon to take a statement.'

'Good,' said Stokes, 'and while you're there, Jackson, buy yourself a new shirt, will you? I know you've been up most of the night, but I can smell you from here – or is it you, Potter?' Both pleaded innocence.

'What are those books you seized from Dennis's flat, Kent? Let me see them. *The Roll of the Dice*, *The Cincinnati Kid*, *The Only Game in Town*, *Positively Fifth Street*. They're all gambling books. Did Bob the Merc gamble as well? Anybody know?'

No one did.

'Did you find any Kamikaze books at Dennis's home, Potter?' Potter looked lost. 'I'll take that as a *no*, then,' continued Stokes. 'Where's Dennis's wife and kids, anybody know? She's got to be able to throw some light on this case. I want her found, and now. Jackson, when are we expecting printouts of the telephone calls from all the relevant numbers?'

'Hopefully within three weeks, sir, it's been given top priority,' PC Jackson replied.

'Is that what they call top priority these days? My mother-in-law gets hers in ten days. Mind you, the way she can nag, it's no great surprise. So, Potter,' said Stokes, examining the sealed plastic bag containing the box of bullets. 'What conclusion did you come to about these thirty-four bullets?'

'What conclusion, sir? What do you mean? It's a box of bullets.'

Stokes dropped his head and blew out heavily. 'How long have you been in the CID, Potter?'

'Six months, sir.'

'Well, you see, Potter, this is the way it is in the CID. You're meant to use your brains and not just your brawn. If you find a box of bullets sunning themselves on the killer's kitchen table next to a packet of Rice Krispies, you're entitled to draw a few inferences.' Silence from Potter.

'Anybody else got a clue? Jackson, what do you say?'

'Well, sir, the full box should have fifty bullets, so there's ten missing, assuming there were six in the gun when Dennis turned up at the Bailey—'

'There were,' Stokes interrupted, impatiently.

Jackson started awkwardly rubbing the back of his neck in search of inspiration. None was forthcoming, but he gave it his best shot. 'It leaves ten missing, so perhaps he was given an already-opened box of forty bullets instead of fifty?'

'Oh, dear me, anybody else got any ideas?' asked Stokes. Silence reigned. 'Alright boys, I'm going to put you out of your misery. Look at the full picture. Dennis is no criminal by trade.

He doesn't rob banks and he's no drug dealer. So, it's likely that whoever gave him the gun gave him the bullets as well.' All agreed, with silent nods. 'Of course, he could have been given a box with only forty bullets to begin with, but what's the more likely explanation – anyone?' Deadly silence.

'I've got it, sir.' Jackson had finally arrived. 'Practice.'

'Well done, Jackson, you'll go far. At least if someone shows you to the well you're capable of helping yourself to a drink. Yes, ten bullets used for target practice. But where? It certainly wasn't Maynard's back garden. Any other inference from the bullets, men?' A further uncomfortable silence followed.

'But, sir,' started Potter, 'surely the finding of the box of bullets must be a good point for the prosecution at his trial?'

'Normally, I'd agree with you, Potter, but there's nothing normal about this case. Let's hope all's revealed in the interview. His brief, Stanford, is with him at the moment. He's not my personal choice for Lawyer of the Year. So, this is the way I see it. Dennis knew we would search his home and we'd find the bullets because he allowed himself to be arrested at the scene. So, it proves that hanging around after the crime wasn't a sudden impulse or feeling of remorse, but part of his plan. He never wanted to escape. He's cleverer than I thought. He's playing an open game, and planning the tactics of his trial even before the killing. But why not run away? Why, why, why? I just can't fathom it. Jameson, what the hell is that Harrods hamper doing here? It's not Christmas yet.'

'£30,000 guv, in mixed notes. I found it in Maynard's home under the staircase,' replied Jameson.

'I wonder what poor bastard had to fork that out to save his skin,' replied Stokes. 'Dennis's brief is sure to make a meal out of that at the trial – just you wait and see.'

Stokes rummaged in his pocket and shamelessly removed a handful of grey tablets. 'You see these, men? They're calming tablets. Apparently not quite as effective as cannabis, but there you go. My missus gets them for me and insists I take a couple before we go round to her mother's for Sunday lunch. You're meant to take one or two of them at moments of great stress – and make no bones about it, a murder interview with Stanford sitting in is certainly such a moment. I'm taking four. Let's hope they last.'

He lifted a glass of water to his lips and gulped down the tablets before standing up and marching out of the room, now fully armed for battle.

Chapter 7

A Killer's Tale

Dennis's second police interview began late, at 9.30 a.m. His meeting with Stanford had taken quite a while. Four men sat in a windowless, stuffy room, some 8ft-square, with an air-conditioning system that had never worked. A filthy threadbare grey carpet lay at their feet. Covering some of its shame was a 4ft by 2ft table clamped to the floor. Two of the four chairs in the room were bolted down to prevent suspects from getting over-animated under questioning. The only decoration on the walls was a panic-alarm bar running round the whole room, horizontally about 3ft from the ground. A video camera gazed down unsympathetically from high up in the corner, straight into the face of its new target, and a clumsy, bulky CD player sat on the table. The door was padded on the inside to avoid any overheated questioning or a reluctant confession being overheard by handcuffed detainees who might be passing by at an inappropriate moment.

Personally, Stanford hated these police interviews. His clients rarely talked, but the police banged on and on anyway – sometimes for hours. Even worse, in recent years, for serious cases, all interviews were videoed so the lawyer had to give the impression that he was actually listening, rather than wondering what his wife was cooking up for dinner or how the hell he was going to pay his VAT at the end of the quarter. But, then again, not every interview was as interesting as this one was bound to be.

Stokes and Detective Inspector Neil Worthington sat on one side of the table and Dennis and Stanford on the clamped chairs opposite. The camera was switched on and Dennis was given the usual police caution – to the effect that he had the right not to answer questions but that it could be used against him at trial if he did not. (Stanford had jokingly told Dennis earlier that morning that one of his regulars had succinctly defined it as, 'Buggered if you do and buggered if you don't.')

After the caution, Stanford cut in before any questions could be asked. 'As you know from the custody record, Mr Dennis spent many hours last night writing, and I'd like him to read what he wrote into the record. The jailer was kind enough to give him some paper, which did not prove to be quite sufficient, and so he had to finish off his account on a toilet roll. It's very detailed, as you will hear. After he finishes reading it, I have advised him not to answer any questions at all.' Stanford then turned towards his client and said, 'Do you intend to take this advice, Mr Dennis?'

'Yes, I do,' was the reply.

'Mr Dennis,' said Stokes, not best pleased by Stanford's opening gambit and blood pressure on the rise, 'do you fully understand the seriousness of your situation? This is a murder inquiry with the use of a firearm. Of course, your solicitor can advise you, but it's your decision, not his. You take the consequences later – not him. Surely you must appreciate that it's in your best interests to answer our questions?'

Stanford answered for his client. 'Thank you for your advice, Mr Stokes, but with respect, you really can't play for both sides. What is it they say? Never ask a barber if you need a haircut.'

Stokes didn't much care for Stanford's bruising analogy. 'Mr Stanford, I'm just making it absolutely clear to your client that, since he was arrested at the scene and has admitted to the killing, he should come clean and allow us to investigate everything fully – in his own interests.'

Here we go again – the usual patter, thought Stanford. But he wasn't going to allow himself to be drawn into some academic debate about the pros and cons of playing ball with the police in interview and merely answered, 'Can my client start reading his statement now, Mr Stokes, please?'

'Yes,' was the deflated response. What else could Stokes say? The interview would be played to a jury.

'Please start reading it, Mr Dennis,' said Stanford. 'I know it's very stressful for you, and if you want a break at any time I'm sure the officers will oblige. Won't you, Mr Stokes?' Stokes just nodded. Stanford was already playing to an invisible gallery.

Nervously, running his hands through his hair and taking a deep breath, Dennis began:

I wasn't born with a silver spoon in my mouth. My parents were poor. We lived in a two-bedroom council flat in Islington. I suffered a lot at school because I was small and overweight and I couldn't pronounce my 'r's properly. I think that's what made me so keen to succeed in life.

My father worked as a printer at the *Daily Express* and my mum as a cleaner there. We never had a car. My parents had never been on a holiday abroad and didn't even own a passport. But they were honest and law abiding. I did alright at school, never top of the class, but I was quite a good chess player and ended up being captain of the chess club at fifteen.

I left school at sixteen with four O-levels. My parents wanted the best for me and had saved a little bit to give me a good start. I was always keen on cooking and ate too much, probably as a comfort. They sent me to a cookery school in Crouch End as my dream had always been to run my own restaurant. I was there for over a year and turned into quite a decent cook. I got a job at a small French bistro in Muswell Hill. I began by washing plates and laying tables and doubling up as a waiter when the restaurant was busy, then later helping out with the cooking.

After eighteen months, I was sacked because I was caught taking home the leftovers without permission. Everybody was doing it, but the owner decided to make an example of me. My parents were horrified because I had lied to them and told them that this was one of the perks of the job and the owner didn't mind. But, sometimes, I was taking home more than just the leftovers.

I was now nineteen and getting any decent job in a restaurant without a reference was hopeless. I was so ashamed, as my parents had skimped and saved to send me on the cookery course. I was desperate to try and make something of my life and to get away from home – I had nothing to lose. So, I decided to forge two references from local restaurants in Islington and applied for a job in the kitchen on the Cunard Line and went for an interview in Southampton. Being fat, they could see I obviously liked my food, and my two letters were terrific forgeries prepared by an old school mate who was more than capable on the typewriter. At the end of the interview, they said they would check up on my references and let me know. I doubt they ever did because I got the job and spent eight years on seven different ships: first as a dog's body, then as a waiter and, eventually, as a cook, before reaching the giddy heights of sous chef. My time at sea was a real education as I met people from all different walks of life and saw so many interesting places.

Then I had a real stroke of luck. When I look back on it now, I think it was the only good thing that ever happened to me, workwise. Once, on the way back from New York, one of the passengers, who had a lovely wife and three children, always had his dinner in his suite and every night ordered an Arnold Bennett omelette as a first course. This was a speciality of mine and I used to bring it to his suite personally, together with the rest of the family's evening meal. It turned out he owned two restaurants in Shepherd's Bush in London and was about to open a third one in Notting Hill, specialising in Mediterranean cuisine. He offered me a job at a good salary and I jumped at it. I would be in charge of the kitchen.

So, now at twenty-seven, I had my own little one-bedroom flat near my parents in Islington and some money in the bank. His restaurants thrived and so did I. Ten years later, he made me the general manager for all his restaurants – all six of them! He also gave me a small shareholding in the company. How proud my parents were.

I married late at the age of thirty-nine and my wife Linda is a wonderful woman who deserves better. We have two boys, Donald and Damien, now aged eleven and thirteen. We are a very close family and I adore them all.

Some two years ago, I finally persuaded my parents to apply for passports and treated them to their first ever holiday abroad – ten days in Mallorca. But that turned out to be the worst thing I ever did. The night before their return flight, there was a fire on their floor in the hotel because some drunken idiot had fallen asleep and left his cigarette burning. The whole floor was ablaze. My parents' room was opposite his and they were burnt to death, together with five other holiday makers. Their charred remains were flown back to London and I had to identify them both at the morgue.

Dennis, clearly distressed, put down the pages he was reading from. Putting his head in his hands, he stared down at the table. 'Could I please have a glass of water? I just need a few minutes to recover.'

'Let's have a break for five minutes,' suggested Stokes, himself moved by what he had heard, although he couldn't begin to see what possible relevance it all had to turning up at the Bailey with a gun. The two officers left the room and Stanford poured them each a glass of water.

'How am I doing, Mr Stanford?' asked Dennis in a weak voice, once the door had been closed.

'Just fine. You've got a good tone to your voice, but you're speaking too fast – particularly at the painful bits. Don't be in such a hurry to get it over. Try and read a bit slower.'

Ten minutes later, the interview continued.

My boss was a really good man. He'd been born in Portugal and worked his way up himself in restaurants from nothing, so we had a bit in common. He gave me a month off from work to try and recover from the horror of my parents' death. By this time, me and my family had moved to a three-bedroom flat in a nicer part of Islington, and but for this tragedy everything was looking rosy. But I simply couldn't recover. I was drinking heavily and visiting casinos to try and escape from reality.

I returned to work a month later, but my boss could see I'd completely fallen apart. I was arriving smelling of whisky late at work every day, and I had lost the respect of the staff. The standard of the food and the service were really suffering. He let it ride for a few weeks before, in tears, he told me that we could not carry on like this together. He bought my shares off me for a handsome sum and even paid me three months' salary as well. He gave me a gold pocket watch as a leaving present for all my years of service. He told me to keep it for my two boys as an heirloom and never to sell it unless I really had to. I think it was worth quite a lot because his only hobby was collecting vintage pocket watches.

Well, I blew the handsome sum and my savings as well. My wife begged me to stop gambling, but I just couldn't. I was hooked and needed to escape as the thought of what had happened to my dear parents kept returning, time and time again, day in and day out, and all because I'd organised a holiday for them.

For months, I did nothing but drink and gamble and get home at about three in the morning. But, finally, I tried to pull myself together and took a job with an old school pal who ran an estate agency and who had never let me down. Actually, the same one who had forged the two letters for me before I got my job with Cunard years earlier. Anyway, after I had been working with him for about a year, I betrayed him and diverted three sales commissions into my own bank account as I was desperate to pay off some of my gambling debts. When he found out he sacked me – who could blame him.

Now we were in real financial trouble. We had our home, but it had a large mortgage on it. Linda threatened to leave me, but she still loved me and I never thought she would. She had to get a job to help keep us. She started working in a beauty salon in Kensington four days a week.

By now, my kids were no longer in private school, my wife was the only breadwinner and of course the mortgage was badly in arrears, plus I still had debts all over town. Linda said that they had to be paid off, even if we had to sell our home and move to a poorer area. She is a very proud lady and said she couldn't go on being ashamed to look her friends in the face.

And so it was I made the biggest mistake in my life – and I've made a few. I started asking around the casinos as to who might lend me some money. One of the other regulars at the Victoria Casino was obviously a criminal of some sort. We weren't really friends but often sat around talking. He opened up when he'd had a few drinks and told me how he'd invested in some form of underhand dealing, with wonderful returns of 400 per cent over three months. It seemed to work for him because he always had plenty of money, although he too was a big loser at the tables.

He told me if I could raise £50,000 cash he could turn it into £200,000 very quickly. He never gave me the details, and I didn't really want to know, although I had my suspicions what was going on. Of course, I didn't have the money, but he was so convincing that it was a sure thing that I began to believe him. Then I remembered that an old customer at the Notting Hill restaurant who I was still in contact with had needed money to pay for his daughter's wedding. He couldn't borrow it from the bank and had gone elsewhere. I rang him up and he gave me two names. I met the first, but he would only loan against the security of jewellery or a car and such. So, I tried the second, who was described as 'Bob Maynard from south London somewhere'. I rang the number, but it was dead. I mentioned the name to my mate at the casino and he gave me a look of horror. I remember his very words: 'You don't want to be getting into bed with Bob the Merc.' Anyway, I was so desperate that I kept on nagging. Finally, he said he would see what he could do to get his number. About a week later, he gave me a number, telling me that if I rang it someone would contact Maynard for me.

So I did. A meeting was eventually arranged in a restaurant in Eltham. Maynard looked the part: big, broad, shaved head and a flashy dresser. A real hard man. He always spoke in a whisper, as if he was afraid someone was listening, and you could hardly hear what he was saying. The long and short of it was that if I wanted to borrow £50,000, it would be at

10 per cent a month. I had already given some details about my situation when I spoke to his go-between on the phone. But when I met Maynard face to face, it was obvious he'd already made his enquiries about me. He knew I was married with two young kids, my wife's name and that she worked in Kensington. He made no bones about telling me that his customers always paid in full, sooner or later, and I was not such a fool as not to understand why. But it was all or nothing for me by then. The thought of easy money and repaying my huge debts blinded me as to what I was getting myself into. All I could see were my wife's red eyes and the shame in them.

Of course, there was no agreement in writing, but Maynard's last words to me were, 'I don't take any prisoners – understand?' Three days later, early on a Saturday morning, as promised, a motorbike arrived with a parcel – no signature required.

My newfound casino buddy met me at my local pub and took the money away, promising me £200,000 within three months at most. I was already working out who I was going to pay back with the £135,000 profit I'd be left with after repaying Maynard the £50,000, plus £15,000 interest.

Well, things didn't work out as planned. About two months later I heard that my casino buddy had been arrested for money laundering and was in prison. I wanted to visit him. I was desperate to recover at least my investment. But you can't go and see a prisoner unless he asks for you.

After the three months were up, I had to explain to Maynard that I couldn't pay. We met in a pub off the Walworth Road, south London. I asked for more time. I even told him the truth about what I'd done with the money. He didn't believe a word and thought it was just a cover story. 'Sell your home, mate,' was all he said. 'Don't blame me for this mess, you knew what you were getting yourself into.' He then asked how my kids were getting on at school. It brought me out in a cold sweat.

Six weeks later, we met again and I told him that he could do what he liked but I wasn't selling my home, it was all we had left. He stared at me and you could smell the evil in him. 'We'll see about that,' was all he said, and he left. I didn't take his veiled threats all that seriously. After all, what good would it do him to hurt me? It was money he was after. I prayed that he would take the loss in his stride and move on.

For two weeks nothing happened and I told my wife that Maynard must have written off the debt. She didn't believe it and wanted me to go to the police, but I had nothing, he hadn't directly threatened me.

Most days, I would take a long walk in the local park at Highbury Fields because I had no job and there was little else to do. One afternoon, I was just about to go back home when I saw two men walking towards me. I would say they were in their thirties. I thought nothing of it until they stopped right in front of me and asked me if my house was on the market yet, and shouldn't I be at home because my kids would be returning from school and my wife was still at work. They warned me that walking in the park alone was a risky business. After a few moments, they wished me a nice day and walked off.

Stupidly, I told this to my wife and she threatened that if I didn't go to the police she would take the kids and run away to her sister in Southport. The very next day I went to Islington Police Station. A young CID officer saw me and I told him about the threats, but of course I left out that I invested the monies I got from Maynard in some sort of crime. He told me he would discuss it with his boss and asked me to come back the next day.

This time, a detective inspector was with him. He was very understanding, but he said the police really didn't have a case against Maynard as he hadn't threatened me directly and the two men in the park could never be traced. Nor could a jury ever be sure they were connected to Maynard as I had so many other debts. They gave me an emergency number and told me to keep them informed if anything else happened.

The inspector knew exactly who Maynard was and called him a really bad egg. He even joked that he wasn't exactly known for enforcing his debts through the Royal Courts of Justice.

When I got home I didn't tell my wife the whole truth about my meeting with the police, nor about the emergency number. I was afraid she would take the kids and leave. I just told her the police didn't have a case, but that we shouldn't worry as these sorts of people wanted money not blood, and when they see anyone stand up to them they eventually back off. But I was afraid to open the front door at night, even to the pizza delivery man.

Three weeks went by and I was beginning to think that my nightmare was over, but of course it wasn't. One afternoon, the telephone rang just after 4.30. A pleasant voice on the other end said, 'Good afternoon, Mr Dennis, I thought you would like to know, we've picked up your kids outside school and we've bought them an ice cream and we're going to give them a lift home – such lovely boys – so polite. Don't worry, we'll have them home shortly. You're still at the same address, aren't you?' Then he hung up.

I was frantic with worry and rushed out the front door. My two boys were walking along the road towards me eating ice cream. There was no car to be seen. It turned out that nothing had happened and it was all lies about my boys being picked up. But the message was clear. They were watching and giving me a final warning.

I went around to the police station that night. This time, they called in an even more senior officer, named Glendenning. He told me that Maynard was a ruthless villain and always kept himself in the background when it came to the dirty work. As I was leaving, he put his hand on my shoulder and told me to leave it to them. The police wanted to catch Maynard red-handed and make it stick. If they swooped too early, and without hard evidence, it would come to nothing and they would be forced to release him without charge. He said they'd be watching my home. They wanted to bug my phone, but I flatly refused because I had hidden the ice cream episode from my wife and I feared if I had told her about the phone call it would have been the last straw, and she definitely would have left.

Two days later, Mr Glendenning rang me and asked me if it was OK to talk. Maynard had been arrested on an early morning raid at his home for blackmail and threats to kill. This was in connection with a completely different police inquiry to mine. Apparently, he had sat in the interview without saying a word. They had charged him all the same because they had a twelve-page statement from a witness. That was the good news. The bad news was that he'd been granted bail because the judge thought the prosecution had a pretty poor case since his witness statement was full of inconsistencies and he had previously been bankrupt. The officer tried to comfort me by saying that even a man like Maynard would heed the warning and it was likely to be the end of my troubles. He said that if anything else happened I should let him know immediately. He thought it was high time to tell my wife everything. I said I would think about it. But I never told her the full story. Anyway, he made it clear that the police would be keeping a close watch on Maynard and I could sleep easy. Maynard could well afford the loss.

I wanted to believe him but still found myself checking the locks at home three times a night. Any noise from the street after midnight gave me a real chill. My wife could tell I was a bundle of nerves and kept saying I was hiding something from her and that she had a right to know. I just said that my nerves were shattered but I would soon be OK. Of course, she never really believed me. It was terrible to see her distress. She cried herself to sleep every night. I could see our kids sensed something was badly wrong, but what could I say?

Dennis stopped reading again. 'Officer, I'm sorry, but can we have another short break. I'm feeling a bit faint, there's no air in this room.'

'Certainly,' replied Stokes, 'we'll leave the door open so

hopefully you can catch a breeze. Would you like a cup of tea, Mr Dennis?'

'That would be great, thank you.'

'How many sugars does your client take, Mr Stanford? I'm sure he's told you.'

'Three,' chanced Stanford, whilst trying to hide a smile.

As soon as the officers had left, Stanford put his forefinger to his lips to stop Dennis from speaking. The officers were just down the corridor. Fifteen minutes later, he called the officers back and Dennis, tea in hand, carried on with his tale:

The threatening letters from the building society were piling up. We were way behind and I could do absolutely nothing about it. Finally, we were left with no alternative but to put our flat on the market, and it was sold about a month later at a knockdown price.

After paying off the mortgage, we had virtually nothing left. We were now living in a small two-bedroom flat in Palmers Green, owned by my wife's boss, and only paying about half what the rent should have been, as a favour. We were living hand-to-mouth.

I got a job as a minicab driver and used to work sixteen hours a day to try to make ends meet. One day, my company received a call from a customer asking for me in particular. The customer said that I'd collected him a few weeks earlier from Heathrow Airport. I was told that I had to pick up a Mr Frank Thomas from the Spice Club in Brewer Street, Soho at 11.10 p.m. and drive him to Chelmsford. I was using an old

Mercedes E-Class that I was renting by the week. This was a good job and I was pleased to have it.

When I arrived at the club, two men were already waiting outside and told me to take them to the centre of Chelmsford. We drove through the city, onto the M25 and then the A12. It was a quiet drive, but after a while I found it a bit odd that the two men in the back were not talking much to each other. I started to look at them in my rear-view mirror. One of them eventually caught my eye and said in a flat tone, 'Do you recognise us?' Then it clicked and chilled me to the very bone. I was pretty sure they were the same two men in the park a couple of months earlier. I pretended I didn't know them, but they could see all too plainly that I was lying.

'Yes, you recognise us alright,' said the other man in the back, 'and we recognise you, Mr Dennis.' He added, 'Sold your home, eh? Taken the money and not paid your debts. Not a clever thing to do – ask your doctor, he'll tell you.' The other one then said, 'Not so much fun in Palmers Green, is it, Mr Dennis? Much nicer in Islington – don't you think?' My mouth went dry and it was a wonder that I could keep on driving in a straight line. By now, we were on the A12 and it was almost deserted. 'Pull over and stop,' the first one said. He seemed to be the boss. I was terrified and I thought they were going to kill me. 'Pull over now, Dennis,' he shouted. I had no alternative, although for a moment I thought of smashing the car and making a run for it, but I was even too scared to do that.

'Stay in your seat and switch off the engine,' was the next command. I felt like a robot and did as they said. The man on the nearside got out and climbed in the front next to me. Then, to my horror, he pulled out a gun from his jacket and waved it around in his hand. 'Want to play a little Russian roulette, Mr Dennis?' He looked deadly serious.

He turned to his mate in the back and said, 'Tell him what your favourite film is.' The reply came, 'Oh, *The Deer Hunter*, great Russian roulette scene.' 'Me too,' said the one with the gun. 'How about you, Mr Dennis? You've gambled on everything else – fancy a little Russian roulette?' I thought I was as good as dead. Then he put the gun to my temple and pulled the trigger. Nothing happened. I thought I was going to faint.

'OK, bad luck, let's give it a second shot,' he said and pulled the trigger again. Again, nothing. 'Oh, dear me,' he said calmly, 'let's try a third time.'

Suddenly, a car with its headlights flashing pulled up about twenty yards behind. I thought it must be the police or some do-gooder thinking we'd broken down. I couldn't believe my luck. But it didn't seem to bother the two men and they both casually got out of my car. Just as the man from the front was leaving, he leaned over and said, 'Two weeks, Mr Dennis, two weeks. The money plus interest in full, or you won't be ordering any more pizzas for your kids.'

Then came the strangest thing of all. As he was just about to walk away, he opened the passenger door and said, cool as you like, 'How much?' I had no idea what he meant. He repeated 'Yes. How much, Mr Dennis? The minicab fare?' I didn't know what to say, but before I could speak, he added, 'OK, let's give you a real nice tip and call it £100.' He pulled out a bundle of money and counted out five £20 notes, before tossing them onto the passenger seat. 'You see, we pay our debts, Mr Dennis – not like you. We won't be seeing each other again – or rather you won't be seeing us again – understand my meaning?'

Then they casually strolled off and got into the car behind, which sped off into the night. I think it was an Audi and that there was an N and an 8 in the number plate, but even that I'm not sure of.

I don't know how I got home in one piece. My heart was thumping and my mind racing. What to do? Maybe I should have driven to the nearest police station, but I feared if Maynard was arrested because of me I would certainly be killed, whether he was charged or not.

I wanted to give up my job, but then my wife would certainly know something terrible had happened, so I decided only to work daylight hours. Anyway, I doubted whether Maynard would use the same trick twice. But my wife could tell there was something terribly wrong. She had become very thin over the months and had lost well over a stone. She was on sleeping pills and tranquilisers as well.

Five days later, she left. The strain was unbearable for her and I don't blame her. I found a note at home, which is too personal and hurts me too much to repeat here. She took the boys with her. I pleaded with her on the phone to come back. I missed her and my boys terribly and I broke down each time I spoke to them on the phone. But in my heart of hearts I wanted her to refuse, as I was afraid for their safety. I was even afraid to visit her at her sister's up north in case I was being followed. I knew she wasn't coming back until I'd cleaned up my mess.

But what could I do? To go to the police again might easily make matters worse. To let Maynard kill me? I was almost past caring, but I was not going to let him hurt my boys or my wife, and going to the police again might end up being a fatal mistake.

Well, I decided to make a final effort to settle the matter once and for all. I only had one valuable possession left – the gold pocket watch given to me by my old boss before we parted. It was the last thing in the world that I ever wanted to sell. I wanted to leave it for my boys. But I was left with no choice and sold it in a hurry for £8,000 cash. I'm sure it was worth far more, but I couldn't put it up for auction and wait three months to be paid out. I would give Maynard £6,000 from the sale, which, of course, was a fraction of what I owed him, and keep the other £2,000 to help make ends meet. I needed that money.

I found out where Maynard lived. I went round on a Sunday morning because I was pretty sure he'd be in. If he was out, I was going to ask anyone who answered the door what time he'd be returning.

I drove to his home in Dulwich with the £6,000 packed in £1,000 bundles of £50 notes. His home was like a fortress: security gates, cameras, dogs. When I rang the bell, he came out and we ended up talking through the locked gates. He was shocked to see me and told me that I had taken a bloody liberty coming around to his home and asked me how the hell I knew where he lived anyway. I tried to act strong and said,

'Never mind that. I'm not having any more of your threats. Here's £6,000 and that's it.' He took the money, but then he said, 'This is a piss in the ocean to what you owe me. You've got until next Thursday to bring me the rest or you'll be a goner. And I know your wife and boys have left you, but I'll find them and when I do... Well, the less said the better. I don't want to lose my appetite for my Sunday roast!' He warned me that if I went to the police, my wife and kids would go missing – never to be seen again. And then, just as I was leaving, he said, 'Next Thursday, at the latest – Friday's too late. I won't be in anyway. I've got a short visit to the Old Bailey – they're dropping a couple of charges against me. My brief tells me that the prosecution's star witness has suddenly taken a keen interest in his own health.' He didn't have to explain what he meant – it was all too horribly clear.

You might call what I did revenge and say that I shouldn't have taken the law into my own hands. But I couldn't just stand by waiting for some terrible disaster to hit my family. What would you have done if you were me? I really had no other choice.

The rest you already know.

'Anything to add?' asked Stokes, matter-of-factly. He'd heard a few sad stories in his time and viewed them all with the deepest suspicion.

Stanford answered firmly on behalf of his client, 'Nope, that's it, thank you.'

'Right,' said Stokes, 'we'll take a break and change the disc. There's a good number of points raised in your client's statement which I'd like to discuss with my officers before we continue. Twelve noon OK with you, Mr Stanford?'

'Fine.'

'I'll keep his original statement and give you a copy,' added Stokes.

'Of course,' said Stanford. 'But, shouldn't we be giving the original an exhibit number, Mr Stokes? We don't want to be losing it – do we?'

'NW/1,' was the begrudging reply from Stokes as he switched off the CD recorder. 'Happy now, Mr Stanford?'

'Verging on ecstatic!'

Chapter 8

A Frustrating Affair

‘You know what that wily bastard Stanford's just done?’ fumed Stokes. 'He's running rings around us, and what with that bloody camera in the room, I had no option but to sit there like a cold plate of baked beans and take it.'

'Ah, but he does it so politely,' said DI Worthington, adding salt to the wound, as they both queued for a much-needed coffee in the canteen.

'That's the worst of it,' replied Stokes. 'He deserves an Oscar for the Best Farce Production – does he get my goat. You know what this means? When we get this case into the Bailey, we, the prosecution, will have to introduce Dennis's statement as part of *our* case. We'll have to play this David versus Goliath pantomime of a video to the jury and give each member a transcript and all. There won't be a dry eye in the house. And now, in our next interview, we won't get a word out of him. And I'll give you odds of 10:1 that at the trial Dennis will trot out the old cliché, "Well, what's the point of having a solicitor if you don't take his advice – I've never been arrested before." I can hear it already. Well, there you have it. Thank the Lord I'm retiring in nine months' time. I've been on the job too long – far too long. And what was that imbecile of a custody officer doing giving a pen and paper to a murder suspect? Look where it's got us,' said Stokes. 'And what the hell did I have to listen to his whole life story for – four O-levels, good chess player, Arnold Bennett omelettes – I ask you?' he added, shaking his head angrily before sighing.

'But let's stop feeling sorry for ourselves and get down to brass tacks,' said Stokes, whilst ordering a bar of Milky Way. 'Get me this Glendenning fellow on the phone – I'm going to roast him alive. His team were meant to be watching Dennis for his own safety. How the hell does he roll up at the Bailey and blow Maynard away without them knowing he's there? That's going to look great in court. And make me a copy of Dennis's statement; I want to mark it up before our next interview,' added Stokes through a mouthful of chocolate, whilst Worthington was eyeing up the spaghetti Bolognese for an early lunch. 'And whilst you're at it, fetch me some headache tablets – strong ones. Oh yes, and before I forget. Get onto the minicab company Dennis was working for, you've got the details in the paperwork from his home. I want the date of his so-called trip to Chelmsford and the Russian roulette nonsense checked out on the ANPR to see if the cameras picked up his car's number plates along the way. If they didn't, we've got him by the balls for sure – it'll blow his whole defence to pieces!'

* * *

At noon, as arranged, the interview continued. Dennis, slumped in his chair, looked a spent force. Stanford wanted it over as soon as possible, but Stokes, now with his shirt sleeves rolled up, tie and jacket removed, was ready for business. Dennis had had his say; now Stokes would have his. 'Before I start, Mr Dennis, let me say we both sympathise with the tragic loss of your parents and I won't be asking you any questions about your early life.' Dennis nodded his thanks. Then he started giving Dennis a grilling.

'Where did you get the gun?' – No reply.

'Have you ever handled a gun before?' – No reply.

'Did you practise with it before you took it to the Old Bailey?' – No reply.

'How many bullets came with the gun?' – No reply.

'Assuming there were fifty in the box originally, what happened to the missing ten bullets?' – No reply.

'Do you think it's in your best interests just to read out your statement and then not to answer any questions?' – No reply.

'What have you got to hide by not answering our questions?' – No reply.

'How did you find out where Maynard lived?' – No reply.

'Why didn't you go to the police immediately on the night when you claim you were threatened with a gun on the A12? Surely that would have been in your best interests?' – No reply.

'What crime did you think your investment of £50,000 was going to be used for? Or do you actually know and you're simply not telling us the truth in your statement about this?' – No reply.

'What's the name of your casino buddy with whom you claim you invested £50,000? What prison is he in?' – No reply.

'Why did you stop your written account before the shooting itself?' – No reply.

'Where did you get the idea to dress up as a barrister?' – No reply.

'Besides killing Maynard, you had several other options: going to the police, moving out of London or even moving abroad, don't you agree?' – No reply.

'Did you think you had the right to take the law into your own hands?' – No reply.

'Did you tell your wife of your intentions? Or were you afraid to because you knew she would stop you and might go to the police herself?' – No reply.

'Why did you need to fire two shots? Did you mean to make sure you killed him?' – No reply.

'When we speak to your wife, will she be able to confirm your account of earlier events?' – No reply.

And finally:

'Who recommended Mr Stanford to act as your solicitor?'

Stanford couldn't let this one pass. 'How's that question relevant to innocence or guilt, Mr Stokes?'

'Well, Mr Stanford, I don't mean this discourteously,' replied Stokes, trying his best to appear a little reticent, 'but your firm is well known for acting for – er – some of the less-savoury members of our society. Perhaps the person who recommended you to Mr Dennis also helped supply him with the gun and bullets, or Maynard's address, or both.'

'An interesting proposition, Mr Stokes. Whom do you suggest he instructs if not a criminal lawyer – a dentist?'

Two hours later, Dennis was produced before the custody sergeant. The charges of murder and the firearm offences were read out to him, to which he replied in a crestfallen whisper, 'I really had no other choice.'

Chapter 9

What's in a Name

_____

1956
___

It was a Friday evening, and the five-year-old boy was in bed asleep, dreaming about owning a dog like Lassie. His father had promised him one for his sixth birthday, which was eight months away. He couldn't wait. His mother was in the front room of their little two-bedroom house, knitting him a thick navy-blue pullover for the winter. His father had gone across the street to the local pub, as he always did on a Friday night after a hard week's work.

It was a lovely summer's evening, and the little boy had his bedroom window open. The street noise never bothered him. When he couldn't get to sleep it comforted him to know that other people besides him were still awake.

But that night, there seemed to be more noise than usual and it woke him up. He heard shouting and screaming from the street outside. He crept out of bed and stood staring out the window. He couldn't believe what he saw. Tears streamed down his cheeks and he ran out of the room crying, 'Mummy, Mummy!'

It was a night that he would never forget.

*   *   *

Saturday morning. Jake was up early to make his monthly visit to Portobello Road Market, his jacket stuffed with crisp £50 notes. There, he would ease the misery of others at street corners; buying up jewellery and watches from the down and outs and bargaining away at the antique furniture shops for the odd piece of Chippendale.

His phone rang. It was Ernie. 'As you asked, Jake, I've contacted my man at the Yard and we'll have the killer's name by late this afternoon.' Curious as Jake was to know, he had a more important matter at hand – namely, haggling with a young Polish girl, who looked like she could do with some ready cash, over what he could plainly see was a magnificent pearl necklace.

'How much do you want for it?' asked Jake, trying not to look much interested.

'I don't know,' she stuttered. 'How much do you think it's worth?'

'Ma'am,' said Jake, putting on his best American drawl, 'I can't be a buyer and a seller – if it ain't got a price, it ain't for sale.' It was a trick that never failed.

'£1,200?' she ventured, finally having plucked up the courage. Jake puffed and turned his eyes towards heaven. Another cheap trick.

'Nice piece, but the pearls are not really top class,' lied Jake, whilst examining the necklace as if it was a bunch of overripe bananas – his next gaslighting trick. '£750,' he offered decisively, whilst removing a wad of notes from his donkey jacket to give her the flavour. 'Take it or leave it' – Jake's epilogue.

She took it.

That afternoon, Jake was at White Hart Lane with his son, Jake Jr, to watch Spurs play the old enemy, Arsenal. Spurs were 2–1 up with fifteen minutes left to play. The ground was rocking to 'When the Spurs Go Marching In', and Jake and his son were in great voice. Having finished singing, he was busy telling all around his views about his team's latest signing ('45 million quid and can't kick with his left foot!'), when his phone rang. It was Ernie again.

'Dennis, that's the fella's name – I've never heard of him.'

'What's that, I can hardly hear a word you're saying, Ernie. I'm at the Spurs – I'll ring you back when I get home.' What did Jake care what the killer's name was? Bob the Merc was dead and Spurs were winning. What more could he ask of life?

Later that afternoon, he was stretched out in front of his TV at home, watching *The Dam Busters*, for at least the thirtieth time, and occasionally drifting off, with Greaves and Gilzean snoozing at his feet. What was that hero's name that Ernie had told him? It began with a D and had an E lurking in it somewhere, was all he could remember.

Denton? Dennard? Dennison? Dennis?

He sat up with a jolt and started sweating. Grabbing his phone, he rang Ernie. 'The fella who shot Bob, what's his name again?'

'Dennis.'

Jake started to sweat a bit more. 'What's his first name?'

'David.'

'How old is he?'

'In his early fifties, I think. Why? Do you know him?'

'Have a nice evening Ernie – I won't be.'

He switched off the TV and poured himself a stiff bourbon.

Chapter 10

Such Much!

1958

The little boy was now seven years old and not so little any more. He lived with his mum in a council flat near Tower Bridge. He was always in trouble at school for fighting, and he was teased because he was so big and clumsy for his age, no good at sport and because he wore a pair of state shoes, which meant you were really, really poor. He only had one shirt for school and his mum would lovingly wash and iron it every night.

She worked part-time in the local second-hand bookshop and ironed shirts at night for locals to help make ends meet. Each weekday, she would walk him a mile to school and would always be there waiting, come rain or shine, at 4 p.m. sharp, to pick him up, with a packet of Spangles or pear drops. Friday was his favourite day as he would be treated to a Mars bar.

He wasn't very good at his lessons, except for English. He had been such a lonely boy that he had sought solace in books. How proud his mum had been when he came home one day with a water pistol he'd won for coming top of the class in the spelling quiz.

73

He used to fall asleep each night listening to a lullaby from his mum. Then she'd leave the light on in the narrow corridor dividing their rooms. In the middle of the night, he'd creep into the warmth of his mum's bed.

He never had a dog to keep him company.

* * *

'Is that Mr Stanford's office?'

'Yes, it is,' Joanne answered on the intercom.

'Well, I've come to see Mr Stanford.'

'Is he expecting you?'

'No, he certainly isn't,' Jake barked into the speaker. Jake didn't make appointments, any more than he did queuing.

'Well, you'd better come up anyway.'

Jake arrived on the fourth floor about ten minutes later. The lift was out of order. He looked like he'd just run a marathon. 'A glass of water, love, please,' he croaked. 'As you can see, I'm not exactly in Olympic shape at present.'

Joanne doubted he ever had been, what with his pot belly hanging half out of his short-sleeved shirt, almost horizontally. She deposited him in the waiting room, where he slumped gracelessly but gratefully into a leather armchair.

'I'll ask Mr Stanford if he can see you.'

'You do that, love. And tell him it's worth his while. It's about this Dennis caper.'

'And your name, please?'

'Davenport's the name – Jack Davenport.'

Joanne found Stanford in his office poring over a selection of photographs of lorries coming and going at a bonded warehouse in Walthamstow, with smuggled spirits onboard. He had his phone on loudspeaker and was talking to a lady with a strong Chinese accent.

'You top criminal lawyer, London?' the voice on the phone enquired.

'That's not for me to say, madam.'

'I need top criminal lawyer, London. You do common assault cases?'

'Hard to make a living doing common assault cases, madam.'

'I tell you my story,' she continued, undeterred by Stanford's apathy. 'I have penthouse in Chelsea Harbour.'

'Oh, yes,' cut in Stanford, finally showing some interest. 'I definitely specialise in common assault cases. It's very important we meet today – 4 o'clock this afternoon, madam?'

'Adrian, there's a gentleman waiting to see you,' said Joanne once the call had ended. 'I know he doesn't have an appointment, but he told me it's to do with the Dennis case.'

'Is it, now! What's he look like?'

'Large, very large, probably in his sixties. Overweight – enormous stomach. Wearing shorts and a shirt, two sizes too small for him, and a big Rolex on his wrist.' Joanne had learnt to be observant.

'So, I presume it's not Chief Superintendent Stokes, then?' joked Stanford. 'What's his name?'

'Jack Davenport,' replied Joanne.

Stanford looked surprised. 'Well, well, what an honour.

Mr Big in person. I wonder what he wants. I think I'll go and look at him myself.' Stanford was, as ever, a cautious man. Better to size such a man up first and then decide on a plan of action.

A few moments later, Stanford entered the waiting room. Jake had made a reasonable recovery, and his face was stuck into a glossy holiday magazine. He looked up and was first to speak. 'Never go on a cruise, Mr Stanford. Mark my words, you're stuck with the same crowd for days and it's potluck if they're your sort. You have to pay it all upfront and, worst of all, it attracts the nosey types who can't wait to ask you your business. I tell them, "I mind my own business and I suggest you do the same!"' Jake paused before continuing with his mini lecture. 'Yes, and I'm giving you this advice for free, which is something I guess you don't know very much about,' he sniggered. 'The name's Davenport – Jack Davenport,' he stated, James Bond style, whilst rising to his feet and holding out his giant right paw. 'But you can call me Jake – anyone who's anyone will tell you who I am. Anyway, I've come to see you about Bob the Merc's case.'

Adrian was tempted to respond that unfortunately Bob the Merc didn't have a case, on account of his being decidedly dead, but restrained himself, as he didn't yet know his surprise visitor's agenda. 'Come in to my office.'

'Well, I'm a man of few words, Mr Stanford, so I'll get to the point,' said Jake as he lowered himself into an armchair, having first nosily looked around Stanford's large office, taking in the oak-panelled walls, the drinks cabinet, the rosewood desk sporting an oversized burgundy leather pad and a few too many files; there to convince any new client that the lawyer had plenty of work, and not to bargain with him over his hourly rate.

'I've made a few enquiries, as I always do, and I understand you're Dennis's brief,' said Jake.

'Correct.'

'I guess the case is going to cost a pretty penny, what with your fancy offices and all.'

'Correct again.'

'Got the money for his trial yet?'

'Why do you want to know?'

'It's like this. Me and some of the boys are not averse to a bit of charity for a worthy cause. We haven't completely given up our membership of the human race – so here I am. What I want to know is how's Dennis going to pay for his case? I know you don't do any of this legal-aid-feeble-paid nonsense. I don't want any sleepless nights because I haven't done my duty. As you might have guessed by now, Mr Stanford, I'm no angel from heaven and I'm no Rockefeller either – I'm not caked up, but what's right is right. Bob the Merc was no friend of mine. I won't be carrying his coffin at the funeral. Your client needs the best. We don't want him rotting in prison for the next thirty years because he's been sold down the river by some second-rate brief at the Bailey.'

'Very reassuring.'

'And, as I've said, I've put out a few feelers. You acted for an old mate of mine, Ronnie Tomkins, a couple of years ago, and you got him out of a real bit of *stuch* for giving his mother-in-law a couple of slaps. He swears by you, calls you Stan the Man.'

'Ah, yes, I remember it well. The poor woman was in a coma for three days. Amazing what damage a couple of slaps can do.'

'Yes,' Jake continued. 'And talking about damage, I know Dennis is skint. What's the damage going to be?'

'Damage?' quizzed Stanford.

'Yes, Mr Stanford. And don't start adding on any VAT either. We will be paying in holding-folding – no receipts necessary, *comprende*?'

Stanford *comprended* only too well and decided to take a strong line. 'Now, Mr Davenport, let me tell you my position. The situation with the funds, I admit, is all a bit up in the air at present. Your hero has a few relatives who might chip in, when push comes to shove, although personally I doubt it. And anyway, what they can offer is not going to cut much ice.'

'How much all in?' interrupted Jake, impatiently. 'No extras, all upfront. Give me your best shot so that I can report back to the boys and remind them of their roots.'

Stanford pondered. 'Alright, I will. Top QC, junior and me: £250,000 all in,' before adding emphatically, 'plus VAT.'

'How much?'

'Such much!'

Jake's eczema started itching. 'Three hundred large – Jesus, I'll have to sell my Bentley – I might even have to get a job. I tell you what, do the case on legal aid and I'll give you a lumpy bonus if he gets off. How 'bout that?'

'Sorry, not interested, Mr Davenport. First, it's against our rules. Secondly, I can't see him getting off. And thirdly, as you already know, I don't do legal aid cases.'

'Never?'

'Never.'

'So, what happens if some poor bastard with a worthy cause comes your way?'

'I'm afraid I would send him and his worthy cause on his

way. Anyway, shooting someone dead in cold blood is hardly a worthy cause. This is a business, not a charity.'

'So, be charitable for once, Mr Stanford.'

Stanford could see he wasn't getting his point home. 'Do you like cowboy films, Mr Davenport?'

'Love them.'

'OK, so it's like this. Sitting Bull is riding on the plains. His wife is walking behind him in the searing heat. He's approached by a cowboy he knows, who says, "Hey, Chief – how come in a heatwave like this you're riding your horse and your wife has to walk?" Sitting Bull gives the cowboy a look like he's deranged, shrugs his shoulders and says, "She ain't got no horse!"'

Finally, Stanford had got his message through. There was a long, silent standoff, with Jake shaking his head in disbelief at the price of injustice. 'Let's call it £200,000 all in, and I'll see what I can do.'

Stanford recognised a poor bluff when he saw one. 'No, let's call it £300,000, Mr Davenport, and you'll dine out on the kudos for years to come. You'll be the toast of your manor.' Kudos was not a word which featured in Jake's everyday vocabulary, but the point was not entirely lost on him.

With difficulty, Jake raised his bulky frame from the armchair and started pacing around the room. Finally, he spoke. 'You're a hard man, Mr Stanford. I could do with you in my team – and that's for sure.' They started staring at one another, each giving the other the power of silence treatment. Jake was first to crack. 'OK, OK, I'll see what I can do – no promises, mind. I'll be back with my answer in a couple of weeks, max. Let's hope your lift's working by then, as I may have something very heavy with me.'

'Yes, a heavy cheque will do nicely, Mr Davenport.'

Jake failed to see the funny side. He didn't do cheques. 'But, if there's a deal, we'll want the best mouthpiece money can buy. We'll want a stallion, so don't bother looking around in the donkey corral. No has-been, no wannabe, no double-barrelled ex-prosecution la-di-dah merchant, and no water-carrier either. We'll want somebody real lively. Do we understand each other, Mr Stanford?'

'We certainly do, Mr Davenport, we most certainly do.'

Chapter 11

What Price Salvation?

The boy was getting dressed for school. His mum always laid out his breakfast on the kitchen table ready for him. Frosties and a sliced banana and a wrapped-up peanut-butter sandwich for lunch.

But on this morning, the table is bare – except for a letter.

* * *

'So, let's get down to business, boys.' Jake pulled the cognac bottle towards him and poured himself an unhealthy dose.

As usual, it had been an excellent dinner at Luca's on the Old Brompton Road. Jake was a regular on Friday nights with his team – lads' night out. For some twelve years, his ample frame had occupied the corner seat, at a corner table. He was, without doubt, their best customer. He had become a regular after reading that whenever Pavarotti had been in town he rarely dined anywhere else. Jake, therefore, assumed that Luca's must serve what he chose to call 'proper portions'. Two years earlier, to celebrate Jake's ten-year patronage, a dish had been named in his honour: *Nodino Grande da Giocomo*. It was an exquisitely flavoured veal chop large enough to feed a pride of lions. He and his cronies ate heartily, drank nothing but Cervaro, Tignanello and Hine Antique and Jake never bothered to check the bill – that was for cheapskates. And, oh yes, he always paid in cash, usually with a mixture of foreign currency thrown in, and Luca the owner never daring to question Big Jake's suggestion as to the appropriate exchange rate.

Actually, the real name of the restaurant was Il Consigliere. Luca had good reason to call it that – his father had been one. But, when Luca turned sixteen, over to England he went. His father was certainly not having him in the family business, or anywhere near it. Anyway, the name was good for trade – how the public love the scent of Italian danger; albeit that the only danger on view at Il Consigliere was the prices. Dining there was an expensive thrill. Jake never called the restaurant by its real name – he couldn't pronounce it properly anyway. To him, and any other cognoscenti, it was simply and unmistakably Luca's.

The air conditioning in Il Consigliere was at best variable – in winter you'd cook and in summer you'd freeze. But what did it matter? The atmosphere was terrific and the noise level stratospheric – it rocked. No one need concern themself as to whether their conversation would be overheard; you were lucky if you could hear yourself speak. The restaurant was permanently packed. Dining there was not a meal but a banquet. If you hadn't a reservation, don't bother turning up. Unless your name happened to be Jack Davenport.

Il Consigliere had been open for donkey's years. It had the personal touch. Luca waiting to greet you as if you were a long-lost friend returning from a year's safari and the heady aroma of basil, rosemary and garlic the moment you entered set the trailer as to what lay ahead. The speciality pasta dishes cooked at your table, the trolley of desserts being wheeled around – both, of course, major attractions to Jake. The round tables, the oak carver chairs, the crisp white tablecloths and serviettes, the scarlet-red wallpaper all blended seamlessly with the scratchy vintage recordings of Caruso, the power of Pavarotti and the molasses crooning of Dean Martin playing in the background, accompanied by the harmonies of the hirsute Italian waiters, who patrolled the tables making sure glasses were never empty.

But the standout features were the oil paintings on the walls. They were all related to cinema legends with an Italian flavour. From Mastroianni and De Sica, Pacino and De Niro, to the cur-vaceous beauties, Loren, Cardinale and Lollobrigida. Jake called them his *bits on the side*. Unsurprisingly, each painting had a price tag underneath – Jake's idea, and for which Luca gave him half the profits. The largest (and most expensive) painting hung behind Jake's chair: the scene in *The Godfather* where Brando tells Pacino, 'Listen, whoever comes to you with this Barzini meeting, he's the traitor.' Jake knew all about traitors. He had no problem replacing any of the purchased paintings; Jake had arranged the services of a master Spanish forger in Fulham, whom he'd nicknamed Speedy Gonzales. One week after a sale, the same painting was back on view – usually at an even higher price to reflect demand. Jake's study at home was crammed with the pictures. Not that he studied much there, except the colour of the wrapper on a fresh box of Cohibas or the label on a bottle of old Macallan.

But this particular night out was a Tuesday, not a Friday, and the other five diners at the table were no longer members of his team. Now, they each had their own teams. Their achievements would never be listed in *Who's Who*, but in the criminal corridors of power they were all household names.

Five days earlier, Jake had rung each one of them with a dinner invitation. He had a unique way of requesting the company of others:

Tuesday night – 8 p.m. – Luca's – be there – I don't give a toss if your daughter's getting married or your wife's in intensive care – be there anyway.

Truly a villain's three-line whip. As expected, the turnout was 100 per cent. The six of them sat huddled at his table, Jake's formidable frame presiding.

'Now, I know you boys are all thinking that there's no such thing as a free meal, and I'm sorry to tell you you're absolutely spot on,' began Jake, finally taking the plunge on hearing Caruso's 'O Lola' playing softly in the background, whilst Luca cleared the dessert plates of homemade tiramisu and zabaglione. 'So, let me get the elephant out of the room and put you out of your misery. Bob the Merc's caught a bullet or two. Personally, I celebrated the occasion with a bottle of Krug, and last Sunday found me in church for the first time in twenty years, offering prayers of thanks. My missus, God bless her, thinks I've finally gone straight. She's plonked her grandfather's copy of the Bible on my bedside table. But, in a way, she's hit the nail right on the head and let me tell you why. There's a podgy little fella called Dennis nicked for Bob's murder and caught red-handed to bargain. Not enough to shoot him dead, he does it outside the Bailey. Now, this fella's looking at a serious amount of porridge and I don't like it. No, I don't like it one little bit. We all know that Bob the Merc was a real nasty bit of goods, and frankly he's been a pebble in my shoe since I came out of Borstal. Well, now he's brown bread and let's all toast to that.' No one appreciated the accidental pun, but they all raised their cognac glasses and wet their throats.

'Dennis has a wife and two kids and we're going to help him. If there's anyone here who thinks otherwise, let him say so right here and now.' No one moved a muscle – no one dared to. But all five listeners started to sweat – charitable donations were not their forte.

'Last week I went to see his fancy brief at his fancy office in the West End and we had a nice little chat about the cost. But you boys needn't worry because he's got the money for his trial.'

This was indeed good news and well received by Jake's five guests, who started to breathe a little easier.

'Yes,' continued Jake, now in full flow. 'We can all relax because he's got all the money he needs.' Jake poured himself a second cognac before continuing. 'It's in our pockets!' The words rang in the ears of his guests like a shrill unstoppable fire alarm. They were fearing the worst and Jake hadn't disappointed them. 'Three hundred large, that's £50,000 each – cheap at the price for a ticket to heaven.' Not a murmur from his guests.

'And another thing,' added Jake, to pre-empt any sickening

attempt at mitigating circumstances. 'I don't want any bollocks that you can't afford it right now, that your wife has her heart set on a new kitchen or that your money's tied up with the Albanians. Let's call it the price of redemption, so you can all put your heads peacefully on your pillows tonight and dream of angels for the first time in your miserable lives – won't that be a relief?'

'But, Jake, he's dead meat from what I've seen on TV,' butted in Franky, the eldest of Jake's former team and now their self-elected spokesman.

'That's why I went to church last Sunday,' retorted Jake. 'You should try it yourself, Franky. Not that one visit will cut you much slack with what you've been up to lately: blackmailing that Cabinet minister over his taste for schoolgirls.' That shut Franky up.

'I've got my reasons, but that's none of your bloody business,' Jake continued. 'You're each in debt to me from years ago for way over fifty grand. I'm calling in my markers on you here and now, and then we'll be quits. Rake in your loans; mortgage your villas in Marbella; visit casinos and change up your unholy stashes of €500 notes; cancel your Mediterranean cruises with your floozies; put your wives and daughters out on the streets for all I care. I don't give a monkey's what you do, but I want the money by noon Sunday, resting snugly in my safe at home – in full. Remember the old days – you've all drunk deep at my well.' Jake was finished with his piece.

Then, abruptly, leaving his guests reeling, Jake stood up and ambled into the kitchen as if he owned the business, looking for Mama, who was personally responsible for cooking any dish that entered his cavernous mouth. Kissing her warmly and wetly on both cheeks, he slipped $300 into her apron pocket whilst mumbling something about treating herself to a well-deserved new coat for Easter.

'Luca, the bill if you please,' he called out in a satisfied, almost melodic air, as he waltzed back to his table whilst removing an indecent bundle of mixed currency from his back pocket. 'And remember, as always – no VAT!'

Chapter 12

Enter *The Man to See*

On the same Tuesday evening that Jake was reminding his former cronies of their roots, one Patrick 'The Edge' Gorman QC was on the other side of town, delivering a *Facts of Life*-style lecture at the London School of Economics.

'There's a killer sleeping peacefully in each and every one of us – anybody who disagrees, raise your hand.' Some 150 hands flew up in the air in a hurry.

Gorman cast his eyes around his shocked audience, pleased to note that he had their rapt attention. *Not a bad opening gambit*, he thought to himself. He'd never had any real appetite to perform this cabaret in the first place, but here he was and all because three months earlier he'd successfully defended a student accused of sexual assault by being a little too familiar with a rather attractive jurisprudence lecturer after a tutorial. The boy's super-rich father was a governor at his son's university and wouldn't take *no* for an answer. Three times Gorman had politely declined, and three times the stakes went up, until Gorman persuaded himself that even he had his price.

Unsurprisingly, the old theatre in the college was packed,

partly because of the emotive posters planted all over the college under the heading 'The criminal within us all – an evening with the legendary defender Patrick Gorman QC', but mainly because the small-print read: 'To be followed by a champagne reception'. This, of course, provided a sure-fire guarantee that no one would be slipping out early.

'Yes, there's a killer lurking in all of us,' Gorman repeated, undeterred, as if he were addressing an Old Bailey jury. Then he looked around for a suitable case for treatment. 'You, young man,' he called out, pointing at a skinny, bespeckled, naïve but academic-looking fellow sitting in the front row, pen and notepad eagerly at the ready. 'So, you're incapable of killing anyone under any circumstances, are you?'

'Definitely,' was the immediate, indignant response.

Gorman allowed himself the hint of a smile. He'd picked the right target.

'Got a girlfriend?'

'Not at the moment, unfortunately.'

'Well, let's face it, that's understandable.' Laughter all around.

'What's your name, my good fellow?' asked Gorman, now adopting a bedside manner to make amends for his unkind quip.

'Douglas.'

'Well, Mr Douglas Do-Right, stretch your imagination and let's say you did have a girlfriend. I know it's unrealistic, but just for the sake of argument – OK?' More laughter, whilst Douglas bowed his head and nodded. What else could he do?

'And let's imagine you're crazy about her. She's gorgeous, sympathetic, intelligent and even cooks you a hot meal every night when you arrive back at the flat you share, no doubt in your particular case you having been burning the midnight oil in the law library. And, to your horror, you find her stark naked, tied down on your bed, bleeding from her nose and bruised around her eyes. She's gagged, terrified and being raped. What would you do?'

'I'd call the police and let the law take its course,' squeaked Douglas.

'Would you indeed! OK, and suppose, to add insult to injury, the rapist is in your year and tells you to piss off and that your girlfriend's a dirty whore who's been giving him the eye for weeks and what she needs is a real man, not a boy?'

Now Douglas sat bolt upright. Four hundred eyes gazed at him in anticipation, but his lips remained sealed.

Gorman decided to turn up the heat a little. 'Your sweetheart, your one and only, being brutally raped in your own bedroom, and you're being treated with derision – nay, like a piece of shit who is boxing way above his weight – you're going to call the police, are you? Your blood's boiling and you want revenge and right now. What are you going to do?'

Finally, Douglas found his voice, and a loud one at that. 'I'm going to grab my cricket bat and smash the bounder over the head with it – then I'm going to get you to defend me!'

At a stroke, the boy had become a man, and many in the audience rose to their feet cheering, clapping and banging their chairs in solid support.

'A wise choice, if I say so myself,' said Gorman once the applause had subsided. 'Got a rich father?' Gorman just couldn't resist it.

Douglas reddened visibly. 'He's a stockbroker, but I doubt he'll be a rich one by the time you're finished with him.' That put Gorman in his place and he had to suffer the loudest applause of the evening.

'Good on ya, Douglas, I've been asking for that – we'll make a barrister out of you yet,' replied Gorman, good-naturedly. 'Now, let's take that vote again. All those who agree that there's a killer dormant in each one of us – stand up. All those who disagree – stay seated.'

Gorman stared around, well pleased with his powers of persuasion.

It was a close call.

'Now,' said Gorman, well aware that he had his audience virtually brainwashed. 'Before I move on to the sordid subject of blackmail, let's see if I can whet your appetite for it. Hands up those of you in favour of moving the champagne reception forward and we have it right here and now – whilst I'm speaking.'

The verdict was unanimous.

* * *

Patrick Gorman QC might eventually pass away from any one of a hundred diseases, but his dying from overwork would attract extremely long odds.

He came from a lower middle-class background. His parents were fortunate to obtain a council flat in Swiss Cottage, so he saw the good life all around, which gave him some ambition, as long as not too much hard work was required.

His success as a barrister was not just because he was bright, but because he was quick-witted and had a razor-sharp sense of humour. More important than both, he was popular and clubbable: a guaranteed route to success at the Bar, without the need to adopt some hyphenated surname designed to deceive all around that you can trace your family roots further back than Barking High Street. But if Big Jake remembered his roots, so did Patrick Gorman, and his local fishmonger was treated with the same respect as any judge he might find himself seated next to at some dreary legal dinner.

He'd been lucky all his life. Born clever, good schooling, boyish face into middle age. But his biggest break was to have a pupil master who was regularly led by the legendary Victor Drummond QC, so he saw the great man in action in numerous trials. If you couldn't succeed at the Bar after walking in his shadow for a year, you were a donkey and should seriously consider investing in a saddle.

Stanford had first seen Gorman in action in a drugs trial seven years earlier. He stood about 5ft 10in. tall, with a luxuriant mop of fair hair parted in schoolboy fashion and a pair of twinkling green eyes giving the impression that he noticed everything and never missed a trick. You couldn't fail to be impressed by his pace, clarity, lack of pomposity and, perhaps most importantly, his court presence and enormous charm. And he had a pretty good grasp of the facts as well, despite his being hell-bent on giving the impression that he was bone idle. If he had any real weakness, it was his insistence in introducing humour into every case, even when there was nothing at all funny about the crime or his client. He was, in short, a breath of fresh air in a profession riddled with status, gossip, one-upmanship and clichés.

Gorman and Stanford became good friends, as well as winning their fair share of cases together.

At a dinner party the very next day, after he'd received a standing ovation at the London School of Economics – having convinced his audience that, when push came to shove, the majority of them were potential killers, blackmailers and thieves – Gorman's eyes were glazing over. His wife, Roberta, had ignored his entreaties from the outset not to accept the invitation. 'We've got to go,' she protested. 'It's five weeks away so don't scream and shout now.' He had warned her in dark tones, as he always did, that, barring a fortunate fatality, the dreaded day would eventually arrive.

Earlier that evening, they had had a flaming row at home. 'Do I really have to go? – she's your friend, not mine – I'm not in the mood – I've got to be up at five tomorrow – I really must prepare my closing speech – you know I'll only sulk all night.' She had heard it all before. He might as well have been talking to the doormat.

'You can't abandon me at the last minute,' she pleaded. 'Do you really expect me to go alone? Martha will think you're too important to go to her home. Is your work more important than me?' And finally, the inevitable crocodile tears. He had lost. This, of course, wouldn't stop him from sulking all evening. For a start, her old school friend Martha was a terrible cook. Worse still, she had gone out of her way to invite six other guests: three girlfriends of hers and their lacklustre husbands who could have bored for England. The conversation over dinner had been so dull that he found himself talking more than usual. He'd rather hear his own voice than those of the other guests.

'Yes,' he told them under interrogation during the meal, 'I'm no better than a tart. Clients pay me for my wares and I do what I can to please them. No, I don't have nightmares when a guilty man gets off, possibly due to my expertise. In fact, I confess it gives me quite a thrill. No, my ambition isn't to be a judge and, if I was one, I would certainly support hanging in a good number of cases. Yes, I agree the legal aid system is a shambles but that's no concern of mine. No, I don't do pro bono work – I have two kids at private school to support. Nor do I prosecute – it doesn't get my mojo working. Yes, perhaps most of my clients are guilty, but not everything in crime is black and white. In fact, the majority of cases fall into a grey area – and that's my territory.'

Oscar Wilde once said, 'To get into the best society, nowadays, one has either to feed people, amuse people or shock people – that is all!' Patrick had been invited to amuse and shock. Martha was there singularly to feed. He never understood why the people who couldn't boil an egg were always the ones who insisted on holding large dinner parties. The first course was a soup, orange in colour with a few croutons scattered around to give it definition. Martha claimed it was pumpkin. What had happened to good old-fashioned mushroom soup? What is this modern nonsense of serving up a soup that has to be orange or green at a party? The main course was sea bass – what else? A simple grilled kipper would have put her desert-dry rendering to shame. The dessert, however, was very much to Patrick's liking – sherry trifle. She claimed it was homemade. He doubted it. He had a strong suspicion that she had purchased a couple of trifles from Marks & Spencer and injected them with a little sherry herself.

'Did you really make this pudding?' he teased her.

'Of course I did. Can't you tell from the taste?'

He couldn't.

The evening wore on relentlessly. He eventually switched off from joining in the conversation. He felt he had the right to; after all, he had performed his cabaret, which was why he had been invited in the first place. He was entertaining himself by considering whether, if given the choice, he would have preferred to sit through one of George Percival's never-ending prosecution closing speeches rather than attend this dinner party, when his phone rang. He went into the hall to answer it. By now it was nearly 11 p.m. and Martha's husband was busy pontificating on the long-term advantages of investing in residential property as opposed to a pension, whilst Martha was laying out her plans for a new conservatory on the dining room table.

He glanced at the number on the telephone, it looked familiar. Such was his boredom that he would have welcomed a call from the executioner at the Tower of London to jolly up his evening.

'Pat, it's Adrian here. Sorry to ring so late, are you still up?'

'Physically, yes. Mentally, no. What's up?'

'I'll tell you what's up. You may have read about it in the press. Mercenary Bob Maynard's been murdered, or should I say slain, and I'm defending the hero who's been charged. I'm not in funds yet, but there's good prospects. Anyway, I thought it would be right up your street.'

'You thought right, it certainly is.' Pat was perking up already.

'I'm booked in to see him at Belmarsh Prison on Friday at 5 p.m., and I'd like you to come with. How are you fixed?'

'I'm fixed very well. If you can pick me up outside the Bailey at just gone 4, I'd love to. I read a bit about it in the papers. It sounds hopeless. What's his defence?'

'Let's discuss that on the way to the prison.'

'OK, but what's his best point?'

'You are!'

Totally reinvigorated by the call, Pat walked back into the dining room looking for a receptive audience to which he could recount his good news.

He found one.

Chapter 13

A Done Deal

_____

1960
___

It was no dream. The boy, now nine years old, was sleeping in a large freezing room with a damp stone floor and no heating. It was so cold that in winter he always slept with his clothes and socks on and made hospital corners on his bed with the thin and grimy grey blanket.

There were thirteen other boys in the dormitory. Some of them cried themselves to sleep every night. But they were kinder to him than they'd ever been at his school. They had all learnt the basic facts of life the hard way.

He never spoke to any of them about how he came to be there, and he never cried. He'd cried enough already.

*   *   *

'Is Mr Stanford in?' Joanne recognised the bark through the intercom immediately. It was unmistakable: husky, brusque and booming.

'Come in, Mr Davenport.' A minute later, Big Jake wafted into the offices.

'Thank the Lord you've had that bloody lift fixed, I was dreading the walk,' was Jake's ungracious greeting on arrival. He had arrived empty-handed and wearing a floral pair of shorts to match the sunny weather.

'Mr Stanford will see you in a minute or two, he's just finishing off a meeting.'

'Good, I'll have another butchers at those holiday brochures while I'm waiting.'

Fifteen minutes later, Stanford's door opened and a middle-aged couple walked out behind a young boy of about seventeen, looking suitably admonished. The parting words from the father were overheard by Jake. 'Do your best for my boy, Mr Stanford, he's learnt his lesson, he's really a good boy at heart. He'll never be back.' Joanne led Jake into Stanford's office.

'Underage sex or drugs, which is it, Mr Stanford?' asked Jake on entering, whilst nodding his head in the general direction of the departing clients. His first guess was correct.

'You've got a keen eye, Mr Davenport, let's leave it at that. Take a seat.' Jake did not. Instead, he pulled a grubby piece of paper out of his pocket, unfolded it and held it up with the writing facing Stanford. It read:

'CAN WE GO FOR A COFFEE?'

Stanford got the drift. 'Joanne,' he announced as they both walked out of the office, 'Mr Davenport's been kind enough to invite me for a coffee. I'll be back in about twenty minutes or so.'

'At the most,' added Jake.

'Sorry for the dramatics,' apologised Jake as they sat facing each other at the local Pret A Manger. 'It's a dot on the cards the Old Bill have got your offices bugged up over this Bob the Merc business. Now, as you can see, I've come empty-handed, but me and the boys are still right behind you. I'm no bullshitter, I don't make promises I can't keep. Write me down your bank details, I'm going to arrange the transfer of the monies as agreed next week. No sense paying in cash if you insist on charging VAT. There's just one condition.'

'What might that be?' enquired Stanford, fearing the worst.

'No one's to know I'm paying for the case – and I mean no one,' replied Jake, giving Stanford a challenging stare. 'Not Dennis, not the barristers and certainly not the Old Bill. I mean no one, are we agreed?'

'That's your prerogative, Mr Davenport. You have my word.'

'Your word's good enough for me, Mr Stanford – let's hope for both our sakes it remains that way,' replied Jake whilst nodding approvingly.

But Stanford's curiosity got the better of him. 'Tell me, Mr Davenport, why are you paying for this case?'

'What concern is that of yours, Mr Stanford? Trust me, I've got my reasons and you'll get your money. You're running a business, not a charity – remember?'

Then Jake picked up his cappuccino, which had been sitting patiently on the table for a good ten minutes as they'd been concluding their deal. After taking one noisy slurp, he marched up to the counter and shouted, 'Miss – this coffee's stone cold – what sort of a joint are you running here?'

Chapter 14

Ice Station Zebra

B elmarsh Prison sits in a sprawling complex next to a Crown court with a tunnel joining the two. It's as inconvenient a journey from anywhere near central London as one could possibly imagine and is referred to with little affection as Ice Station Zebra. It's as if the authorities, in their wisdom, had searched for the most inaccessible piece of land known to civilised man and plonked a prison and court complex on it. Driving from the Old Bailey to Belmarsh Prison late on a drizzly Friday evening is not generally considered to be one of Britain's most scenic experiences – the colour green does not spring to mind. But it gave Stanford ample time to discuss the case with his counsel, whilst he read a transcript of Dennis's lengthy interview statement.

'Well, if it isn't Mr Gorman and Mr Stanford! We've got the A Team here tonight alright – and a Friday evening appointment an' all. Bob the Merc's case, I shouldn't wonder. Am I right, Mr Stanford?' enquired the prison officer on their arrival.

'As always, John,' replied Stanford. 'How's your boy?'

'He's doing fine now, thanks to you. That lecture you gave

him seems to have done the trick. You know he calls you Uncle Adrian. By the way, it's been two months now and you still haven't sent me your bill.'

'Give us a large room for our meeting, John, and we'll call it quits,' replied Stanford affably.

'Yes, I've got the corner room nicely cleaned up for you already, Mr Stanford.'

When they arrived at Room 6, having been photographed, fingerprinted and frisked, and having had the inside of their shoes checked, Dennis was already waiting. Stanford introduced his illustrious QC. 'How are they treating you here, Mr Dennis?' Gorman had a knack of breaking the ice gently.

'Not too bad, better than I thought. Actually, I'm quite popular here. A few inmates have come up to me, patted me on the shoulder and thanked me. They've stuck me in the hospital wing for the moment, where they put everyone on a murder charge when they come in until the doctors decide they're not crackers.'

Gorman liked the look of his new customer. Washed and shaved for the occasion, notepad at the ready and a straight talker with a gentle, clear voice. *We'll get on just fine*, he thought.

'I've read your long statement in your police interview and it's very good – yes, very good, as far as it goes.' Gorman paused. 'But the problem is, it doesn't quite go far enough. It doesn't deal with how you got the gun and the bullets, and what gave you the idea to kill Maynard outside the Old Bailey. Of course, his wife will be the prosecution's main witness at the trial. You can leave her to me. I don't know what knowledge you have of our legal system, but at first blush there are really only two possible defences open to us.'

'Acting in self-defence for the murder charge and acting under duress for the gun and bullets charges,' interrupted Dennis.

Gorman was impressed. 'Well, I can see you certainly haven't wasted your time here since you arrived, Mr Dennis.'

'There's not much else to do. This place is crammed with know-alls, who are only too willing to tell you how to run your case and who should run it for you. One of them's got an old copy of this legal book called *Archbold*, and he lent it to me the other night.'

'I can think of better bedside reading,' quipped Gorman. 'Now, look, it's still early days, of course, and we won't get the full prosecution evidence for about another six weeks, but I already have a shrewd idea of how I'd like to run this case. So, at this stage, I don't really want you to tell me about anything that might be missing from your police statement. Do you mind, Mr Dennis?'

'Mr Gorman, Mr Stanford tells me you're the best and so do half the prisoners here, but they can't afford you. So, you play my case exactly as you want to, that's good enough for me.'

Music to my ears, thought Gorman, who was never averse to a thick helping of flattery. 'Thank you for that, Mr Dennis. I wish my wife was here to hear you say it; then I might get a little bit more respect at home. But you can't have everything in life. Actually, there are two points I'd like you to clear up for me. First, where did you get the notion to dress up like a barrister? I'm dying to know.'

'Well, the truth is, when Maynard told me that he had to be at the Bailey on Friday morning, I went to visit it the next day and I saw three or four barristers with their wigs and gowns on, smoking outside the front door. If I went there in my normal clothes, the police might have become suspicious about my hanging around and, anyway, he might have recognised me before I could shoot him. So, I took a taxi to the Bailey and put the wig and gown on, which I'd bought, before getting out.'

'That's going to sound great in the witness box. And secondly, why on earth did you take off your wig before firing the second shot?'

'It sounds heartless, but I wanted to make sure that Maynard knew for sure who was killing him before he passed on.'

'Another great reply!'

The three of them then spent an hour or so going over the case. Just as they were leaving, Stanford said, 'By the way, Mr Dennis, you still haven't told me how you got hold of me as your solicitor – I'm curious to know.'

'After the case, Mr Stanford. I promise to tell you after the case. All I can say now is that it was from an impeccable source. And I'd like to ask you, Mr Stanford, who's paying for my defence? Who's this mysterious benefactor?'

'Ah, yes,' replied Stanford, eyes twinkling. 'I too have my secrets.'

* * *

'What did you make of him?' asked Stanford as he and Gorman were driving back to civilisation after the conference.

'Well, leaving to one side that he's a self-confessed forger, thief, fraud artist, gambler, drunkard and shot a man dead in cold blood, he's not a bad fellow.'

'What do you think his worst point is, Pat?'

'Taking off his wig before he shot him a second time.'

'And his best?' asked Stanford, whilst eyeing up his QC at the traffic lights just before the Blackwall Tunnel.

Gorman needed no time to consider. 'As you yourself told me, you happen to be looking at him!'

Chapter 15

The Life and Crimes of Bob the Merc

Bob the Merc wasn't born with a silver spoon in his mouth either; nor did a succulent roast chicken ever fly into it.

He was an only child. His father was an original East Ender from Stepney – an honest, hard-working family man and a faithful husband, but always verging on broke. By the age of fourteen, he was running a protection racket on a sixth-former in charge of the school tuck shop. Kicked out of home at seventeen for stealing meat from his own father's butcher's shop and selling it to the local restaurants, he took to mugging and made a tasty income with a flick knife as the tool of his trade. After some intensive Borstal training, he eventually made his debut at the Old Bailey at the tender age of nineteen, charged with blackmailing a publican over an affair with a pretty young barmaid. 'Two years,' said the judge. 'This is meant to be a deterrent sentence – but I doubt if it will deter you.'

The judge was right. Eighteen months after his release he was back in court, this time for threatening to kill his landlord in Woolwich, who had changed the locks on his flat because he was six months behind on the rent. Three years was his sentence this time.

By the age of twenty-nine, he'd eased his way into drug smuggling – ordering kilos and sometimes paying only for grams. By now, he had his own handpicked team from the various prisons he had patronised. He had a sharp eye for staff. At thirty-five, he had amassed quite a tidy sum and was flagged up in Scotland Yard's records office as one to watch. When three of his team were caught red-handed on the beaches of Torquay unloading a hefty consignment of cocaine from Colombia, he was nicely tucked up in bed at home in London. One of the three had been chased along the beach by HM Customs and, before being nabbed, was seen to throw away his mobile phone. On its recovery, the last number dialled was Bob's and they raided his home at dawn.

'Now, Mr Maynard, why would you be receiving a call at 3.15 in the morning from a man on the beach in Torquay?' he was asked in his police interview. 'Did he want to discuss England's poor performance in last night's Euro qualifier? Or perhaps he desperately needed your advice on whether to invest in some South African mining stock?' There was, of course, no credible answer, and Bob had just about enough sense not to try and provide one.

He stood trial with the others and even forked out for a top defence brief. It proved to be a sound investment. 'Members of the jury,' his barrister intoned in his closing speech, 'in this England of ours you really cannot convict a man of drug smuggling simply because he receives a call at 3.15 in the morning.' His three mates went down – but he walked.

Finally, Bob came to his senses. Drug smuggling involved trusting too many people, and he didn't trust anybody. So what to do for a living? He had a sizeable amount of cash at his disposal, but it wouldn't last for ever and inflation was rampant. The answer was obvious – loan sharking, of course. It stared him in the face. You lent out money and when debts were not repaid on time, with 10 per cent interest a month, you threatened your customers – or, even better, their families. Occasionally, it suited you that some unfortunate really couldn't pay. Then you dished out your own deterrent so that other debtors would suddenly discover they were not quite as poor as they had claimed. And this is how it was that he came by the nickname 'Mercenary Bob Maynard', or more colloquially, 'Bob the Merc'. And boy was he proud of it.

His wife was no angel either. They had first set eyes on each other during a prison visit when she was on the next table seeing her father, who was serving ten years for manslaughter. It was love at first sight for Bob. A peroxide-blonde bimbo in tight leather trousers, 5in. heels and eyelashes on stilts, telling her father how tough it was for her in the real world and how it had been three long years since she had tanned herself up like a leather handbag at the Marbella Beach Club.

On his release from prison, he drove straight round to her home and took her off on a weekend to Paris. If she was not already high maintenance when they met, she certainly eased into the condition with aplomb, marshalling the art of knowing the price of everything and the value of nothing. Céline was the exotic name she was blessed with on birth, and she rarely shopped anywhere else. By the time of Bob's celebrated passing, she was truly his soulmate, and he never loan-sharked any money before taking her counsel. She was his partner in crime as well as in bed.

Bob was not just a vicious loan shark; there was more to him than that. He had his hobbies as well. When he was not in Zurich counting his coins, he could be found in his study at home reading biographies and watching TV. But not any TV. Bob the Merc was selective in what he read and watched. He had a unique knowledge in two specialist areas: criminal biographies and gangster films.

Were the TV programme *Mastermind* limited to his specialist subjects (with no general knowledge round), he would have been a strong contender for champion. He often dreamt of his performance in the programme.

'Your name, please?' John Humphrys would ask.

'Robert Maynard, otherwise known as Bob the Merc.'

'Occupation?'

'Err – I'm in the loan shark business.'

'Special subject?'

'The life and times of Al Capone.'

His other choice would have been *The Godfather* trilogy, which he watched several times a year. Ask him about any line in the three films and he would answer with alacrity. Like, 'Who said "mind the kids" whilst backing out of a drive?' He would answer, 'Clemenza', without pausing for breath.

Naturally, his home was the largest in the street. Prudently, it was in his wife's name. Amazingly, it was a gift to his wife from a Swiss lover. If he was unlucky enough to be asked by the Inland Revenue how it was purchased, he had his pack of lies at the ready. The truth was somewhat different. It was in fact a back-to-back arrangement with a dishonest Swiss banker, who had financed the purchase subject to a little sweetener in the form of a 25 per cent surcharge.

Bob and Céline had two sons. The older one had seen the light at the age of eighteen and decamped to Australia never to be seen again. Bob Jr, however, was sent to private school. He seemed to be doing just fine until two days before his GCSEs, when he was caught in a midnight raid stealing the history papers from the headmaster's study, leaving Bob Jr no choice but to follow in his father's murky footsteps.

By the age of nineteen, he was in regular employment as the enforcement branch of his father's burgeoning empire. Compassion was not uppermost in his limited range of qualities. A few years before his father's timely death, there had been a spate of burglaries in their street. One day, an innocent young neighbour had casually asked Bob Jr how it was that their house was never burgled and his (which was half the size of theirs) had been done three times in a year. 'Respect,' Bob had answered, 'respect and a shrewd knowledge of the terrain.' The neighbour only understood what Bob Jr was talking about when he saw reports of his father's murder on TV.

So, Bob Jr and his mum were left in control of the family empire and, to borrow the words of John Wayne, neither of them were in the forgive and forget business.

Chapter 16

The Guvnor

'Hello Jim, Adrian here, I'll be with you at 12.30 sharp as agreed. We'll do the deal by 1 and then we'll go and have a schnitzel at Ciao Bella – what do you think?'

'Great idea, Adrian. See you then.'

Jim Garrett was the senior clerk at Everest Chambers, deep in the heart of Chancery Lane. Thirty gossiping barristers all under one roof, specialising in defending rich, hapless types, who couldn't possibly have murdered, robbed, defrauded, raped or pillaged, but who had nevertheless run into some serious misunderstandings with the authorities.

The use of the title *clerk* would be a gross misnomer to Jim's elevated position. The epithet *guvnor* was far more appropriate. After all, it was he who decided who did what and for how much – and he took a neat 5 per cent for his troubles, win or lose.

His work required specialist skills: the common touch, knowing the market, flattering solicitors and buying them plenty of lunches to ensure their future goodwill. It was said that all legal gossip stained his desk before the Lord Chancellor's. Jim was indeed accomplished at his job.

But Jim was all too aware that there was no more than a smattering of criminal barristers whom Stanford would trust to defend Dennis – perhaps five, maximum. One was in his chambers. But Stanford wouldn't be looking for some Oxbridge intellectual or a fraud specialist. No, Stanford wanted Patrick 'The Edge' Gorman QC and nobody else. Stanford would not be an easy man to bargain with in this particular case because he knew he had a fine piece of property to market. Any member of the Criminal Bar would have willingly carried out 250 hours of community service to get their hands on such a brief. But had Stanford not made a fundamental tactical error in taking Gorman to a conference at Belmarsh before they had agreed the fees? This would surely give Jim the edge in the market-style bargaining that was about to take place. Nevertheless, over-pitch the price and Stanford might walk away and go elsewhere. A certain delicacy was required.

'OK, Jim, let's get this sordid business over with, I'm feeling peckish already,' said Stanford, having taken his seat, looking confident and relaxed with his legs stretched out.

'How's he paying for his defence?' was Jim's opening gambit.

'Let me worry about that, Jim, but I can assure you it's not with legal aid certificates.'

'This case could drag on, Adrian, it could run three weeks.'

'Three weeks!' countered Adrian. 'If it lasts three weeks, I'll make a loss on it. Two max, possibly only seven or eight days.'

'I was thinking £90,000 to take the brief and £5,000 each day after that,' said Jim, matter-of-factly. 'This case is right in the public eye, and there'll be an enormous amount of stress involved.'

Stanford was ready for him. 'Yes, yes, yes, we'll include a pain and suffering element in the fee, particularly bearing in mind who's prosecuting.'

'And who might that be?' enquired Jim.

Stanford started to chuckle. 'George Percival – or so I've heard.'

'Oh my God, Percival the Persecutor! That pompous, long-winded, arrogant, conceited clever dick will drag the case out for weeks.' The pound sign started resetting northwards in Jim's brain. 'This is a different ball game altogether. Do you know, in a recent case against Mr Gorman, one of the jurors sent the judge a note asking whether Percival was in love with the sound of his own voice and, if not, why did he have to repeat everything three times? Well, apparently the judge read out this note to Percival in open court, to which Percival stood up and spluttered, "I'm lost for words." Mr Gorman was heard to say in a loud aside, "Well that's a first!"'

'Who's Percival leading?' asked Jim.

'Nick Denning.'

'Down and Dirty Denning. My God, what a team! This is going to be one tough fight. It sounds like they've both been hand-picked to do a demolition job. This case is no stroll in the park.'

'If it was, I wouldn't need Pat, would I?'

'Very true,' conceded Jim. 'Do you know Mr Gorman's very fashionable in Hong Kong at the moment? He's got plenty of highly paid work out there,' Jim added, as if there was a possibility that he might refuse to take the case unless the fee was tip-top.

'As a matter of fact, I do know,' replied Stanford. 'He lost no time in telling me all about it on our way to the prison. He also told me he hates being in humid Hong Kong on those long, boring fraud cases, and if it wasn't for the money, he'd prefer to be doing a bail application at Uxbridge Magistrates' Court. Do you know, he takes his own salamis with him as a reminder of home?'

'Unfortunately, I do. He sends me to Terroni's to buy them for him before each trip.'

'Who's he going to lead in the case?' asked Jim. 'I was thinking of Miles Hartford-Jones. He's a safe pair of hands and twenty years' call.'

'I wasn't,' said Stanford, leaning back in his chair and folding his arms in defiance. 'Let's face the facts – how can I put it politely – he's not exactly seeded at Wimbledon. I'm not looking for a safe pair of hands who'll treat this case as a sinecure and doze through most of it. I'm looking for somebody "real lively" – to quote the words of an interested party. I'm thinking of young Daniel Jacobsen. He's got the energy of the innocent. Listen to this. Two weeks ago, he turned up in my office after that case he'd won for me at Kingston. "I thought you might like to hear the result in person,"' mimicked Stanford. 'He virtually stole the line straight out of *The Winslow Boy*. I like him a lot. He's plucky and ambitious and, most importantly, he's also a winner – I'll take him. Now, let's cut out all this fancy footwork. You know exactly the figure I'm thinking of, and I know exactly the figure you'll settle for. Shall I go first?'

Jim nodded. What choice did he have?

'£100,000 all in, and half for Jacobsen, whether it lasts a day or a year – no extras. I've even included an additional £15,000 as a merciful gesture because Percival's prosecuting. That's my first and last offer – are we all done?'

Jim puffed and panted, but he knew when he was beaten. 'Let's go and have that schnitzel,' he muttered meekly. 'Lunch is on you!'

Chapter 17

A Simple Plan

'He's going to do him tonight – it's got to be tonight.'

'What's the hurry?' asked Bob Jr. 'Why tonight?'

'He's going to be moved out of the prison hospital wing at any time.'

Bob Jr was sitting with Lenny, his right-hand man, in a bar in Soho late on a Sunday afternoon. A consoling bottle of Johnnie Walker Blue Label sat between them on the bar – leaking speedily. Bob hadn't taken the death of his father well – not well at all. Furthermore, he was not prepared to trust Dennis's fate to twelve good men and true at some eventual trial at the Old Bailey. Anyway, it wasn't good for business for Dennis to be sitting pretty in prison, still breathing.

'What's the plan?' asked Bob Jr.

As it was all his own idea, Lenny was pleased to tell him. 'He's got that lunatic Scottish Angus in the same wing as him. He's waiting trial for killing two coppers in the getaway from a blagging at a bureau de change on the Edgware Road. He's never going to see the light of day. He was caught, sawn-off shotgun an' all, jumping into a stolen BMW outside the door.

He's worried about his missus and will stop at nothing for a few extra quid for her.'

'What's the deal?' As Bob Jr was paying, he wanted chapter and verse.

'£2,000 upfront – we've paid it to his brother already – and another £8,000 when Dennis's heart stops beating, which should be tonight.'

Bob Jr frowned, indicating that he thought the price was a bit steep, bearing in mind that Scottish Angus had no current alternative employment. 'How's he going to do him?'

'He's going to break his neck with his own hands in the showers. He's going to make out Dennis insulted him and he lost his cool. What's it matter, Scottish Angus is dead-meat anyway.'

'Does he know who's behind this?' Bob Jr was keen to ensure that his name didn't feature in the affair.

'He thinks it's being organised by some Italian mafioso who's owed £150,000 from Dennis's gambling debts, and that the Italian wants Sicilian justice, and now.'

'Good thinking, Lenny – who told him this?'

'I sent an old mate of mine in on a social visit with a false passport and a toupee. You can count on me, he knows how to keep his mouth shut.'

Bob Jr concluded the meeting, paid the bill and stood up to leave. 'Right, if this goes well tonight, I don't want to see you for at least a month. I hope to read about Dennis's last moments in tomorrow's early edition of the *Evening Standard*. If not, I'll want to know why. He's got to go.'

Bob Jr was truly a man of few words.

Chapter 18

A Rocky Investment

1964

The thirteen-year-old boy didn't like Mr and Mrs Elcock very much, nor their house in Croydon. He didn't like calling them by their surname or their first names – and certainly not Mum and Dad.

Mr Elcock always seemed very distant and although his wife tried to be nice, he never really thought she meant it. It was as if whenever they looked at him, they were saying to themselves, 'We've made a terrible mistake.'

* * *

When Jake heard the news, through the ever-reliable underworld grapevine, that Dennis had nearly taken his last ride in the prison showers, he went apoplectic.

'Three hundred large I've invested in this caper and some crackpot Scotsman tries to top him. Just imagine if he had. My money would be up the spout and that poor bastard would never even have set foot in the Old Bailey. Some investment that would have been. We should've had him protected in prison from the beginning. I'm losing my touch, Ernie, I told you a few weeks ago, it's time to draw stumps.'

The two friends were once again trawling around Kenwood, this time on a sunny Sunday morning. Ernie had gone round to Jake's home in Primrose Hill to break the news gently before the walk. He found Jake in the bath with his five-year-old grandson, Jack Minimus Davenport – his favourite place in the whole wide world. They were both busy pushing ducks around and tucking into a plate of peanut butter sandwiches – smooth, of course – with the crusts lovingly removed, so as not to disturb Minimus's delicate milky-white teeth, or Jake's overworked digestive system. Two glasses of Cherryade stood by, together with Jake's long-suffering wife, Daisy, caring for their every whim.

As usual, Jake was giving his devoted grandson a Sunday morning lecture about the facts of life. 'Now, listen up, Minimus – when you grow up you do exactly the opposite to what I did. You stay at school 'til you're eighteen, choose your friends carefully and earn your own money from a steady job. Take it from Grandpa, you'll never enjoy spending money unless you've earned it yourself.' Jake had given the very same lecture to his son, Jack Jr, year in, year out when he'd been a kid. It had worked. His son ran a car rental business with his wife in Bromley and had never set foot inside the Old Bailey.

Daisy, listening at the door, had heard it all before – Jake the preacher! He had met her in a Wimpy bar near Leicester Square when he was just out of Borstal. He'd been a regular there when he noticed that she started serving him double portions. She was blonde, skinny and pretty, with a great East End sense of humour. He asked her to the flicks and they were married six weeks later. She turned two blind eyes to his business ethics – he was simply incorrigible. Schiller, the German philosopher, put it best: 'There's no man so evil that some woman and his dog won't still love him.' But when all was said, Jake was still a family man and when, at Sunday lunch, during his preaching, his family threw glances at him which translated into 'take a look at yourself', he would answer, self-pityingly, 'a man with no vices has few virtues' – not a bad defence at that.

'What the hell happened, Ernie?' whispered Jake as their walk began.

Ernie, of course, had the full inside story. 'Apparently, Dennis was taking his daily shower, with no more than a bar of coal-tar soap for protection, when this enormous Scottish fella came lumbering up from behind, grabbed him by the neck and started throttling him. But before he'd finished his dirty work, two prison officers arrived on the scene, looking for Dennis to move him to a normal wing. It had taken the prison doctors five weeks to decide that the Scot wasn't a head case. The alarm went off and six officers piled in to pull him off. He then claimed that Dennis had called him a fat Scottish bastard and told him his wife was having it off with half the local rugby team. They've moved Dennis into the SEG unit for his own safety, cosied up with the grasses and pervs.'

'Poor sod,' replied Jake. 'This is Bob Jr's work of course, no doubt about that. I want him protected – understood? Find out who we know in that prison and tell them to put the word about that if Dennis suffers so much as a scratch on his pinkie, they'll be given a good seeing-to. And make sure that my name stays right out of it. Tell them Dennis was in debt up to his eyeballs to the Dunlop brothers from Manchester and killed Maynard on their behalf. Tell them what the hell you like, but I want no comebacks – understood?'

'Of course I do, Jake – leave it to me.'

'I will,' growled Jake. 'And for God's sake, keep him in one piece – I want a trial, not an inquest. I've paid top dollar well in advance for the tickets. Now, if you don't mind, I'd like the show to go on.'

Chapter 19

A Curious Cellmate

The minutes drag by if two of you are locked up together in a 10ft by 8ft poky cell for some twenty-three hours a day in Belmarsh – the land where time stands still. Dennis's case papers were scattered all over the room. Prosecution photographs, witness statements, Dennis's interviews and the pathologist's report. Dennis was now in the normal wing. His trial date was still months away. But he had been fortunate indeed with his cellmate, one Paul Samson, awaiting trial for a massive bank fraud, extradited from Marbella together with his wife, who had siphoned off millions on his behalf.

Samson had had a good education and had risen high in the City fast. But money became his god and so he started running in blinkers, counting his coins and not his mistakes. 'When you defraud a bank out of millions, no one goes without supper,' soon became his motto, which was the white-collar crime equivalent to a hitman saying, 'If I don't take on this contract killing, somebody else will – so he's dead anyway.'

Samson was good company. He was sympathetic and generous with his smuggled food parcels, alcohol and mobile phone

– courtesy of an impoverished prison officer. But he was also a worried man. He was in his early forties and could take a prison stretch. But to come out to nothing, and for his wife to lose her £5 million home in Notting Hill if she went down, was a bit too much.

'Who's going to give me a job when I get out? And what good would it do me anyway? I'm used to a mega-bucks life-style. I'll have to go back to crime, there's really nothing else for it,' he would moan daily.

One boring Tuesday afternoon found the two inmates in their cell having just woken up from killing time with a siesta. 'Mind if I read your case papers?' asked Samson, whilst cutting them both a thin slice of smuggled carrot cake.

'Be my guest,' replied Dennis, shrugging his shoulders. 'Perhaps you'll see something I've missed.'

'You can read mine if you like,' said Samson, pointing towards thousands of pages stacked 3ft high in the corner of the cell.

'No thanks, I've got plenty to read as you can see.' Dennis was fast becoming a world expert on the works of Frederick Forsyth.

Samson picked up a thick bundle of Dennis's case papers and got down to work. He had 5 million good reasons to.

Chapter 20

An Interim Enquiry

1966

The fifteen-year-old boy with the thick, curly black hair looked much older than he was. He could easily have passed for eighteen. He spoke better than a lot of boys his age because reading books had always been a comfort to him.

He was a very hairy boy and had already started shaving twice a week. He worked in the docks and the markets, he cleaned cars, unloaded lorries, stole and slept wherever he could hang his hat. But he was free.

He used to lullaby himself to sleep, humming softly the tune 'I've Got Sixpence' that his mum, sitting on his bed, would sing to him every night when he was a kid. He still saw her face in his dreams.

* * *

'Is Mr Stanford in? And, before you ask, I haven't got an appointment.' Joanne buzzed Jake in without replying.

He arrived carrying a box of Godiva chocolates for Joanne

in one hand, and a magnum of Petrus 1989 in the other, recently fizzed up from *falling* off the back of a lorry. 'I've come to enquire about my investment,' he said as he was shown into Stanford's office, plonking down the magnum on the desk with scant respect.

'Well, there's just two weeks to go before the kick-off, but we're ready,' Stanford replied.

'What's this fellow Gorman like? I hear he's a bit of a comedian. Personally, I'd prefer it if he was a magician. Are you sure he's the right man for the job?'

Stanford just shrugged his shoulders. 'Well, he's the best there is. His nickname at the Bar is "The Edge", because that's what he gives his clients. Come to the trial and you'll see for yourself.'

Jake turned down the invitation in a hurry. 'Err, no, I won't be there in person for obvious reasons. Let's just say I'll be well represented. Who's the judge?'

'Ah, yes, we've drawn the short straw there – Mr Justice McIntyre.'

'Mack the Knife!' exclaimed Jake. 'He's the reason for the overcrowding problem in London's prisons. God help our man if he goes down. Who's the pros?'

'George Percival.'

'Any good?'

'Long-winded, but tip-top.'

'What's the evidence looking like?'

Stanford gave him a potted version. 'Well, there's really not much evidence to worry about. Just a video of our man in fancy dress pulling a gun out and firing two shots at a target he couldn't miss if he was blindfolded, followed by a confession stating that he did it and didn't regret it. But, besides that, it should be plain sailing.'

Jake started laughing. 'Very good, Mr Stanford, very good. You're filling me with more confidence with every word.' Jake stood to leave. 'I won't be seeing you again until after the trial. If Dennis gets off, I'll bring you the other two magnums from this case.'

'Great, my cellar could do with a bit of replenishing,' replied Stanford affably, as he stood up to walk Jake out. 'I look forward to our next meeting then, Mr Davenport, and let's hope it's a celebration. Either way, it's going to be interesting. I just can't wait.'

Jake gave the lawyer a defiant stare, whilst nodding his head ever so slowly. 'Nor can I, Mr Stanford, nor can I.'

Chapter 21

Bad News

_____

'I'm sorry to say, Mr Dennis, we've got some bad news for you.' There was one week to go before the trial, and Gorman and Stanford were again seated in the legal visits room at Belmarsh – this time with Gorman's junior barrister, Daniel Jacobsen, making his debut. 'We've just received some more evidence from the prosecution, and it doesn't make pretty reading.'

'Oh, yes, what is it?' Dennis, showing obvious concern, sat forward with both his elbows leaning heavily on the table.

'Well, firstly, the computer expert's report on your iPad has finally arrived. To get to the point, it seems you were googling the law of self-defence on three occasions in the week leading up to the Russian roulette incident. I suppose that means you were telling porkies at our first meeting when you said you'd read the law up in prison.'

'OK, I'll admit that was a little white lie, but it's not a crime to look up the law, is it?'

'No, of course it's not, any more than walking around with a rope is before you hang someone. But it doesn't help. It looks like you were carefully considering your options.'

'And what's the second bit of bad news?'

'A statement from your former cellmate Paul Samson – it's devastating.'

'What? What's he got to say? He's not a bad bloke.'

'Isn't he? Well, in short, he says you told him you made up the whole Russian roulette episode.'

'He said what?' Dennis couldn't believe what he was hearing.

'Yes, he said you allowed him to read your case papers and you discussed the case endlessly together.'

'That's true, absolutely true, but I never told him anything of the sort,' said Dennis, eyes bulging.

'Well, the prosecution are calling him to say that you did. God knows our case has enough problems without his evidence.'

'Someone must be paying him to lie. What a thing to do,' replied Dennis, shaking his head in disbelief. 'I just can't believe it.'

'How long were you cellmates?' asked Stanford, calmly.

'About two months or so. Then they suddenly moved him out to Wandsworth Prison. Now you mention it, he never kicked up a fuss about being moved. I should've spotted something was wrong then,' said Dennis, making an effort to recover his composure whilst covering his forehead with his right hand. 'Can I see the statement?' Gorman gave him a copy. Dennis read it, mumbling expletives under his breath.

'Well, now, Mr Dennis, Percival's going to suggest you needed to bolster up your account so that Maynard's threats would appear even more horrific than they actually were. And so, you educated yourself with your iPad, your imagination ran away with you and you invented, very craftily, what happened on the trip to Chelmsford.'

'I did no such thing,' replied Dennis, now almost shouting, widening his eyes and staring his lawyers straight in the face. 'What sort of a creature have I been sharing a cell with? This is going to finish me – and that's for sure.'

No one disagreed.

'Well, Mr Gorman, how're you going to deal with it?'

'Good question.' Gorman sounded anything but confident.

'Yes, but what's the answer?' Dennis sounded desperate.

'Another good question.'

Chapter 22

Enter Mack the Knife

Mr Justice Magnus McIntyre had a more pressing matter on his mind than presiding at some distasteful underworld murder trial after the weekend. He had skimmed through the case papers after dinner at home. Some middle-aged crank had got carried away and shot dead a notorious loan shark. *'Addita contumelia ad injuriam,'* he mumbled to himself repeatedly – scholar that he was. Yes, to add insult to injury the deed had been done outside the very citadel of justice and the defendant had the nerve to be fighting the case. Outrageous! He should be pleading guilty, and any respectable defence counsel would have told him as much, in no uncertain terms. But no, a couple of weeks of court time was going to be wasted listening to what really amounted to no more than an elongated speech in mitigation; the defence playing a sonorous violin in a minor key to the jury, in the hope that they would return a wholly perverse verdict. Well, it was simply not going to happen – not with him presiding, anyway. And who was this defence QC – Gorman? Never heard of him. A fashionable hired gun, no doubt. He'd soon show this upstart who was calling the shots.

On the plus side, he had George Percival prosecuting. His former pupil was now the head of his old chambers, packed with the righteous and indignant, who rarely defended. What more could a judge ask for? True, Percival was pompous and suffered from his own incurable disease – logorrhoea – but he was a superb cross-examiner, and he would give this do-gooder short shrift. Yes, McIntyre concluded, the verdict was entirely predictable.

But McIntyre was in the throes of a major personal crisis and could think of little else. His wife, Frances. They had been married some thirty years. She too was a lawyer, in fact a law lecturer at King's College London until her retirement some five years earlier. They had never had children because both of them had been too busy with their careers. Their initial flames of passion, sparked during a liquid chambers Christmas party, were now flickering embers.

He became a judge at forty-seven and found himself dispatched all over the country trying murder, rape and bombing cases. He had few pastimes. He didn't ski, sail or golf. He cared nothing for football or rugby, preferring to immerse himself in books on ancient history in his spare time. To him, restaurants were a waste of hard-earned money and even the theatre was, like most claret, hugely overpriced and, on the whole, disappointing. But he *was* a bridge player. And any visitor to his home would have seen the shelf in the toilet decked out with books on the subject. Rubber bridge for high stakes was not for him. It was vulgar and attracted a flashy crowd at his club. Duplicate bridge was his game, where you pitted your wits against other tables in the room. But that was really it: a great academic lawyer, a top duplicate bridge player and a bullyboy on the Bench. Not a very lovable mix.

In the first month following his appointment to the High Court Bench, McIntyre had to sentence a seventeen-year-old tearaway for robbing an old man at knifepoint at a public convenience by the Thames late at night. At the hearing, the boy's mother sat at the back of the court, crying from start to finish. He had her heart-rending letter in his hands: 'Never had a father … easily led … no education…' She was a house cleaner by day and spent five nights a week cleaning offices. She had been forced to move home three times in four years.

He called upon the boy, asking him if he had anything to say before he passed sentence. The young lad said six words: 'My father died in the gutter.' This was the most moving mitigation the young judge had ever heard in his 25-year career at the Criminal Bar, and he spared the boy prison. More fool him, because not a year later the same boy graced his court again, this time for attempted murder and armed robbery at a petrol station in Park Lane. From that day on, he was a monster on the Bench.

One of the more humorous aspects of life at the Bar is the nicknames attributed to judges by barristers – usually wholly accurate and always deeply insulting: 'Penal Pete' – 'Father Christmas' – 'Ice-Cold Alex' – 'No Bail Bertie' etc. featured regularly in robing room gossip. Mr Justice McIntyre had the best of all – 'Mack the Knife'. There was no grey area in the law for him, and lengthy speeches in mitigation resulted in nothing but lengthier sentences. A suspended sentence was not an option. Indeed, it was said by some that the only suspended sentence McIntyre might welcome involved the use of a rope.

He was even at the butt-end of his own personal joke, which white-wigged young barristers would be treated to when telling elderly statesmen that they had a trial starting in his court. 'So, Mack the Knife was the judge in a capital murder case a week after hanging had been abolished. The defendant was duly convicted and the judge called for the black cap – which all judges donned before passing a sentence of death. The defence counsel rose nervously to his feet in astonishment and said, "My Lord, I am bound to inform you that capital punishment was abolished as of last week." "Not in my court!" roared Mack the Knife.' No one liked this joke more than McIntyre. He took pride in being known as a hard-hitting, heartless judge. In truth, there was very little else that made him memorable.

If ever a radio programme was produced in the vein of *Desert Island Discs*, but instead of asking the guests their favourite pieces of music they were asked the names of eight people they would least like to be stranded on a desert island with, Mr Justice McIntyre would become a household name in no time at all. Many a barrister would willingly throw themselves to the mercy of the waves in a tempest rather than face the prospect of sharing dry land with Mack the Knife for the rest of their lives.

His wife was a very different gravy. Attractive, in a simple, understated way, modest, good company and loved by all her students. She had married him at a tender age for his brainpower and not his looks. He had Brylcreemed black hair with a parting as straight as a ruler. He was 6ft tall with an aquiline face and no creases because he rarely laughed. On the Bench, he was a powerhouse and took no truck from anyone. In his court, the burden of proof was reversed. You were guilty when the trial started and, irrespective of the verdict, guilty when it finished.

But, for the moment, reluctantly, his career had to take second place. Frances, how could she do this to him? Had he not been a faithful husband? Had he ever so much as looked at another woman? In fairness, few had ever looked at him – save in horror from the dock. Did she lack for anything? Had he not, just a couple of months earlier, taken her himself to the Selfridges sale and allowed her to buy not one but two pairs of Italian shoes and a new coffee percolator? And how was he being repaid? With egregious treachery. But what to do, what to do?

And what had aroused his suspicions? That very Thursday, when he arrived home after court, Frances was out. She was attending her weekly cookery course. He had gone up to their bedroom to fetch his cardigan with the intention of taking up his regular seat in front of the fire with a bridge book and a glass of Madeira. His eyes had noticed an empty glass on the bedside table. He was by nature a stickler for tidiness and was taking the glass downstairs to the kitchen when the waft of alcohol drifted into his nostrils. After a cursory forensic examination, he reached his conclusion – whisky! He hated whisky and if ever he drank, it would be a glass of red wine, port or Madeira. So, what was an empty glass of whisky doing on his bedside table? *'Res ipsa loquitur,'* he mumbled to himself – yes, the facts spoke for themselves. Neither he nor his wife drank whisky, so, who did? Charles! Yes, Charles drank whisky. Charles, his old school friend who stayed with them regularly when he was up in London with his wholesale leather goods business. Charles, who had still been at home that very morning when he had left for court at 7.30 a.m.

So, why was a glass smelling of whisky, which was his friend Charles's chosen drink, occupying a prominent position on his bedside table? Further investigative work was called for. McIntyre went directly to the drinks cupboard in the lounge to examine a bottle of Black Label he had brought back from the duty-free at Paris Airport a week earlier when he and his wife were returning from a weekend visit to her elderly uncle. Someone had opened it, and it was no longer full.

The evidence was starting to stack up: whisky glass in the bedroom; recently bought whisky bottle opened; Charles's drink of choice was whisky. Did this amount to a case to answer? *No*, he found himself ruling, *insufficient evidence* – even in his court. And so, with great reluctance and after the deepest considera-tion, McIntyre decided not to broach the subject with his wife on her return home that night. Further evidence would have to be served so that he would have a watertight case. But from where?

Suddenly, it hit him and he allowed himself a self-satisfied smile at the prospect of nailing the case.

Yes, he had a plan.

Chapter 23

Halfpint – the Supersub

_____

1968
___

All he could see were iron bars, sagging brickwork and nasty people –
some much older and in uniform but mostly his own age and dressed
as he was. All he could hear was shouting and the rattling of keys. All
he could feel was regret at being caught – but not remorse. He only
had himself to blame.

He vowed he would never return – never.

*   *   *

'Ernie, get hold of Halfpint. Tell him the usual place – 5
o'clock sharp tonight.' Jake slammed down the phone.

Halfpint had been in charge of Jake's – how should one call
it? – *SOS* or *Special Operations Services* for countless years. He
stood 5ft 3in. small in his Cuban heels, and the largest part of
his body was his brain. Jake had cruelly nicknamed him Halfpint so long ago that he would have difficulty remembering
what his real name was if his very life depended on it.

They had first met years earlier at Le Caprice, behind the Ritz hotel. Halfpint had taken his wife there to celebrate their fifteenth wedding anniversary. He had saved up for the occasion for over six months from the laundrette business he ran in Peckham. Jake was there with a few of the boys, noisily celebrating the profits from a large haul of hijacked spirits, when this skinny little fellow in an old grey suit – straight out of Weaver to Wearer – ambled up to their table, cool as you like, and politely asked them, almost in a whisper, if they wouldn't mind 'turning down the volume a bit'.

Jake couldn't believe what he was hearing. Big Jake being told to shut it – what a liberty!

'Say that again – Halfpint,' dared Jake. So Halfpint did.

'My missus and I are out celebrating our fifteenth wedding anniversary, and I'm sorry to tell you that you're ruining our evening.'

'Yes, yes – well, we're out celebrating too,' Jake roared in reply. 'And I don't mind telling you it's not a wedding anniversary!' But later, Big Jake couldn't resist a noble gesture – particularly with his team present to see it, not to mention a good number of onlookers – and he sent a bottle of Bollinger over to Halfpint's table. No one had dared to put Jake in his place for years. And, anyway, what could he do about it – knock the man spark out in a swanky West End restaurant?

At the end of the evening, Halfpint came over to Jake's table again, this time to thank him. The two of them got talking and Jake could see that this plucky, polite and diminutive south Londoner could be of real value to his many sordid enterprises.

A second meeting was arranged with just the two of them present. In hushed tones, Jake explained the nature of his nefarious activities and Halfpint jumped at the chance of receiving a fat brown envelope here and there.

Halfpint was not a regular member of Jake's inner sanctum but was always available sitting on the bench waiting to be called upon in a crisis, especially when a little delicacy was required as opposed to brute force. He was, in short, Jake's *supersub*. If a consignment of motherless goods had gone astray and Jake had a shrewd idea of their likely whereabouts, Halfpint would be summonsed with instructions to approach the errant party and persuade him to return them forthwith to their genuine wrongful owner – namely Jake. Halfpint had a way with words.

'Now,' he would say, 'there must be some misunderstanding. My guvnor's a reasonable man, but I've been telling him for years that he really must do something to control his temper. It's frightening, believe me. I've seen it for myself – sometimes it just gets uncontrollable. But you needn't worry, I've assured him this is all going to end peacefully – and by tomorrow, 4 p.m. I'm right, aren't I? He's waiting to hear from me later tonight. I know he won't be disappointed. I'm due to meet him as soon as he finishes his anger-management class. Personally, I'm very worried. I'm not at all convinced these classes are doing him any good. But I am going to bring him good news, I hope?'

Or, if Jake hadn't received his anticipated cut from a deal: 'My guvnor suggests we all have a friendly meeting to sort this little matter out. I told him there's no need for any rough stuff – it's not my way. But, of course, I'm not in charge – I'm just the messenger. Still, if you're willing to pay over what's due, there's no problem. There'll be no need for a meeting at all. What do you say – are we still friends?'

Oddly enough, the fact that Halfpint was so diminutive and painstakingly polite seemed to work wonders. It was deeply unsettling and very effective.

'Halfpint, I need your help,' Jake said as the two of them settled down to a late afternoon tea at the Langham Hotel near Regent's Park. This was their usual meeting place, and it had been chosen with care as the tables were set wide apart, which avoided eavesdropping. Anyway, Jake never needed an excuse to eradicate a plate or two of smoked salmon sandwiches followed by a couple of Old Cuban cocktails in the Artesian Bar.

'There's a trial coming up at the Bailey next week,' continued Jake, eyeing up the pastries. 'For reasons I can't begin to understand, the Old Bill think it's a criminal offence for someone to have rubbed out Bob the Merc. You may have heard about it?' Halfpint nodded. 'Let's just say I've a passing interest in the verdict and I want to even the odds a little. So you'll have to get your laces done up pronto, Halfpint – I'm calling you off the bench. Now, listen up,' Jake leaned forward and started whispering, 'here's what I want you to do…'

Chapter 24

Percival Sets Out His Stall

The best view of proceedings in Court 1 at the Old Bailey is undoubtedly from the dock. You sit high up, as befits your star role, and look the judge straight in the eye. Better still, nowadays, if anyone for some absurd reason should wish to assault you, you're protected by a thick glass screen. Unsurprisingly, this ringside seat is not much in demand as a vantage point as after the show, most occupants do not depart for an early supper at Sheekey's but a late one at Belmarsh Prison, where the service is somewhat lacklustre and the wine list decidedly limited.

For this particular show, the courtroom was packed. The pre-trial publicity had resulted in a long queue forming at 9 a.m. for the limited public accommodation in the circle seats. The stalls were reserved for the trial lawyers, the police, the press and, of course, the jury, as well as out-of-work barristers, dreaming about their eventual debut in this most holy setting.

But this theatre of dreams is in a different league to any found on Shaftesbury Avenue. For a start, the gallery seats are free and dished out on a first-come, first-served basis. Secondly, you never see the same show two days in a row. But, best of all, no one knows for sure the ending or, sadly in modern times, when this might be. It's also in such demand that it has been running continuously for centuries; far longer than even Agatha Christie's *The Mousetrap*. Everyone is thrilled to be there except one person – the defendant!

*   *   *

Enter George Percival QC for the prosecution. Percival was a fiery advocate who never minced his words and went straight for the jugular. He was a bit of a one-trick pony; no humour in court and a tad too much morality when out of it. He never defended. The very notion of someone getting off who might be guilty was beyond the pale. Still, he had a formidable presence, never giving an inch, taking every point – good or bad – and suspecting every opponent of foul play, particularly Gorman. His preparation was meticulous, verging on anal. In short, he was a walking textbook who ran on batteries not blood.

He was in his mid-fifties, about 5ft 8in. tall, with thinning and greying hair, a thick neck and a fat stomach to match, which he covered masterfully with a tight waistcoat. He suffered from a ruddy complexion which turned a deep shade of aubergine when mauling some hapless defendant under cross-examination. He wore horn-rimmed glasses, which he regularly used as a prop by removing whenever he made what he thought was a good point, or his opponent made a bad one – so the jury knew his views without his having to open his mouth. He had a nervous habit of removing his wig and mopping his brow, especially when he was seated and having to listen, without interruption, to a classy defence closing speech. He had a lamentable track record against Gorman, which he never talked about and Gorman never stopped talking about. Three losses on the trot – a statistic he was desperate to correct, and surely now was his chance. Dennis's defence was fanciful.

Oddly enough, Percival was a superb mimic and often entertained barristers in the Bar Mess by imitating many an Old Bailey judge. His showpiece, when Gorman wasn't around, was impersonating him. His *pièce de résistance*, taken from an actual case against each other, was his pretending to be Gorman arrogantly standing with his hands on his hips and with an incredulous look on his face.

'Officer, are you seriously suggesting, under oath to this jury, that my client's first words to you, as he stood there in his Calvin Klein underpants in the freezing cold at 6 a.m., right next to the front door which you and your team had just smashed in, were "I've been expecting you lot for weeks – what kept you? Let's have a friendly chat over a plate of scrambled eggs and then I'll give you all a nice going-home present?"

"Yes, indeed they were."

"You didn't find any eggs in the kitchen, did you, officer – during your somewhat vigorous search?"

"We didn't look for them. We were more interested in looking in his safe."

"Did you find any eggs there?"

"No, we didn't."

"Aha!"'

*   *   *

Now, in Court 1, as Percival began his opening speech, humour was not on the menu.

'Ladies and gentlemen of the jury,' he began, 'let me set out my stall and give you a trailer of what this case is all about.'

Stall, trailer! That's a laugh, thought Gorman, sitting next to Percival in the front row. Percival's modest *stall* was always the size of a supermarket and his *trailer* the epic length of *Ben-Hur*. 'Remember this,' Gorman whispered into the ears of his solicitor, Stanford, sitting in the row behind him, 'for a speech to be memorable it doesn't have to be everlasting!'

Any of the great prosecutors of the past would have opened the case in twenty minutes, at most, mused Stanford. Unarmed man shot dead outside the Old Bailey. Defendant, dressed as a barrister, waits at the scene and admits to the shooting, then claims he did it in self-defence and under duress and the rest you will hear from the witnesses. There you have it. Stanford had done it in his mind in about fifteen seconds.

But such precision wouldn't look good in print, nor would it merit Percival's name being splashed all over the front page of the *Evening Standard* that very night. And so he spoke for the best part of two hours, spiking his so-called *trailer* with the following lines:

Murder in cold blood…
    Premeditated to the nth degree…
    We are not living in the Wild West…
    We have something called the rule of law in this country…

Can't take the law into your own hands…

Not suggesting that Maynard is someone with whom you would want to go on a summer holiday, but he has a right to life just like you and I…

Dennis must have nerves of steel…

Just think about the pre-planning necessary, members of the jury – purchasing a gun, bullets, probably practising with the missing bullets, the cunning bluff of dressing himself up as a barrister and hiding the gun inside a brief.

If your life is in danger, members of the jury, you go to the police, that's what they're there for. If necessary, you go there two or three times or even more – you don't buy a gun instead. Nor, might I add, do you start studying the law of self-defence on your iPad.

Compare Mr Dennis's behaviour to our traffic system. When the lights are red, you have to stop, you don't say, 'Oh well, there's no cars about so I'll drive through' or 'I'm late for work so no one will mind' – you have to wait for green. But not Mr Dennis. He decides that the red light is only a suggestion to stop, and it's OK to make his own mind up and drive through them. If the lights are broken, you may have to use your own discretion. But the lights were not broken in this case, members of the jury, the police were still there – waiting for Mr Dennis to try and help him. But he didn't want their help – that's the last thing he wanted. Dennis wanted Maynard dead – and that's something with which the police would not have obliged him.

And, members of the jury, it's worse than that. He doesn't just buy a gun and keep it under his pillow at home at night in

143

case he's attacked, or even walk around with it tucked inside his trousers – no, not this defendant – he rolls up at this very building and fires not one bullet, members of the jury – hold onto this – but two bullets at point-blank range.

We on behalf of the Crown say there can only be one verdict in this case and I do not have to spell out to you what that is.

Finally, much to the relief of all, and with an exaggerated mop of his brow, Percival sat down.

'Who's your first witness?' asked Mr Justice McIntyre after Percival had placated himself with a glass of water.

'Céline Maynard – the deceased's widow,' answered Percival.

The judge turned towards Gorman. 'Will you conclude your cross-examination today?'

Gorman rose to his feet. 'I have a good number of questions for her, my Lord, as you might imagine, but I won't be all afternoon.'

'Good,' replied Mack the Knife, before adding, 'I have to break off a little early today – 3.30 at the latest. I've an important appointment I have to keep elsewhere.'

Now, where might that *elsewhere* be?

Chapter 25

Céline the Queen

'Madam, before Mr Gorman begins his cross-examination, would you like a break or a drink?' asked Mack the Knife kindly.

'Oh, yes, I'd love a gin and tonic, my Lord!' replied the witness enthusiastically.

'Yes, wouldn't we all, but I'm afraid I can only oblige you with a refreshment of the same colour – water.' Concealed smiles from the jury box, but not from Gorman. The judge was stealing the thunder from his *grande entrée*.

Céline Maynard had already been in the witness box for some forty minutes, recounting the terrifying events outside the Bailey where her beloved husband had been slain before her very eyes. Percival, as was his wont, had taken her through her eyewitness evidence at a snail's pace. By the time she'd finished, even Dennis had felt sorry for her. She was suitably dressed for the occasion in virtually flat shoes, a black suit and a cream silk shirt, with a simple leather handbag to match. Even her makeup looked restrained – and no mascara. Her appearance was in stark contrast to the flouncy outfit she'd been wearing on the CCTV footage at the scene of the killing.

For his part, Percival was dreading Gorman's cross-examination. He knew only too well what was coming – character assassination, as it was known in the trade. When you had little to offer for a defence this was par for the course. You kept well away from the facts of the case and slaughtered the deceased's character. It was standard practice, like playing for time when you are a goal up in a football match by keeping the ball near the corner flag towards the end of the game.

'What did your husband do for a living, Mrs Maynard?' was Gorman's starter for ten in cross-examination, after the witness had refreshed herself a little.

'Do for a living? I'm not sure what you mean.'

'Not sure what I mean, Mrs Maynard? Let me put it another way. How did your husband pay the bills? How did he make ends meet? Tell us, please,' asked Gorman in his most moderate tone.

'Well, I didn't really get involved in his business affairs. I was just a housewife. He did this and that – you know – a deal here and there.'

'Thank you for being so specific, Mrs Maynard, now everything's clear! You were married for what, well over thirty years, is that right?'

Céline just nodded.

'So, surely after all that time you must have had a pretty good idea what your husband did for a living.'

'Not really, I never interested myself in such matters, if you know what I mean.'

'No, actually I don't. Where did you first meet?' Gorman had no idea what the answer might be – but what the hell.

Céline hesitated and then, 'We met at Wormwood Scrubs Prison.'

Gorman's eyes starting popping. 'Wormwood Scrubs! That's not a mixed prison is it, Mrs Maynard?'

'No, I was visiting my father there.'

'Oh I see, so your father worked there. Was he the governor or a prison officer or probation officer or what?'

'No, he was an inmate,' mumbled the witness, 'and so was my husband at that time.'

'So, your father was an inmate, was he? Oh, I'm sorry to hear that. I won't ask you what for, it's absolutely nothing to do with this case.' (*The hell it wasn't*, thought Stanford sitting behind him.)

'The family home, Mrs Maynard, it's in your sole name, isn't it?'

'Yes,' came the delayed reply.

'How long have you lived there, please?'

'About fourteen years.'

'And how did you pay for it, Mrs Maynard? Six bedrooms, four bathrooms, quiet road, good area – it must have cost a pretty penny.'

'Do I have to answer that question, my Lord?' asked Mrs Maynard. 'I can't see what it's got to do with this case.'

'Nor can I,' grunted McIntyre from his seat high up in Court 1.

'Quite improper, in my submission, my Lord,' protested Percival.

The jury and the witness were sent out of court for a short while, whilst Gorman told the judge that he intended to suggest to Mrs Maynard that her husband had been a vicious loan shark, trading on fear, and had built his crooked empire on it.

'Now, Mrs Maynard,' continued Gorman on the jury's return to court, 'you were about to tell us how you paid for your home.'

'It was a gift,' she replied without much enthusiasm, and with even less conviction.

'Very generous indeed, no doubt, but from whom?'

Céline looked distinctly pale. 'A lover.'

'A lover! How understanding of your husband! To agree to live in a house bought for you by a lover. Now, where might this lover have come from? Your imagination or your husband's, Mrs Maynard?'

'No, not my imagination, he actually came from Zurich in Switzerland.'

'And his occupation, Mrs Maynard?'

'A banker.' The answer was manna from heaven for Gorman.

'A banker! So, let me get this straight, a Swiss banker, with whom you were having an affair, decides to buy you a house, and your husband says, "OK – that's fine, let's go and live in it"! I suppose the banker paid for it from a Swiss account, did he, Mrs Maynard?'

'I can't quite remember the details,' she offered.

'Did your husband, by any remote chance, have an account at the same bank, or was his at another Swiss bank, Mrs Maynard?' joked Gorman.

'I don't really understand what you're getting at.'

'Do you not? Very well, let's move on. Did you ever go away on holiday, Mrs Maynard?'

'Occasionally.'

'How occasionally?'

'Well, Easter, the summer and sometimes Christmas.'

'Would that be Cornwall, Torquay, the Lake District or where?'

'Well, actually we went abroad – we liked travelling.'

'Just give us last year, if you please. Easter?'

'Miami.'

'Summer?'

'South of France. Not in a hotel. We've got a little villa there in Antibes.'

'Has this little villa got a view of the sea, by any chance?'

'Yes, it has.'

'And a little swimming pool, no doubt?'

'It was there when we bought the villa, ten years ago.'

'I'm sure you've got no idea of the price you paid for it, so I won't ask you,' added Gorman, cynically. 'Christmas?'

'Barbados.'

'A nice eclectic mix, if you don't mind me saying so. So, your husband, living in a house bought for you by a Swiss lover, who just happens to be a banker, took you on three exotic holidays last year alone. Is exotic a fair description, Mrs Maynard?'

There was no reply. Gorman didn't expect one.

'The police found some £30,000 in mixed denominations under your staircase in an old Harrods hamper. What was that, Mrs Maynard – pocket money?'

'Bob always had money lying around the house; he didn't really trust banks.'

'Tell us what credit cards your husband held, Mrs Maynard.'

'He didn't have any.'

'So, he was a cash merchant then, was he?'

'He didn't owe any money to anyone either,' she retorted.

'Is that right, Mrs Maynard? Well, what about the Inland Revenue? Did your husband pay his taxes, Mrs Maynard? Did he have an accountant?'

'Now, if there's one thing I never involved myself in, it was my husband's tax affairs.'

'Unfortunately, neither did he, according to the Inland Revenue records given to us by the prosecution – they can find no trace of him. But I can tell you where he's very well known, Mrs Maynard, and that's on the Police National Computer. Now, you must know something about that. After all, you met him in prison, as you've just told us.' Gorman held a list of Maynard's criminal record in his hand. 'Now, let's see,' he said. 'Your husband made his debut in crime at the Old Bailey at the age of nineteen. Well, I call it his "debut in crime" but that might not be quite fair. It was, in fact, the first time he was caught. Two years for blackmail, I believe, is that right?'

'I hadn't met him yet.'

'Quite right, quite right, my mistake – let's move on. When you first set eyes on each other at the Scrubs, while you were visiting your father, why was he there? Threats to kill a landlord, wasn't it?'

'He told me the trial was a disgrace – he was innocent an' all,' she protested.

'So, the jury got it wrong did they, Mrs Maynard? Fair enough. Three years, I believe. And then a few years later he was the only defendant to be found not guilty in a serious drugs smuggling case, wasn't he? Did the jury get that wrong too, Mrs Maynard?' The jury liked that one.

'And then, of course, and I'm sorry to have to put this to

you, but on the day your husband was shot in this very case, the prosecution had to throw in the towel against him on charges of blackmail and threats to kill. You and your son were watching on from the public gallery, weren't you?'

Céline took out a handkerchief and dabbed her dry eyes masterfully. 'Yes, we were,' she mumbled.

'Then you heard the prosecution counsel tell the judge that the main witness for the Crown, a Mr William Churchman, refused to give evidence out of fear, and had also turned down police protection, saying, he'd "feel safer in a Siberian labour camp" – and later took three months' imprisonment on the chin for his troubles.'

Before the witness could answer, Percival flew up from his seat. 'My Lord, that is absolutely inadmissible as Mr Gorman knows very well – and now it's too late to correct it.'

'Yes, I agree,' said the livid Mack the Knife. 'That should never have been put, Mr Gorman, without my leave, which you never asked for – quite disgraceful.'

Gorman had his cheap alibi waiting. 'Well, my Lord, it was said in open court by the prosecution in that case in answer to a specific question from the judge, and his three-month sentence is a matter of record.'

'Move on – move on immediately,' replied the judge, scowling at Gorman.

Gorman did, but the damage had been done. 'Now, let me tell you where my questions are leading to, Mrs Maynard. I'm suggesting to you that your husband was in business, and a very profitable business, as you well know. He was a loan shark, wasn't he?'

'A loan shark? What's a loan shark? I don't know what you mean.'

'Don't you, Mrs Maynard? Well, let me tell you so there's no mystery. A loan shark is someone who lends cash in high sums to desperate people at ridiculous rates of interest. If they eventually can't pay back, they may well be given more time to pay with possibly even higher interest rates. If they still can't pay, they're threatened with violence or worse and then it gets carried out. In other words, I put it to you that your husband was a ruthless criminal living the high life on the misery of others. This is how I suggest your home was paid for, and your three holidays a year. And that is why the Revenue has no record of him. Loan sharks don't pay tax.' Then, in a quiet soothing tone, he added, 'But you know all this, Mrs Maynard, don't you?'

'No, I certainly do not.'

'Let's try another avenue. Give us a typical week in your husband's life – any week you like, Monday to Friday.'

Silence reigned.

'Well, Mrs Maynard? I'm waiting. I ask you once more, what did he do for a living? Did he have an office, staff or a job? How did he pay for your exotic holidays? How much money did he give you each week to keep the house and to dress you? Would you care to answer any of those questions?'

Still no response.

'OK, I won't press you. Let's move on. I see from the police photos of your home there's a convertible Mercedes in the drive. Latest model, I believe – yours?'

'Yes. It was a present from my husband on our last wedding anniversary.'

'A cash deal, I suppose?'

'It was a present.' The witness was becoming indignant.

'Now, let me ask you about your sons, Mrs Maynard. You have two sons, don't you?'

'Yes.'

'I don't mean to hurt your feelings, Mrs Maynard, but where's your older son, Donald, now? He must be about thirty-three.'

'In Australia, I think.'

'Where in Australia?'

'I don't know, I'm afraid.'

'When did you last see him?'

'Fifteen years ago.'

'And when did you last speak to him?'

'Fifteen years ago.'

'So, we can safely assume that he's not in the family business. Do you want to tell us why he left home at eighteen and fled halfway across the world to Australia?'

'No, I don't.'

'Very well then. Now, your younger son, Bob Jr, I believe.'

'That's correct.'

'He must be thirty-two, is that right?'

'Yes, he is.'

'In business with his father, wasn't he?'

'He helped him out sometimes.'

'Now, on that we agree, Mrs Maynard. I put it to you, your son did whatever he was told to do. He was the enforcement branch of your husband's loan shark business, wasn't he?' pressed Gorman.

'It's not fair to say things like that when my poor boy's not here to defend himself.'

'Yes, I noticed he's not here, Mrs Maynard. He could have been, couldn't he, if he'd wanted to – sitting quietly at the back of the court listening to proceedings? Mr Percival for the prosecution sitting right next to me has heard me make my case plain – namely, that your husband was a loan shark by trade and your son his dreaded enforcer. So, if I'm wrong, the prosecution could call your son to put us straight. Did the police take a statement from your son, Mrs Maynard?'

'No.'

'Did they try to? After all, he witnessed the shooting with you.'

'Yes, I think they did,' she answered begrudgingly.

'So, I assume he refused to cooperate, is that correct?'

'You'll have to ask him, won't you?'

'Well, if the prosecution call him to tell us about your husband's business affairs, I most certainly will, Mrs Maynard. Bob Jr isn't a great believer in the tax system either, is he, Mrs Maynard?'

'I really don't know, but he has no criminal record at all – so there.'

Gorman was waiting for this moment. 'Well, let's not get carried away – he's been charged four times, but he's never actually been convicted. That's the uncomfortable truth, isn't it, Mrs Maynard? Grievous bodily harm – twice – plus money laundering and attempting to pervert the course of justice. Is that a fair résumé, Mrs Maynard?'

'He's a good boy really, trust me.'

'It's for the jury to decide whether they trust you, Mrs Maynard. I would simply observe that if that's really the case, your son has nothing to fear by coming to court and telling us all about the family business, does he?'

'That's up to him,' she replied curtly.

'Just one last matter, Mrs Maynard, and then I'll be finished. What was your husband's nickname?'

'Nickname? What do you mean nickname?'

'He was known as Mercenary Bob Maynard, or otherwise "Bob the Merc". Is that true or false?'

The witness looked ill at ease. 'I've heard people calling him by that name, but I never really knew why.'

'Did you ever ask him why?'

'Yes, he told me it was just a silly joke.'

Gorman rowed in with another of his trademark speeches. 'Oh, yes, to him it may well have been a silly joke, but his customers didn't find it funny, did they, Mrs Maynard? Not at all funny.'

Then Gorman sat down, giving the crucified witness no chance to answer.

Percival rose speedily to his feet. 'No re-examination, my Lord,' he announced in a tone which, cynically translated, meant, *get her the hell out of here*.

Dennis's defence was up and running.

Chapter 26

Rough Hands

——————

At 9 a.m. on the dot on the first day of the trial, Halfpint was in pole position in the queue for Court 1 at the Old Bailey. He had risen at 5 a.m. to dress for the show. It had taken him quite a while to dye his greying hair jet-black and to give it a greased look, as well as to adjust to perfection a false closely cropped beard and moustache. He was wearing his favourite brown Cuban heels, a plain white shirt and a navy cardigan bought for him the previous Christmas by his niece. By the time he'd finished he looked like everyone's favourite uncle.

When the court's doors finally opened, he took an aisle seat in the back row and watched on intently as the names of the twelve jurors were drawn at random from a pool of twenty. Seven men and five women took their places. The five women were summarily dismissed from his reckoning. No, it was the seven men who were on his radar. Two of them, wearing suits and ties, were immediately discarded. A third in a thick brown jumper with the *Daily Telegraph* crossword puzzle sticking out of his jacket was quick to follow. That left four candidates. Two were very young. One looked like he couldn't tell a razor blade from a rubber and the other had a serious case of acne. Never get a kid to do a man's job. No, he stood by his *Titanic* principles: women and children off first!

That left just two contenders. Now, which one should it be? No rush, he had all day to decide. He cast his eyes on one of the other dramatis personae: the judge. 'Madam Clerk,' he heard him whispering, 'it's already stifling in here. Please ensure the temperature is lowered by at least five degrees straight away.' The judge then turned to the jury and told them that although Court I was indeed an historic venue, it was often too hot and had the worst acoustics in the entire building. *What an old fusspot*, thought Halfpint.

Whilst the prosecutor was busy setting out his extensive stall in his opening speech, Halfpint was concentrating on the body language of the two remaining candidates on the jury. The first was in his mid-thirties, wearing a claret-coloured cashmere polo neck and sporting what looked like a gold Cartier tank watch on his wrist. He was elegantly groomed and gave the impression of someone who led an easy life. When Percival reached the part of the opening speech dealing with the killing itself, the juror looked truly horrified – mouth opening wide, eyes closing in disbelief – before pouring himself a welcome glass of water. *Not for me – a real mama's boy*, thought Halfpint.

Now, six of the seven men on the jury had been deemed unsuitable but the last one gave cause for hope. Early forties, two days' facial hair growth, thick curly brown hair with no parting, about 5ft 10in. tall, light-blue faded jeans, dirty brown boots, sleeves rolled up to the elbow, sitting there with his arms folded, taking everything in, but outwardly showing nothing. He had a clear, hardened, ruddy complexion. It was that of a man who spent a good deal of time working outdoors, as opposed to in an office of some sort.

Halfpint started eliminating. Doctor, dentist, lawyer, accountant, estate agent, schoolteacher – all dismissed in one fell swoop. The man's hands appeared rough, a bit grimy and he had a muscular build. Yes, he had a job that involved working outdoors, Halfpint concluded. But what? A builder, plumber, roofer, car mechanic? All possible. There was also something about his general poise that persuaded Halfpint he was more than likely self-employed – even better!

Finally, when the judge rose early to keep his 'appointment elsewhere', a minor incident occurred, which made Halfpint's decision easy. On standing up to leave court and whilst putting on his donkey jacket, a rolled-up newspaper fell out of Rough Hands's pocket. Halfpint, true professional that he was, leaned forward, straining his eyes to see what it might be. The *Racing Post* – a betting man! Now that was indeed a stroke of good fortune. What more could he have asked for?

'He's my boy,' Halfpint mumbled under his breath. 'He's my boy alright.'

Chapter 27

Elsewhere

'**B**aker Street and make it snappy.'

'Which route would you like, guv?' asked the cabby as Mr Justice McIntyre sat himself down in the back. It was 4.10 p.m. and the judge had some important shopping to do.

'Definitely not via King's Cross – if you get held up in Gray's Inn Road you've crossed the Rubicon and the die is cast.'

The cabby looked at him in the rear-view mirror as though he were a complete nutter. 'Which end of Baker Street, guv?' asked the cabby twenty-five minutes later.

'Here will do nicely,' said McIntyre as the taxi pulled into Manchester Square. Mack the Knife alighted, gave the cabby a tenner and waited for the change – 40 pence! He then went in search of a bank and withdrew £1,000 cash. He shook his head sadly. Had he not become a *cash merchant* himself, just like Bob the Merc? Then he walked up Baker Street towards Selfridges – that was where his iPad had told him he'd find the shop.

Spymaster. A haven for the over-curious, with every surveillance gadget known to man on display. Briefcases with cameras, watches with recorders, bug detectors, encrypted phones – a true paradise for James Bond aficionados. Mack the Knife had seen the shop in a TV documentary on the art of spying in the modern world.

He peered in through the wide window and waited for two large eastern-European-looking gentlemen sporting dark glasses to leave, carrying an unseemly number of bulky bags. Finally, he mustered up the courage to enter. The last time he recalled such embarrassment was years ago in a pharmacy when he furtively enquired about precautionary measures, following a couple of clumsy fumbles with Frances at the chambers Christmas party, where she had given him cause for hope of his first amorous conquest.

'I'm looking for a device which records both sound and video,' he said to the shop assistant, as he cast his eyes around a vast array of gadgetry on display on the shelves of what was a much larger shop than he had anticipated. *My goodness*, he thought to himself, *what sort of clientele does this shop attract?*

'Can you give me a little detail as to its proposed use, sir?' asked the shop assistant.

'Yes. I'm concerned about the regular theft of petty cash from my office, and I want to catch the culprit red-handed.' McIntyre could tell from the look on the shop assistant's face that he didn't believe a word but was quite accustomed to requests such as this one, and that a fair number of such sales were related to infidelity.

'Well, we have several in stock which would fit the bill,' continued the man, 'but the most popular is this iPhone charger. You see, it not only works as an iPhone charger but also films and records any movement in the room.'

'I already have an iPhone charger,' replied McIntyre like a spoilt child.

'Excellent, sir. In fact, ideal – then no one will realise anything has changed. It should work a treat.'

'It won't be a treat for me when I look at what's going to be on it,' answered McIntyre. 'I'll take it.'

'That's £520 please, sir. How will you be paying?'

'Cash,' announced McIntyre promptly whilst pulling out his newly acquired wad of notes from his wallet.

'Here you are, sir,' said the shop assistant, having packed the item in a carrier bag. 'It comes with full instructions, and here's your receipt.'

McIntyre stared at the piece of paper as if the very touching of it would infect him with leprosy. 'A receipt! That's the last thing I need,' he said gruffly as he exited the premises at speed, his expensive new toy buried deep in his coat pocket.

Chapter 28

Two Deadly Duos

‘The name's Pete Lomax – been married for twenty-two years, three kids, runs a tyre shop in the Angel. Loves a flutter – promised his wife a new kitchen and just sold his vintage MGB to pay off his bank overdraft. Now he's stuck at the Bailey trying some poor bugger for murder. He's got one assistant, whom he doesn't trust as he's sure he's selling his tyres for cash whenever he's not around and pocketing the money.'

It was 8 p.m. and Big Jake was once again at the Artesian Bar in the Langham Hotel near Regent's Park, downing his third Old Cuban cocktail, when Halfpint arrived. 'Not bad, Halfpint, not bad for a day's work, and great fancy dress to boot – I barely recognised you when you came in. We'll make a spy out of you yet,' said Jake, as he eased a fat brown envelope into the inside pocket of his jacket. 'How did you find all this out?'

'Having studied the twelve jurors all day long, I made my choice,' Halfpint proudly replied. 'I was waiting as he left the Bailey. He strolled through Smithfield's meat market and stopped off at a bookmaker's to check the results. He came out five minutes later looking like he'd just filed his own bankruptcy petition. Then he walked all the way back to his tyre shop in the Angel – not a customer in sight. So, in I went and asked him if he could give me a price for four new tyres for my old Honda.

'Anyway,' continued Halfpint with aplomb, now crossing his legs and pleased to see he had Jake's full attention – a rarity when he was talking. 'He immediately wanted to know how I'd be paying. "Cash, of course," I answered. We struck a deal at £400 for the lot. I told him I'd bring my car in at 11 a.m. tomorrow, which I knew would be useless to him. Sure enough, he told me that was no good as he was on jury service at the Bailey. So I asked him if the case was interesting. "A loan shark copped it," he answered. "Bloody good show too, I wish it had been my bank manager." And then he went into one about how this bloke's brief was red-hot and had slaughtered the dead man's wife, who was obviously lying her head off all afternoon.

'Then he started moaning about how was he going to run his business when he was stuck at court all day, and it all came pouring out about his financial troubles, his wife's planned new kitchen, his crooked employee and his three bone-idle teenage girls, who were costing him a fortune using his credit card all over town. He had a photo of his vintage MGB on the wall in his office and told me that it had to go to pay off the bank. He was almost in tears. "OK," I said coming back to my tyres, "what about before court?" So, now I'm back there at 8 in the morning. Wally's got the false plates lined up ready for me.'

Jake looked horrified. 'Wayward Wally? I hope you haven't told Wally why you need them? I wouldn't trust him to put vinegar on my chips.'

'Not a word, Jake. I told him I needed them for a car I'm smuggling out of the country.'

'Halfpint, you're a tasty little operator, I'll give you that,' said Jake, looking a little relieved and slapping Halfpint's knee. 'Now, tomorrow, when you get your tyres changed, what's your pitch going to be?'

'Well, I thought I'd tell him that after I left his tyre shop last night, I read a piece in the *Evening Standard* and realised that it must be about his case. I'm going to spin him a yarn about how me and the boys were talking about it in the pub, and what do you know, one of them knew the defendant and he was a really nice guy. I'd say how they'd been at college together on a business studies course, and how this friend had made it big in the stock market and wanted to help him out. I'd slip him an envelope with 5,000 smackers in it and tell him this was shrapnel to Dennis's old college mate, and that there'd be another five large in it for him when our man walks.'

Jake wrinkled his nose. 'What if he goes to the police?'

'He won't, he's not that sort,' replied Halfpint confidently. 'Anyway, he'll probably vote not guilty come what may, so the money won't bother his conscience. But what we're looking for is for him to persuade the others on the jury to do the same.'

Jake frowned. 'All very nice, but how are we going to know what the jury's thinking? If the trial's going really badly, we may have to use some more persuasive measures. After tomorrow I don't want you round at his garage again while the trial's running.'

'Leave that to me, Jake, I've got it all figured out.'

'Right, I will,' announced Jake. 'Halfpint, you're off to a good start – in fact, you're playing a blinder. Ernie will drop you off the money at 6 in the morning.'

Jake then paused and assessed the situation. He picked up his glass and started caressing the edges with his burly lips, as if he was licking the ear of his bit on the side. 'Halfpint, you know you and me could make a deadly duo – your devious mind and my money! Now, get some kip, and for God's sake make sure you turn up with a set of bald tyres tomorrow, even punctures if necessary, or our nag will come a cropper at the first fence.'

'Don't worry, Jake, they're all well below what's legal anyway.'

Jake just sneered. 'That's no great surprise. I'd expect nothing less from a man of your calibre, Halfpint.'

* * *

Whilst Jake and Halfpint had been scheming at the Artesian Bar, Bob Jr and his right-hand man, Lenny, were meeting in the bar at the Little Italy restaurant in Soho. Bob Jr had stormed out of the family home. He couldn't stand any more of his mum's sobbing, or her account of how she'd been roasted alive that very afternoon at the Bailey. He was looking for some comfort and had no one else to turn to.

'You know, Lenny, it's hard to believe, but I've never seen my mum cry before – not even at the old man's funeral.'

Lenny nodded sympathetically.

'This ain't justice,' continued Bob Jr. 'Dennis has got himself a top brief – God knows who's paying for him. Do you know he didn't ask my mum one question about what she saw? Not one bloody question. He went on and on about our house and holidays and the taxman, and even had the nerve to ask her where the hell I was and why I wasn't in court. She felt like she was on trial – not Dennis. Now, what sort of justice is that? She came home, locked herself in the bedroom with a bottle of Bristol Cream, and I couldn't get her out. I had to listen to the whole bloody story through the keyhole.'

'What about our having a quiet word or two with a couple of the jurors? That should do the trick.'

'Oh, a great idea! Three years ago I was up for perverting and lucky to get off. Who do you think the Old Bill will nick if it all comes on top? – Me! No,' Bob Jr decided. 'There's nothing I can do.' He shook his head as if he couldn't believe his own words. 'This is the way it is these days. You shoot a man in cold blood and because he didn't pay his taxes the killer stands a good chance of walking. Well, if he walks, it won't be for long. Mark my words, Lenny, as I live and breathe – he's a dead man walking.'

Chapter 29

One–Nil

———

I ron-Rod Stokes opened the door to the incident room, took a couple of steps in, started sniffing and stopped in his tracks. 'Potter, what's that sickly aftershave you're wearing? You smelt better when you hadn't showered! You must be the only person in the world who smells better when they *don't* shower!'

Potter reddened. 'My bird gave it to me for my birthday, guv.'

Stokes failed to sympathise. 'Yes, I bet she did. She wanted to make sure no other woman ever came near you. I don't know why she's worrying anyway. Do you mind standing at the back of the room?' Potter shrugged and obliged. 'Thanks, Potter, and you'd better sit right at the back of the court today as well. If the judge catches one whiff of you, he'll lower the temperature another five degrees and we'll all freeze our bollocks off.'

'Well, men, we didn't exactly cover ourselves in glory yesterday, and that's for sure. We're 1–0 down already, and today could be worse.' The Iron-Rod was getting to the point. 'That Stanford's a slippery bastard if ever I've met one. Getting Dennis to read out that piece of fiction in our interview was a disgrace.' Stokes started fiddling in his jacket pocket for a few calming tablets before continuing. 'I tell you, in my next life I'm coming back as a defence brief. I'll ride around in a Ferrari, buy a couple of Savile Row suits and take the piss out of the police. And as for his mouthpiece Gorman, he's turning the whole trial into a farce. When he was cracking away at Maynard's widow, you'd have thought he was prosecuting for the tax man. Do you know what he said to me outside court yesterday? "Good morning, Mr Stokes,"' he mimicked. '"Nice to see you're still in harness, when are you retiring?" Then he had the nerve to tell me that I'm on a certain winner – bloody hypocrite. But just wait 'til it's Dennis's turn to go into the witness box. Percival is frothing at the mouth at the prospect. He's a proper old-fashioned centre-forward, and by the time he stands up to cross-examine Dennis he'll have worked himself into a right old frenzy. He's going to massacre him, that's for sure. And he won't have Stanford there to protect him either. Wait 'til he asks him where he got the gun and about the missing bullets and his dressing up as a barrister. Count on me, the verdict will be a mere formality.'

The eight officers, listening in silence, were not quite so confident. Was their guvnor losing the plot?

'Yes,' Stokes reassured himself. 'He's going to scatter him all over the court.'

The tablets were working already!

* * *

Whilst Stokes was salivating at the prospect of Dennis's demise, Halfpint was fully engaged trying to 'even the odds a little', as Jake had put it. He and his dirty old Honda were encamped outside Rough Hands's tyre shop in the Angel. He couldn't afford to be late. The only new items on the vehicle were the false number plates, carefully sprayed in with the leftovers of Halfpint's invaluable hair dye, so that they would blend in with the rest of the jalopy.

At 7.55 a.m., a scruffy, podgy man in his early twenties arrived and stood outside. Halfpint sized him up whilst sitting in his car. *This must be Rough Hands's scallywag of an employee*, he concluded. Scallywag was tucking into a bacon and egg McMuffin, which he followed with a roll-up cigarette for afters. He then started walking up and down the street looking around him and talking into his phone as if there was villainy afoot. *Some monkey business, likely as not*, thought Halfpint. He lowered his window a little to listen. 'I'll be here alone all day – no problems – safe as houses,' were the only words he could decipher and then, finally, 'see you later'. Scallywag rolled a second cigarette and pulled on it hard. 'I wouldn't touch him with a disinfected barge pole,' mumbled Halfpint to himself.

At 8.05 a.m. Rough Hands arrived in an old white Ford van. The shutters were opened and both men entered the shop. Halfpint followed. Scallywag was sent out to inspect the tyres on Halfpint's Honda, and the car was driven into the bay.

Whilst the tyres were being changed, Halfpint grabbed his moment and entered the tiny office with his well-rehearsed speech about reading the case in the newspapers, and Dennis's imaginary old college mate, who wanted to ease the passage a little for his long-lost friend. Rough Hands listened intently to Halfpint's sweet talk and didn't believe a word of it. When a fat, rectangular packet was dropped on his office table together with the £400 for the tyres, Rough Hands suddenly started thinking that the story might be true after all. Either way, £5,000 in advance to soothe his conscience and pay towards a new kitchen was just what the doctor had ordered.

'Now, listen carefully, Pete,' whispered Halfpint. 'I want a daily report on how the jury are thinking, and this is how I'm going to get it.' Halfpint then produced three red biros. 'I can see you're wearing a shirt with a pocket – good. Make sure you wear one every day of the trial – is that clear?' Rough Hands simply nodded, his eyes screwed up in disbelief. 'Now, each day you'll take these biros to court with you. If the trial's going badly for our boy, you'll wear none; one if it's going so-so; two for good; and three for great – got it?' Halfpint repeated it slowly to make sure his mini-tutorial had registered.

'And how can I be sure I'll see the other £5,000 if he gets off?' enquired Rough Hands, fearing he'd be done over for the balance.

'You can't,' replied Halfpint, 'but Dennis's old mate is caked up. £5,000 is a cheap day out at the races for him.' Rough Hands remained unconvinced. 'Let's hope we meet again next week in happier circumstances,' said Halfpint as he was leaving. 'And make sure you've got enough clean shirts with pockets to last the trial, or you'll have to ask the judge for a break while you do a little pre-Christmas shopping,' he joked. 'And another thing, don't lose these lovely biros. I'm looking to buy them from you after the trial. £5,000 for the three – got it?'

Chapter 30

An Expensive Wig

D ay two of the trial began with the prosecution calling their computer expert to tell the jury about Dennis's three *visits* to his iPad to study the law of self-defence. Unsurprisingly, no cross-examination from Gorman, who did his best to look thoroughly bored throughout. No sense in highlighting a bad point.

Then came Derek Portman, the sales assistant from Ede & Ravenscroft, the barrister's outfitters in Chancery Lane which Dennis had visited two days before the killing. 'Yes,' he told the court, 'the man in the dock visited my shop and bought a wig and gown, a white shirt and a collar and tabs. He paid for it all in cash – £837.50, to be exact. Actually, he first asked me whether we sold second-hand wigs and gowns. He looked a little crestfallen when I told him that we didn't. During our conversation, he told me that it was all to be a surprise for his son, who had just qualified as a barrister, and they were the same size in everything.'

'Did you believe him?'

'To tell you the truth, I did. He was very calm and chatty and a pleasure to deal with. He even looked at a few pin-stripe suits but said that they were a bit expensive for him. One thing I do remember is that he was shocked by the price of wigs and asked if they had any second-hand value.'

'And what did you answer, Mr Portman?' asked Gorman in cross-examination. 'Do wigs have a second-hand value? I have a personal interest in knowing.'

'Not if your head's too big.'

'Dear me, Mr Percival will be most upset to hear that!'

'So, mine should sell in a jiffy,' butted in Mack the Knife, joining in the general banter. 'Don't you agree, Mr Gorman?'

'Oh, yes, my Lord, in a flash.' And then in a loud aside, 'To the Chamber of Horrors at Madame Tussauds.' Wisely, a scowling Mack the Knife let it pass. Not all publicity was good publicity.

Next came the CCTV footage of the killing, with Dennis looking like the master of disguise and committing a cold-blooded murder if ever there was one. 'Play the part again where Dennis takes off his wig just before the second gunshot, if you would. I think it's important for the jury to see that sequence a second time,' ordered Mack the Knife. Percival willingly obliged.

Stokes was already feeling better and left his calming tablets untouched. The jury looked horrified at what they saw, but Halfpint up in the gallery was pleased to note that Rough Hands appeared unmoved. *My, my, what a fresh crisp shirt he has on with a shiny new biro in the breast pocket. Better than none*, thought Halfpint.

Percival then called the police officers who were first to arrive at the scene and they recounted how Dennis was standing there nervously pulling on a cigarette when they arrested him. Stokes was starting to enjoy himself, and his mind started drifting towards his well-earned retirement.

The next piece of evidence was to read admissions from the prosecution. The ANPR system had picked up Dennis's car at various spots en route to Chelmsford and also that his minicab company had received a booking for the trip. On occasions, a driver was visible, although not clearly enough to prove who it was. However, there was no evidence available as to whether the back seats were occupied or not. It was also conceded that the time between the two sightings on the A12 was consistent with the vehicle having either stopped at some point or slowed down considerably during its journey. Stokes's hopes in tatters.

The morning ended with the Home Office pathologist being called to give evidence as to the cause of death. Before he really got going, the judge interrupted him. 'Always a pleasure to see you, Professor Williams, but a telephone directory doesn't need an index! I don't think any of us are in any doubt as to the cause of death – two bullets fired at very close range to the stomach and the heart, as we've all seen on the video. Would that be a fair summary?'

'You have it in one, if I may say so, my Lord,' replied the pathologist.

'You may indeed,' replied the judge, nodding his head in appreciation in the direction of the witness. 'Well, if that's the case, I wish you a very good day,' he said, before reminding himself that the defence also had a right to be heard. 'Oh, sorry, any questions, Mr Gorman?'

'No, my Lord. I too wish Professor Williams a very good day. I'm sure he must have more important work *elsewhere*.'

Mack the Knife was lost for a suitable repartee. *Elsewhere* was a touchy subject. All morning, the judge had been thinking about how he was going to deploy his new expensive toy at home on Charles's visit that very week.

Clever dick, thought the judge. *Well, he won't be feeling quite so smug when he hears me summing up this case in a few days' time.*

Chapter 31

Oh the Shark Bites with His Teeth, Dear

'Members of the jury,' began Mr Justice McIntyre after the lunch break, 'we're now going to watch the police interviews of Mr Dennis after his arrest. The prosecution do not intend to play the first interview. Apparently, his solicitor couldn't get back in time from the Cannes Film Festival, and it's an agreed fact that he advised his client on the telephone not to answer any question put to him in what was a forty-minute interview in his absence. More about that, members of the jury, when I come to sum up the law to you at the end of the trial – yes, a good deal more.' Mack the Knife was already sharpening his blade.

Stokes, sitting in court behind Percival, started checking his pocket to see if he had enough calming tablets to get him through the afternoon session. The second police interview, in which Dennis read out his long speech, was the weakest point in the prosecution's case.

Before the video was switched on, Gorman was suggesting

subtitles. 'I wonder, my Lord, if each member of the jury could have a transcript of the interview at this stage – exhibit NW/1, I believe. They'll then be able to follow the video word for word and mark up whatever parts they feel appropriate.'

'Yes, a good idea,' replied McIntyre, 'and perhaps it will help them read between the lines as well, Mr Gorman – don't you think?'

The video was switched on and Dennis's tragic story about how he met Bob the Merc and the terrible threats he received had the entire court spellbound, culminating with the Russian roulette incident on the A12 outside Chelmsford and finally his pleading words: 'I really had no other choice.'

By the time the harrowing video had ended it was nearly 4 p.m. and everyone needed a break.

Gorman was on his feet, wanting to end the day on a high. 'My Lord, bearing in mind the time and the ten-minute break we're about to have, may I suggest we call it a day and deal with my client's last interview tomorrow morning?' Gorman knew only too well that in Dennis's last interview he hadn't answered one single question.

'Yes, Mr Gorman,' replied the judge. 'Another very good idea – for the defence. But in the interests of justice I take the view that the jury should hear all the interviews in one go, so they get the full picture, even if we have to sit late. Don't you agree, Mr Percival?' he said turning towards the prosecutor.

Before Percival could reply, Gorman protested. 'My Lord, I have an important appointment elsewhere myself today which I have to keep,' he lied.

'Well, we won't detain you long,' answered the judge. 'It's

a relatively short interview, as I recall it.' Stokes nodded approvingly.

At 4 p.m., the jury returned to court, Rough Hands now sporting two pens in his shirt pocket. The video of the last interview was switched on: 'Where did you get the gun?' 'Why did you need to fire two shots?' and so on.

By 4.40 p.m., when the day had drawn to a close, it was plain to see from the jury's glances at each other that Dennis's persistent silence throughout the last interview had not gone down well for the defence.

How many biros would Rough Hands be sporting tomorrow morning? wondered Halfpint as he left the public gallery. He reached his verdict before he'd set foot outside the building – *none.*

Chapter 32

Halfpint the Cheapskate

At 6.30 that evening, Big Jake was again anxiously waiting in the Artesian Bar for his daily bulletin on the Dennis trial. He had grown tired of the Old Cubans and had switched to Negronis. Halfpint, punctual as ever, made his entrance and plonked himself on the couch by the window, next to Jake.

'Well?' asked Jake. 'How's our man doing?'

'Swings and roundabouts,' replied Halfpint, matter-of-factly. 'Wet eyes all round when the jury saw him on video telling his sad tale, but his last interview, when he stayed shtum, was a bloody disaster.'

'OK, but more to the point, how did the meeting go with the tyre man this morning?'

'Sweet as a nut. I gave him the money and he barely blinked.'

'Good, so how are we going to know what the jury are thinking?'

'Oh, don't worry, Jake, I gave him another little present which should do the trick.'

'Like what?'

'Well, actually I gave him three pens.'

'Three pens! What were they? Parkers or Mont Blancs?'

Halfpint started giggling. 'No, Jake, nothing so pricey – three biros for a pound from Co-op.'

'Three for a pound?' repeated a mystified Jake. 'What's he supposed to do with those? Write a long confession statement to the Old Bill, or ease his constipation?'

'Just wait and see,' replied a chuckling Halfpint.

Jake's eyes widened. 'You're a real cheapskate, Halfpint, I always said it. What with that old banger of a Honda of yours and your grandfather's Ingersoll watch, you've got deep pockets and short hands. Waiter!' barked out Jake. 'Bring me a glass of tap water for old Scrooge here. He's on a pre-Christmas economy drive, and that's for sure. And while you're at it, bring me an Old Cuban. This Negroni I've been drinking is giving me hot flushes.'

The waiter arrived with the drinks, wondering which one of the two was the real scrooge. 'Here's to the success of our little venture, Halfpint,' said Jake as he lifted his Old Cuban above the tap water and clinked glasses. 'Yes, me drinking an Old Cuban and you tap water says it all, Halfpint – don't you agree?' he added cruelly.

Halfpint pretended to be deeply offended. 'Your tie buys my suit, Jake. I always said it, your tie buys my suit. There, I've said it twice.'

Jake just nodded approvingly whilst eyeing up Halfpint suspiciously. 'Never a truer word, Halfpint, never a truer word. Cheers.'

Chapter 33

To Be or Not to Be

On the third day of the trial, Iron-Rod Stokes arrived for his daily pre-court briefing in fine fettle. 'Here, men,' he called out, pointing to two large bags of croissants. 'Let's begin the day with a little celebration. We've got a new member in our team and he's real hot – the judge! Did you see him put old Gorman in his place yesterday? Important appointment after court – what a lot of eyewash.'

'But you ain't seen nothing yet! Wait 'til his summing up, he'll tell the jury what's what. I can hear it already.' In a deep rich voice, he then intoned, 'Members of the jury, you must cast from your mind all feelings of sympathy and coldly exam-ine the facts. And the facts, you may think, are that this was a cold-blooded killing, carefully planned and executed on British shores – right outside this very building.'

Stokes opened up the two bags and dumped the contents on the table. 'Come on, boys, don't be shy, tuck in. Half are almond and the other half plain.' The eight officers needed no second invitation. A free gift from the Iron-Rod was a rare event.

'Jackson,' continued Stokes, 'get yourself down to the cells

and give Dennis's dear old cellmate Samson a copy of his statement to read. Lean on him a bit so he doesn't suffer a sudden
loss of memory in the witness box. And you can tell him from
me if he's hoping to be moved to an open prison in a year's time,
have his own room, do his own cooking and get a bit of home
leave, he'd better come up trumps. And take Potter with you to
teach him a few basic tricks of the trade.'

'The real cabaret will start this afternoon when Dennis gets
in the witness box,' said Stokes as the officers were munching
away, crumbs everywhere. 'I've brought some extra calming tablets with me today – I thought Stanford might need a few.' He
grinned and produced a handful from his pocket.

'I'll be giving evidence myself later this morning to round off
our case. No doubt Gorman will have a crack at me, but I'm ready
for him. I've not been put out to grass just yet.' Stokes looked
around to see if anyone's facial expression indicated otherwise
before continuing. 'I spent an hour after court yesterday with
Percival going over his twenty pages of cross-examination notes.
He's got every angle covered. It's going to be a bloodbath – an
X-rated massacre. It's going to make the *Texas Chainsaw Massacre* look like *Tom and Jerry*.'

His team were not quite so optimistic. Clairvoyance was not
one of Iron-Rod's stronger suits.

*　　*　　*

'To be or not to be, Mr Dennis, that is the question.' Dennis
had no idea what Gorman was talking about.

Deep down in the cells at the Bailey, Gorman, together with

Jacobsen and Stanford, were having an early morning conference with their client. A crucial decision had to be made that
day, and Dennis alone had to make it.

Dennis had sat quietly in the dock for the first two days watching the trial seesaw. The fierce prosecution opening speech; the
defence's destruction of the widow Maynard; the judge clearly on
the prosecution's side; the horrified faces of the jury as they watched the shooting incident; then the jury pitying him as they watched
him on video reading out his long statement; before, finally, the
all-time low of his remaining silent in his final interview.

And who was there to support him in his time of need besides
his defence team? Nobody. In all the months he'd sat in prison, he
had refused to let his wife and kids visit him for fear of retaliation
from Bob's cronies, who doubtless had spies working for them in
the prison. He'd often spoken to his family on the phone, but he'd
never rung any number connected with them directly. He rang an
old friend who arranged a three-way conversation. No one knew
his wife's whereabouts, and that was how it was going to remain,
at least until after the trial – whichever way it went.

'Yes, to be or not to be,' repeated Gorman dramatically.

Dennis could take no more of this mumbo-jumbo. 'I'll be in
the box this afternoon, won't I, Mr Gorman?'

'That's what we've come to discuss, David,' said Stanford. 'It's
your decision, but I'd like you to listen to what your two barristers have to say, think about it carefully and let us know your
final decision during the lunch break – OK?'

'Adrian,' said Gorman, 'read out that depressing party piece
you insist on drafting in every case to bring us all back to earth.'
And then, turning to his client, 'Listen to the Grim Reaper at

work before you make a decision. Even better, Adrian, give him a copy and let him read it aloud to us, here and now.'

Adrian gave Gorman a quizzical look. 'Do you think that's wise?'

'Well, I've said it now, so let's not make a mystery of it.'

Reluctantly, Stanford handed his client a copy of a table he had compiled, whilst Gorman sat back in his chair, crossed his arms and closed his eyes.

Dennis started to read it out to them.

Pros and Cons – re. client giving evidence

Points for	Points against
• No criminal record, family man, not a professional criminal	• Self-confessed forger and thief
• Killed a nasty piece of work	• Took the law into his own hands, in-depth planning of killing, disguise and use of a gun, firing twice, not self-defence on the spur of the moment, researching law of self-defence three times prior to the killing, took off wig before firing second shot
• Stayed at the scene afterwards	• Stood no realistic prospect of escape anyway
• Did it for his own safety and that of his family	• Duress not a defence to murder
• Sought the help of the police, but to no avail	• Not the police's fault – could have left town (his wife and kids did)
• Read out his life story in his police interview, warts and all	• Not including the killing itself – also, alleged manufacture of Russian roulette incident
• The Edge: Patrick Gorman QC!	• Judge hell-bent on a conviction (just wait for his summing up)

When Dennis had finished reading, Gorman opened his eyes and saw that giving his client a copy might not have been such a good idea: Dennis looked drained. 'Don't worry, Mr Dennis,' said Gorman, 'we won't be handing out copies to the jury or they might not bother retiring! Only joking.'

'Here's where we stand at present, Mr Dennis,' continued Gorman in a more serious vein. 'The case is going OK.' He paused. 'In fact, a little better than I anticipated, if I'm honest. First off, this morning, Samson the traitor will be giving evidence. That'll be interesting. Followed by Stokes. But there's nothing he can add that is going to make the prosecution's case stronger. I'm going to give him no wriggle room. A few sharp points and then I'll sit down. So, the question is, do we call you to give evidence or stand pat? I know that's an expression you well understand, Mr Dennis, if you don't mind my saying so,' he added with a wry smile.

'I thought I was going into the box, Mr Gorman. Why shouldn't I?' Dennis looked very pent up. 'And how's it going to appear to the jury if I don't speak up for myself and tell them Samson's a bloody liar? I'm ready for it.'

'I agree entirely,' said Gorman. 'At first blush, not calling you will look appalling, but that's not the litmus test. The real question is, will your giving evidence improve your prospects, or will our case take a nosedive by the time Percival's finished with you? Will the jury accept your account or think you're slanting the truth and deceiving them? What was it Buddha said over 2,000 years ago? *"If you can't improve on silence – don't talk."* It's a close call, Mr Dennis, a very close call, but all my years of experience tell me not to put you in the box. What do you think, Daniel?' Gorman looked across for support from his junior.

'You'll never improve on what you read out in your police interview,' said Daniel. 'There will be many unanswered questions – true. But, as I see it, some of your answers will only serve to make the prosecution case stronger. Even a rottweiler like Percival can't cross-examine a video. I agree with Patrick.'

'What about you, Adrian?' asked Gorman, angling his head towards him.

'We had a six-handed trial ten years ago or so,' said Stanford. 'Three gave evidence and three didn't. Only three were acquitted, and not one of them had gone into the witness box. It seemed to me that the jury concluded that the three who gave evidence were definitely lying. Although they were still highly suspicious of the three who didn't, they couldn't be sure, so they gave those three the benefit of the doubt and let them off. I think you're better off staying out.'

'Try me out, Mr Gorman,' offered Dennis. 'Pretend you're Percival. Give me a grilling, here and now.'

'Alright, I will. Here's a few wobblers for starters,' replied Gorman, leaning forward enthusiastically on his chair and rubbing his hands together.

'Who taught you how to use a gun?'

'I'm not prepared to say, I'm not going to get anyone else in trouble.'

'Did you load it yourself?'

'Yes, I did.'

'Did you go for target practice with the missing ten bullets?'

'Yes, I went into the woods in Essex – I got the idea from the film *The Day of the Jackal*.'

'Are you intending to call your wife to give evidence? If not, why not?'

'Ask my counsel.'

'Very good answer. You're getting the hang of this game already. Next, why was one bullet not enough?'

'I'm sorry to say that I wanted to make sure I killed him.'

'Why did you stop your written account before the Old Bailey shooting?'

'I was pretty sure it would all be on CCTV anyway.'

'Your family had moved to the safety of your sister-in-law's home up north – a long way from London. If it was safe for them, why not for you? Why didn't you go with them and get a job locally?'

'I would have been in fear that we might eventually be found. In any event, I wasn't sure it was safe for them there either.'

'Did you tell your wife of your intentions to kill Maynard? If not, why not? Were you afraid of what she might say and do to stop you?'

'I didn't want to worry her.'

'Why did you look up the law on self-defence on your iPad? You had your solicitor's details in your pocket when you were arrested. Why didn't you go round to see him before your decision to kill Maynard and ask him whether, under the circumstances, you were entitled to do so in self-defence? Did you fear his answer might not suit you?'

'That's a difficult question to answer.'

'It's meant to be. Next, do you now regret what you did?'

Dennis whistled softly. 'You've left the best 'til last, Mr Gorman. Whatever answer I give just sounds awful.'

'Need I go on?' asked Gorman. 'You were better than I feared, but I can't say any of your answers were brilliant and, rest assured, Percival will do it a lot better than me. Once he gets those crocodile teeth of his into you, he'll roll you around like a baby hippo in the Nile and he won't let go – it won't be pretty.'

They all sat in silence whilst Dennis weighed up what to do.

'It's your call, Mr Dennis, not ours,' added Gorman. 'We can only advise you. If your evidence is a disaster, we'll still be going home for dinner – you might not.'

Dennis stood up and started pacing about the room with his hands in his pockets, staring at his feet, clearly in a dilemma. Finally, he spoke. 'Well, no rush. I'll see you all again down here at the lunch break then.'

The lawyers stood to leave. 'Just one more question, please, Mr Gorman. When did you decide that you didn't want to put me in the box – if you don't mind me asking?'

Gorman did, but what could he say? So he tried the truth for size. 'Before we met when I read your police interviews in Adrian's humble Jensen on our way to visit you.'

'Really?'

'Really!'

Chapter 34

Making the Best
of a Bad Situation

'Any questions, Mr Gorman?' asked Mack the Knife in a self-satisfied tone which really meant, 'Let's see how you get on with this witness – maestro.'

'Oh, yes, a good number, my Lord.'

Paul Samson had just finished telling the jury all about his two-month sojourn with Dennis in B wing at Belmarsh Prison, and how they'd become the best of mates at London's answer to Château d'If. Now it was Gorman's chance to shine.

'Do you consider yourself a cunning man, Mr Samson?'

'Well, bearing in mind my own conviction, I suppose I have to admit that I am.'

'Can we stretch that to sneaky?'

'No, we can't.'

'OK, let's settle for cunning at the moment, then, and see how we get on. Serving six years for a banking fraud, are you not, Mr Samson?'

'I am.'

'Were you happy with that sentence?'

'Well, I wasn't over the moon, but it could have been worse.'

'Yes, a lot worse – a £15 million loss to the banks, if I'm not mistaken.'

'Correct.'

'False bank accounts all over Europe and one in your wife's name. Where's your wife today, Mr Samson?'

'At home, I'd guess.'

'Oh, so she's not in Marbella at the moment then?'

'No, we lost our home there.'

'I'm sorry to hear that. But you haven't lost your home in Notting Hill, have you? It's in your wife's name, isn't it?'

'Yes, as a matter of fact it is. It used to be her parents' home.'

'What a piece of luck. Your wife, Selma, I believe, was extradited back from Spain with you, wasn't she? And charged with being your accomplice?'

'She was.'

'So, what happened there? All charges against her were dropped when you pleaded guilty, weren't they?'

'Well, she was only a pawn in the game really.'

'Oh no – not a mere pawn, Mr Samson, at least a bishop, wouldn't you agree?'

'She only did what I asked her to.'

'That's a novel defence,' replied Gorman, now giving a running commentary on every answer.

'Well, actually it was a bit of a shock to me when my solicitor told me that they were dropping all charges against my wife.'

'Was it really? But, I dare say, not quite as much of a shock as when my client heard what you had to say about him. Anyway, you were going to fight your case but – surprise, surprise – you suddenly changed your plea to guilty three days before your trial was due to begin. And, as you've just admitted, you received an amazingly lenient sentence and your wife walked free as a bird – straight to her £5 million home. So, what pangs of conscience suddenly overcame you to betray the trust of your cellmate and tell the police that he was lying his head off about the Russian roulette incident? You're no lover of loan sharks, are you?'

'No, I despise them, but what's right is right. You can't just kill someone in cold blood, can you?'

'But it's OK to defraud a bank out of millions in cold blood, is it, Mr Samson?'

'Well, it's not quite the same thing. Dennis told me everything about his life and I told him about mine. We were stuck in the same cell and even walked about the yard together every day. We weren't your typical criminals. We were both first-timers. We kept to ourselves.'

'No doubt. But what I am putting to you is that you were staring at least twelve years in the face – and you knew it. The evidence against you was damning – what with your lifestyle, secret bank accounts and villa near the beach in Marbella. And so, you decided to row for the shore and chuck Dennis to the sharks, didn't you?'

'I did nothing of the sort! My statement is absolutely true.'

'You don't know what the truth looks like, do you, Mr Samson? Now, I accept that it may well be that your evil plan wasn't hatched before you'd seen his case papers, but once you'd read Dennis's police interview your eyes lit up – your sneaky mind was on fire – bingo! It hit you, didn't it?'

'What hit me?'

'It hit you that if you told the police that Dennis had admitted to you that he had invented the Russian roulette incident to improve his prospects, and you gave evidence to that effect, all sorts of deals were on the table.'

'Absolute rubbish.'

'And you comforted yourself by thinking, "What the hell, Dennis killed a man, didn't he?"'

'Nonsense, I would never do such a thing – never!'

'You were playing for the highest of stakes, Mr Samson, but you had your price, and so the flag of friendship came a poor second to trade. And trade you did. You traded a pack of lies for a hugely reduced sentence, your wife's freedom and a £5 million home. Not a bad day's work, Mr Samson – not bad at all.'

'That's rubbish. Every word I've said here is true, I swear it on my children's lives.'

'Well, Mr Samson, if you insist on swearing, swear on your own life and not your children's.'

At first, Samson appeared a trifle reticent to take up the offer, but finally took the plunge. 'OK, I swear on my own life.'

Gorman stared deep into the eyes of the witness, and then suddenly without another word sat down and started shuffling through his case papers.

'Are we to take it that you've finished your cross-examination, Mr Gorman?' asked an irritated Mack the Knife.

Gorman glanced up towards the witness box. And then, with as straight a face as he could muster, replied, 'My Lord, I must confess I'm amazed to see that the witness is still alive!'

Chapter 35

No Dogs Barking

_____

'Ever heard the expression "the dog that failed to bark in the night", Detective Chief Superintendent Stokes?' asked Gorman. Iron-Rod was flattered to be referred to by his full title. It didn't happen often, at least not when Stanford was involved in a trial. He was now in the witness box – the last witness to be called by the prosecution before they closed their case.

'Yes, I have, but I've never really been sure what it meant.'

'Ah, it's a famous Sherlock Holmes expression,' said Gorman. 'It comes from the short story "The Adventure of Silver Blaze", so my junior tells me, and he's an expert.' He turned to the row behind with an approving nod towards Jacobsen. 'It means, in the art of detection, where the very fact that nothing happens speaks volumes and is suspicious in itself.'

'Thank you for that, Mr Gorman, I'll make sure I read it soon.'

The judge took a hand. 'Well, you could do worse. Every detective should read it and then we'd have a few more arrests.'

What do you know, thought Stanford, _Mack the Knife actually_ *has a sense of humour.* Then the judge turned towards Gorman. 'Mr Gorman, this anxious parade of your knowledge on the works of Sir Arthur Conan Doyle is most impressive, but this happens to be a murder trial and not a cosy meeting of the Bar Literary Society. So, putting it in the vernacular – get on with it!'

'Right, let's get to the point then, Chief Superintendent Stokes – without further ado.' Gorman then started firing questions at the officer.

'Your team searched Maynard's home from top to bottom, correct?'

'Yes.'

'Spent two whole days there and moved the wife and son out during the search, correct?'

'True.'

'Dug up half the garden – removed bricks above the fireplace and even had blank notepads forensically examined to see if there were any imprints on pages below, correct?'

'Absolutely.'

'Not a bank statement or letter in sight, no business correspondence and, oh, yes, no mobile phone either, true?'

'It is,' answered Stokes.

'And yet, a beautifully furnished home – as the jury have seen in the police photos. Solid oak Smallbone kitchen?'

'If you say so, Mr Gorman.'

'Finest Axminster carpet under foot?'

'True.'

'Bang & Olufsen stereo in virtually every room, including the bathrooms?'

'I believe there was.'

'Any receipts?'

'Err, no, I don't think we found a single one.' Mack the Knife's ears pricked up. *Receipts* were not his flavour of the week.

'No family photograph albums or holiday snaps in the south of France or the Caribbean?'

'No, sir.'

'So, what did you conclude, officer, after you discovered that the deceased was a stranger to the Inland Revenue and, dare I say it, somewhat of a celebrity on the Police National Computer?'

Percival couldn't let this pass and, jumping to his feet, said, 'My Lord, what does it matter what Superintendent Stokes concluded – it's what the jury concludes that matters. This court doesn't transact its business on police opinion.'

'Does it not?' asked Gorman. 'Dear me, I must have been practising under a misapprehension for some twenty-five years now!' Appreciative laughter all around – Gorman was in top form. 'Let me put it more directly to you, officer. It was plain to you, was it not, that the deceased was leading a high-cash lifestyle?'

'I can't deny it,' replied Stokes, before adding, 'but I found no evidence at all that he was a loan shark except for what the defendant told the police before his arrest and after in his police interview.'

'What about his nickname?' cut in Gorman. 'After all, there's never been a suggestion that he was a second-hand car dealer, has there?'

'No, that he certainly wasn't.'

'So, in the six months or so since his death, I assume you've questioned virtually every publican and informant in the south-east to see what Bob the Merc really did for a living. What did you come up with?'

'Well, it's very difficult, people don't want to talk to us, and they certainly won't make a statement,' replied Stokes sadly.

'Not surprising, is it, that people don't want to talk to you – what with Maynard's son on the prowl? In reality, you hit what I believe the police call a wall of silence, didn't you?'

'We did, unfortunately.'

Gorman changed tack. 'Now, let's all enter his study together and see what intellectual treats were on view. Photographs 10 to 18 in your bundle, members of the jury,' continued Gorman, looking across at them. 'No Shakespeare on his bookshelves, no Dickens, no Jane Austen and certainly no *History of the Decline and Fall of the Roman Empire*.' (The very thought of Bob the Merc reading this holy work made Mack the Knife feel nauseous.)

'No, nothing like that, and that's for sure,' replied Stokes.

'Four books on Al Capone, every work Mario Puzo ever penned and well-worn at that. And, in pride of place, bang in the middle, *The Profession of Violence* – the bestseller on the rise and fall of the Kray twins – and, if I may say so myself, an excellent book, although I doubt if my copy's as well-worn as the deceased's. But, disappointingly, there's nowhere to be seen a copy of the deceased's memoirs, which would have blended in rather well.'

'Another opinion, my Lord.' Percival was moaning again.

Gorman pressed on as if Percival had never spoken. 'Now, let's lower our eyes a shelf to the deceased's DVD collection. *The Godfather* trilogy; *The Long Good Friday*; *Sexy Beast*; *The French*

Connection (parts I and II); *American Gangster*; *Scarface*; *Layer Cake*; *Public Enemy Number One*; *Goodfellas* – to name the highlights. And finally, *The Shawshank Redemption*.'

'Jolly good too, I've seen it myself – wonderful ending,' said Mack the Knife, keen to show the common touch.

Gorman ignored the judge's second attempt to lighten the proceedings. 'The common theme, officer – crime – agreed?'

'Agreed,' conceded Stokes.

'£30,000 in mixed denominations found under the stairs in a Harrods hamper. What's happened to that?'

'At present, it's being held for potential seizure by the Crown, as is protocol with large sums of unexplained cash.'

'Anybody climbed out of the woodwork to claim it yet? His wife or son, perhaps?' asked Gorman.

'No, no one at the moment.'

'And finally, officer, one other matter, and only one you'll be pleased to hear.' Stokes definitely was. 'You'll agree, won't you, this is a very unusual case?'

'It most certainly is,' replied Stokes sincerely.

'You've been a police officer for what, thirty years?'

'Thirty-one, to be precise.'

'And I suppose you've dealt with a large number of murder cases in your time?'

'A fair few – I must admit.'

'I guess you've had the misfortune to handle cases where innocent people are shot in a robbery, premeditated murders out of revenge, pub fight murders and the murder of lovers and such?'

'Yes, all of those,' replied Stokes, now virtually on autopilot.

'Well, what about a premeditated killing in broad daylight in front of witnesses, where the killer remains at the scene and lights a cigarette. Anything like that?'

Stokes thought deeply. Now was his chance to stick the knife in. 'No, I can't say I have – a merciless, cold-blooded killing.'

'Yes, no doubt you thought it was on the day you were appointed the senior officer in this case. But you did not think it quite so cold-blooded, I would venture to suggest, once you'd heard my client's account.'

'That's for the jury to decide.'

'Yes, indeed it is,' replied Gorman. And then after pausing for effect, 'that's why they're here. Thank you, officer,' he said quietly, before finally sitting down. For once, he meant it!

Chapter 36

An Unusual Junior

Daniel Jacobsen was on a legal high. To be Stanford's personal choice as junior counsel in the highest-profile murder case of the year, if not the decade, was the greatest compliment he'd received in eight years of practice. And all because he'd given himself the edge by rocking up at Stanford's offices to report the outcome of a trial, rather than emailing him. To watch Patrick Gorman in action burying the deceased's widow and making Stokes resemble a star witness for the defence was a rare treat, and he was being paid for it as well. And all at the tender age of thirty-two. True, when Gorman turned towards him whilst telling the jury that his junior was a Sherlock Holmes aficionado, Daniel had cringed. But to be fair, Gorman had apologised to him after court – too late the hero.

His father had bought him the complete collection of the Sherlock Holmes short stories for his eleventh birthday and he had been hooked ever since. He prided himself on knowing the difference between *seeing* and *observing*, which was fundamental to judging your fellow man. In uneventful moments during the first three days of trial he would spend the time assessing each juror and what their likely occupation might be. Little did he know that Halfpint, high up in the public gallery, was a dab hand at this game too. The only difference was that Halfpint had acquired the knack from hard experience amongst the criminal fraternity and not from the comfort of an armchair.

When Daniel's father had driven him to school as a young teenager, they used to play their own little game. 'Here's an easy one for you, Daniel. That fellow who's waiting for a bus – what do you think he does for a living?' Daniel stared at the striped suit and tie, waistcoat, detached collar, wheeled holdall, *The Times* in hand, confident manner.

'Barrister?'

'Barrister, very good. I agree.'

Years later, on a hot summer's afternoon, after being collected from school, the tables had turned. 'Dad, that elderly man in the short-sleeved shirt and Panama hat, hands in pockets, taking a leisurely stroll across the road towards St John's Wood Station. Why's he going there?'

'To catch a train?' ventured his father.

'Dear me, Dad,' teased Daniel, cheekily. 'You're getting a bit rusty. He's going to pick up the late edition of the *Evening Standard*, if I'm not mistaken.' He wasn't!

When Daniel was nineteen there was an occasion when he had shone at home at a dinner party. One of the guests had asked if he could bring along a Swedish friend who was alone in London on holiday. During the meal, Daniel's father was talking about the difference between *seeing* and *observing* and showing off a bit, suggesting that he could have a fair guess at what the stranger's occupation might be. All listened intently as his father conjectured, narrowing down the possibilities, like a wine connoisseur at a blind tasting, before announcing, 'I venture to say you're in the property business, am I right, possibly a developer?'

Before the visitor could answer, Daniel, who had not yet uttered a word, spoke. '*Was* in the property business – now retired?'

The stranger's eyebrows raised high in surprise. 'Absolutely correct.' Daniel's father was frowning. He'd been outgunned by his own son – and in public.

'How could you possibly know he's retired?' the guests enquired.

Daniel replied, maturely for his age. 'Not wearing a watch – and no watch marks either,' as if this fine piece of deduction was staring everyone in the face.

During the first days of the trial, Daniel had been putting his methods to work in court. For example, he noticed that the judge's mind was constantly wandering. His thoughts were decidedly *elsewhere* and, from the grave look on his face, Daniel concluded he was possibly preoccupied with some personal issue.

Daniel had also noticed that Percival's handwriting was huge and expansive. He concluded Percival came from a rich background, with no concern as to the cost of paper. Conversely, Gorman's writing was tiny and he always wrote on both sides of paper. A self-made man, of course, who was brought up with a *waste not, want not* mentality.

And as for the five women and seven men on the jury, what did Daniel make of them? He was ashamed to admit that he always found women more difficult to work out than men. Not that he hadn't tried. After a year of attempting to chat up girls at the University of Bristol, where he had studied psychology, he had met with little success. However, eventually one of the girls who was on his course had inadvertently come to his aid. Somewhat of a tomboy, she had the habit of wearing masculine trainers to lectures and he commented on them. She replied, 'Just you remember, Dan, you can tell a lot about a woman from her shoes.' He hadn't looked back. Within a few weeks, and after catching the odd episode of *Sex and the City*, Daniel had become a regular connoisseur of female footwear. And he was applying his observational methods in Dennis's case. For example, there was little doubt in his mind that juror number 3 was a housewife, married to a man of considerable means. He began, as he always did, with her shoes. To the average onlooker, they were plain, expensive-looking high heels. Many a man would have missed the flash of crimson red on the soles, but not Daniel. He knew this could only signify one thing – they were Christian Louboutin shoes. Moreover, judging by the still vivid-red soles and the combination of the lady's decidedly authentic but subtle diamond jewellery, they were almost certainly new for the season. The price of such a pair? £500 minimum.

But what about her housewife status? That was simple. The uncomfortable manner in which this lady held the worn-down stubby pencils provided by the court demonstrated that she hadn't written anything substantial for years. Daniel had observed her struggling to arrange her fingers in such a way as to accommodate her false but equally expensive-looking scarlet nails around her pencil. No, this was not a woman used to writing. And, with those nails, she wasn't used to typing either. On day two, she produced a rather masculine-looking, chrome-plated Sheaffer pen from her Mulberry clutch. Given her difficulties with the pencil the day before, Daniel concluded that she must have borrowed it from her husband.

Juror number 6 was an overweight woman in her mid-fifties. She did not wear the weight well, and Daniel assessed that she had probably gained it recently as her face remained relatively thin. On her feet she wore Crocs, the plastic sandal–clog hybrids that are famed for their comfort but not for featuring in *Tatler*. Each morning, as she walked up to the bench you could almost hear her creaking from side to side, and she winced visibly as she lifted her right leg to get up to her seat in the juror's second row. On the first day, she wore a loose-fitting T-shirt and tracksuit trousers. On day two, no doubt having struggled with the icy winds that Mack the Knife insisted on circulating with the court's air conditioning, she arrived in a huge woollen jumper that resembled a sack that hadn't been washed in years. This, combined with the 1.5in. of grey roots betraying her otherwise implausibly auburn hair, completed the picture. Daniel concluded that she was signed off work, having had her right hip replaced. The time off had probably led to the recent weight gain and, sadly, a little depression. The roots in her hair betrayed that she no longer deemed herself to be attractive, and more than once Daniel had noticed her struggling to stay awake during the afternoon session. Too much late TV, probably as a result of insomnia.

To the left of juror number 6 sat a well-kept and simply dressed lady, who, when reading the oath, had no difficulty whatsoever – unlike many of her fellow jurors. She sat bolt upright in her chair, took copious notes and wore her hair in a neat bun each day. She was about thirty-five, slim and tall and wore no makeup at all. Her shoes? Simple pumps, not particularly expensive. Here was someone who meant business. She was keen not to stand out, but was equally used to keeping her appearance neat and tidy. She listened intently and even managed to fix a smile at old Mack whenever he interrupted with an attempt at humour. Quite possibly a schoolteacher, Daniel thought.

The fourth female juror was an older lady, probably in her late sixties. He felt sure that she had fallen on hard times. She wore the same outfit each day, but when she had listened to Gorman cross-examining the widow Maynard about her three holidays a year and her Smallbone kitchen, she appeared to know exactly what they were talking about, as if she had also enjoyed a similar lifestyle. Her shoes and handbag were clearly high-quality but, on the other hand, they were well-worn. Her gold watch was the style that was highly fashionable in the 1970s but not any more. If Daniel had to guess, he would have said that her husband had passed away some years ago and she had been forced into frugality.

The final female juror was easy for Daniel to work out. On the second day, she was sorting out her overpacked purse whilst waiting for the judge to enter. Amongst the contents he noticed a pass card with the logo of a well-known firm of civil solicitors emblazoned across it. Now, this was the sort of firm where even a trainee solicitor could expect to earn upwards of £50,000. But this woman could not have been older than twenty-two. Why would she have such a pass? And wearing such immature, faux-leather boots. She must be a secretary or receptionist.

As for the seven men, the two young ones, Daniel decided, were more than likely out of work. The younger-looking one probably had a nagging girlfriend (he was always checking his mobile phone for messages the moment the court rose). The two older men in suits were very likely self-employed as they looked seriously concerned when the judge told them the case could last up to two weeks. The fifth male juror must live far from the Old Bailey because each day he arrived at court in a really heavy pullover. He didn't travel by car, so he obviously lived quite a distance away and had to leave early in the morning when the temperature had not yet risen and travel in by train, with the *Daily Telegraph* crossword puzzle for company.

A blind monkey could tell that the sixth male juror, in his thick polo-neck pullover and his gold Cartier watch, was a spoilt brat – at best, he worked in the family business, but he had never had to get his hands dirty in his life.

This left Rough Hands. Did Daniel's conclusions take him any further than Halfpint's? On days two and three, Rough Hands was always behind the other jurors when entering court. Daniel concluded he had been to work first and was therefore probably self-employed. Moreover, he was constantly gazing at his watch after 3 p.m. as if he was in a hurry to leave. His fresh but hardened complexion indicated that he largely worked out-doors. But what about his clothes? Had Halfpint missed some-thing? Or rather, what had the eagle-eyed Daniel spotted? He noticed that each time Rough Hands entered court and stood up to leave, his jeans were patently stretched at the knees and also dotted with subtle black grease marks. But, most impor-tantly, the jeans were also *patched* at the knees. This juror clearly did a lot of bending down and, what with the grease marks, it was a near certainty that he was a car mechanic, a plumber or he changed tyres. There were also deep cracks in his boots across the top of the toes, just where one would expect them to be as a result of constant bending. *Big deal*, mused Daniel. *What good would it do him – other than providing the opportunity to show off to the rest of the defence team?*

But, for Daniel, there was something more exotic on view. Nick Denning, who had been hand-picked as the prosecution junior, had been forced to withdraw at the last moment. A bad case of laryngitis. The prosecution team couldn't take the chance of Percival falling ill during the trial and Denning having to take over, croaking all over the place. Miss Angelina Russo, only seven years qualified and a young member of Percival's chambers, had taken his place – and what a beauty she was! Daniel had never set eyes on her before but had overheard the odd bit of cheap gossip in the robing rooms. 'The Sophia Loren of the Bar!' When he cast his eyes on her as she entered the court on the first day of the trial and sat behind Percival, he saw no reason to disagree. A lemony fragrance drifted across the barristers' rows, and it was certainly not coming from Percival! Even Doctor Watson could have worked that one out.

She was about 5ft 6in. tall, with large, light-brown eyes. She had the olive skin, high cheekbones and lustrous, straight auburn hair which seem to be the sole preserve of Italian women. Her diamond-cut legs and curvaceous figure completed the oil painting. There was only one word for her – Daniel was ashamed to admit to himself – *sultry*. She wore a classic Vacheron on her delicate wrist to match the white-gold chain and pendant around her slim neck. *Straight out of Chopard*, guessed Daniel. She had a certain mystique (rarely to be found in the barristers' rows at the Bailey) which fascinated Daniel.

She was no member of the nouveau riche originating from the back-streets of Naples, concluded Daniel. *No, she was old money.* This young lady had class, it flowed from her every expression and movement, as if she was trying to understate her natural beauty and comparatively noble birth. *Sympatico* oozed from her every pore.

But what was she doing in London, donning a barrister's wig and gown, which did little to conceal her thousand charms? Father an Italian diplomat? Or perhaps he had married an English woman. No, her beauty was most definitely from her mother's side. So, why was she in London? Father a lawyer in Italy? She spoke beautiful English, with just a trace of the sort of Italian accent you might overhear from the next table at Harry's Bar in Venice when ordering a hugely overpriced Bellini. Not that Daniel had ever been there personally. Was there not an invisible sign hanging outside Harry's Bar in large print, just above the menu? *No legal aid lawyers allowed!*

Was the beautiful Angelina spoken for? Apparently not. No ring on the exquisite fourth finger of her left hand, nor any suntan marks to indicate a missing ring there either – good news indeed!

Reluctantly, once again, Daniel's eyes turned to Rough Hands. He noticed of course that the man had worn an open-necked shirt each of the first three days of the trial. On the first day there was nothing in the pocket; the second morning there was one pen; the second afternoon two pens; the third morning there were no pens; and finally, on the third afternoon there were two pens again on re-entering court after Stokes had been led around like a dog on a lead by Gorman in his cross-examination.

What's going on here? pondered Daniel. Rough Hands hadn't taken a single note on the paper provided by the court. Why does a juror who never writes down a word sport a different number of pens at virtually every court sitting?

'When you've eliminated the impossible, whatever remains, however improbable, must be the truth,' said Holmes. Yes, he had the answer to his own question before you could utter the word *elementary*. A sign! Definitely a signal, but why and to whom? Daniel gazed around the courtroom. The police? No, ridiculous. The press? Absurd.

Daniel took a quick look over his shoulder towards the public gallery above. Not a great view from where the barristers sat and, anyway, he couldn't start staring at the gallery from his seat. So, he stood up and strolled behind the dock, glancing up at the packed gallery. A mixture of tourists, students, unemployed and… hello, who is this dapper little fellow in the back row trying a tad too hard to look as though he's thoroughly bored? The one wearing the grandfather's cardigan and the starched white shirt. *No, maybe not*, Daniel decided – *a capital error to reach a conclusion without sufficient evidence*. Wait and see was the way forward. He retook his seat just in time to hear Patrick Gorman tell the court some truly startling news as the defence case was supposed to begin.

Iron-Rod Stokes might have chosen a somewhat different adjective to *startling* – something slightly more evocative, perhaps.

Chapter 37

A Brave Decision

'I call no evidence,' announced Gorman at the beginning of the afternoon session on the third day of the trial. There was a noisy rumbling at the back of the court as Iron-Rod Stokes, cursing to himself, fiddled in his pocket for those tablets.

The four words stung all present to the core. The judge then went through the standard warning required by law and asked Gorman to confirm that he had explained to his client the legal implications of not giving evidence.

'Yes, indeed I have, my Lord. I repeat, I call no evidence.'

'Not your client and not any witnesses?' enquired the judge.

'No, none,' answered Gorman emphatically, following the old cowboy adage: *If you've got to swallow a frog – better to swallow it whole.*

Mack the Knife was surprised, Stokes and his team flabbergasted and Percival deeply frustrated. Hours of preparation, twenty pages of cross-examination notes and he could toss the lot in the fire.

Way up in the public gallery, Halfpint's eyes lit up. *He's a Slick*

Willie alright, he thought. *Finish the evidence on a high, that's his game. Wait 'til Big Jake hears the news, he might even stand me a man's drink tonight at the Artesian!*

*   *   *

Percival tore off his wig as if it were infected with maggots and hurled it full-force across the room to relieve his pent-up frustration.

After hearing from Gorman, in open court, that his client was giving a wide berth to the witness box, Percival had retired and gathered the prosecution team together in the solicitors' room on the second floor of the Old Bailey for an early inquest. Angelina, his junior, was there, as were Stokes and three of his team. The court had adjourned for the rest of the day to allow Percival time to prepare his closing speech, now due to begin the following morning.

'That smoothie Gorman.' Percival almost spat out the words. 'Nights I've sat up preparing my cross-examination of Dennis, and I'd have done better to have gone fishing. He never gave me the slightest inkling that he wasn't going to put his client in the box. Frankly, I'm amazed. It's a really bold decision, but I should have spotted it.'

'Why do you think he's done it, Mr Percival?' asked Stokes, whose colour was just beginning to return to his face.

'Well, maybe I flatter myself, but perhaps Gorman feared I was going to make mashed potatoes of his client on all the un-answered questions arising from his police interviews.'

'And why do you think he's not called any witnesses?'

enquired Stokes in a tone reminiscent of a man who had just suffered a family bereavement.

'Who could he call? His wife? Not likely – too risky. Friends? To say what? He's basically a nice fellow? The jury already think that. No, Gorman's done us like a kipper. He's scuttled my boat and it hasn't even set sail.'

'Well, the jury won't think much of it, will they?' chipped in Stokes hopefully.

'True,' replied Percival, 'for about half an hour, and then all they'll remember is the video of his story when interviewed. No, Gorman's dealt us a cruel blow, and there's no point deceiving ourselves.'

Percival was still holding on to his twenty pages of cross-examination notes. He gave them a disdainful look, incredulous that he was still carrying around such junk. Then, in a grand gesture, he tore them in two and started stalking the large room in search of a dustbin – in vain.

'Never a bloody dustbin when you need one,' he muttered, before dumping the torn notes onto Stokes. 'Here, I never want to see them again. Consider them a gift, they're no use to me. Read them to your grandchildren tonight before bed – tell them it's a fairy story. Yes,' he added with a vigorous shake of his head and a dose of self-pity, 'nothing but a sad fairy story, and let's hope it doesn't give them nightmares.' No one laughed.

'Right,' Percival finally declared, 'I'm off to the Garrick to write my closing speech – in the bar if they'll let me. Angelina, I'd be grateful if you would come with to help – that'll give the walking dead there a stir!'

*   *   *

Whilst Percival's heirloomed Osmiroid fountain pen was smouldering at the Garrick Club, Big Jake and Halfpint were comfortably ensconced a mile or so away at the Artesian. Their daily meeting was an hour earlier than usual. Jake's monthly poker game started at 9 p.m. sharp, and nothing, but nothing, was going to delay it. Halfpint was bursting to break the surprising news.

'He didn't put him in the box, Jake.'

Jake widened his eyes in disbelief and jerked his head back. 'Didn't put him in the box? What do you mean he didn't put him in the box? Has he gone mad, got a holiday booked and wants to get this case over pronto or what?'

'I don't know, Jake,' replied Halfpint, 'but the whole prosecution team looked horrified when he told them – and the judge an' all, so it can't have been that bad an idea.'

'Well,' said Jake, after composing himself a little, 'this Gorman fellow's meant to be top-notch, and there's nothing we can do about it anyway. So we'll just have to trust his judgement, won't we?'

'All the same, I wish you could have been there this morning, Jake.'

'No, thank you very much. I've been in the Old Bailey more times than I care to remember, Halfpint. In the bad old days I used to have a season ticket. I've been in the cells, the dock and the witness box, but I've always left through the front door. I never quite made it to the public gallery and I'd like to keep it that way, if you don't mind. I'd be recognised for sure and the coppers would think there's some villainy afoot.'

Halfpint didn't mind. 'Still, Jake, I wish you could have been there. He gave the senior officer a right old drumming about Bob the Merc's bunch of gangster books and DVDs, and even asked him what he knew about Sherlock Holmes.'

'Sherlock Holmes? I thought he died a long time ago,' a mystified Jake replied.

'Not in Court 1 at the Bailey, Jake. No, in Court 1 he's very much alive and kicking.'

'Are you having hallucinations, Halfpint? Next you'll be telling me that Doctor Watson's on the jury,' he said, wetting his lips with a large Negroni.

'What are you drinking there, Jake?' The day's excitement had left Halfpint with a dry throat.

'What's it to you?'

'It looks real good.'

Jake got the message. 'Does it now? Waiter,' he called out, as if he were the bar's only patron, 'bring my old friend here a Coke. It seems he doesn't think much of your tap water.'

But, for once, Halfpint had the last word. 'You're all heart, Jake, I always said it – you're all heart.'

Chapter 38

Mack the Knife Sets His Trap

'Charles is coming for dinner tonight, Magnus. He's stay-ing with us for a couple of days,' announced the judge's wife, Frances, on his return home from court after the third day of the trial.

'Oh, is he? I'd completely forgotten,' lied Magnus persuasive-ly, surprising himself. Truth be known, little else had crossed his mind since the trial had begun.

'I told you days ago. You've been in a trance since that horri-ble trial started. You really must learn to switch off after court. I'm preparing French onion soup, beef bourguignon and a lemon soufflé for dessert. Everything I was taught at the cook-ery course last week. I'm really excited about it.'

Magnus wasn't. *Typical*, he reflected, *she always makes a real effort when Charles is around: candlelit dinner, white tablecloth, French dishes, Frank Sinatra crooning away in the background – I might as well be invisible.*

Frances wasn't done yet. 'I'm worried he may not like it, but I've got to try something new.'

That's rich, thought Magnus, as he opened a cheap bottle

of Mouton Cadet – all his guest deserved. *She's worried about whether he likes it – what about me? Have I been blind! Well, this will be his last supper under my roof.*

Magnus had his master plan all prepared. His iPhone charger was ready for a showdown. He knew how to work it, as well he should – he had spent many a break in proceedings practising in his room. There would be no slip-ups.

And yet, did he really want to see his wife and Charles writhing around entwined on *his* bed? And what of his marriage afterwards – would it survive? Could he bear to live with a woman who had betrayed him so, and with his old school friend?

He had carefully considered his options. First, he could set the iPhone charger up plugged in behind the bedroom side table and angled towards the bed. That way he would obtain a sight and sound recording. But did he really want *sight*? Or he could aim the iPhone charger at the door. That would only capture footage of Charles entering the room and whatever unpalatable sounds followed.

But hold fire, was there not a third option? He could leave the contraption switched off altogether and confront Charles with it the next afternoon after court on his arrival home, before Frances returned from her cookery course. Of course, he would then have no hard evidence at all, but he could pretend to Charles that he had. Charles's facial expressions and reaction would surely be enough, and this third option had the distinct advantage that he would not have to live the rest of his life with the image of Charles whispering honeyed words into his wife's receptive ear, appearing before him like Banquo's ghost.

This third option might salvage his marriage, but was he prepared to deprive himself of hard evidence, however disdainful, in favour of common sense? It was a close call. But who could he consult for a second opinion? No one. To his mind, leaving the iPhone charger switched off would be akin to perverting the course of justice, and this the lawyer in him would not allow – nor the bridge player. He was holding the ace of trumps, and it had to take a trick.

And so it was that when Magnus left for the Bailey early the following morning, the iPhone charger was switched on and recording – facing the bed. In addition, a faint horizontal line had been drawn on the bottle of Black Label in his cabinet downstairs at the same level as the height of the remaining whisky.

The phone charger was surely going to play its part as exhibit A in Magnus's private prosecution. No natural justice for Charles – he didn't deserve it. Magnus was to be the prosecutor, judge and jury. And there was only one appropriate sentence as prescribed by his law – eternal banishment!

Chapter 39

Ace in the Hole

―――――――――

8.30, Wednesday night. Jake was getting in the mood for the game. He was singing along with the late great Dave Van Ronk to the old poker favourite 'Losers', which was blasting out from his B&O speakers. He knew the lyrics backwards. He'd been singing them for long enough – once a month for the past twenty years to be exact – along with Kenny Rogers's 'The Gambler', Roger Miller's 'From a Jack to a King' and the theme tune from *The Cincinnati Kid*.

Jake's Poker Extravaganza. Sacred as any pilgrimage to Mecca, but by private invitation only. Even the production of a certified death certificate wouldn't justify a player's absence. Not hard to guess who was in charge of the guest list. Why shouldn't he be? His lounge hosted the game. A running buffet of rib of beef, cold lobster, mountains of smoked salmon, Californian asparagus, a plate of smelly cheeses to die for and a box of Cohiba Robustos, with alcohol on tap. All provided courtesy of Harrods, Camden Town – stolen goods branch.

Restaurateur Luca's nineteen-year-old son, Juliano, dressed in an immaculate Zegna tuxedo, was on regular duty as the maître d'; tipped handsomely by the winners and pathetically by the losers at the end of the evening.

Seven Edward G. Robinson wannabes sat in plush red-leather carvers at an enormous round rosewood table covered with a green baize, with the eighth chair reserved for the non-playing dealer – Halfpint, sporting his grandfather's pre-Second World War dinner jacket. It looked like it had been to Dunkirk and back.

'Let him deal from the top – let him deal from the bottom – let him deal from up his sleeve – who cares? He's not playing!' Jake's definition of natural justice.

The dramatis personae did not make for pretty reading. Only two of them could be termed professional criminals, but, then again, none of the others were on the shortlist for a knighthood.

- Paul the Perm – had hairdressing salons all over central London.
- Rolex Ron – the best-known face in the Hatton Garden jewellery business.
- Shaun the Shifter – ran bonded warehouses with a somewhat laissez-faire attitude. From his premises everything *shifted* in the dead of night.
- Spike the Spot – in the currency exchange business.
- Trevor the Tout – in the black-market ticket business: a poor seat for a pretty price.
- Ruthless Ricky – also known amongst the cognoscenti as the Lone Ranger. No one knew for sure what he did for a living, but from the ever-present hard look on his face and the absence of an ounce of fat on his body, they suspected

that it involved a gun. He regularly flew in from Monaco for the game.

- Big Jake – everyone knew what he did for a living, but no one dared talk about it.

All shared a common denominator – they ran high-percentage cash businesses.

Jake was a warm and generous host, as long as you played by his rules:

- Any player arriving after the 9 p.m. kick-off to be fined £250, to be given to a charity of Jake's choice (no details ever provided).
- All watches and mobile phones to be surrendered on entry. (This prevented anyone playing for time by only betting on near certainties if they were winning in the wee hours.)
- Game to conclude at 4 a.m (alarm clock to be set and hidden at the back of the drinks cabinet).
- Cash game only – pounds, euros, dollars or shekels – no limit. Western rules prevailed, which meant no credit given under any circumstances – *you put up or shut up* (in God Jake trusted, but everybody else paid cash).
- 2 per cent of every pot to go towards the catering costs (business as usual for Jake).
- Dealer's choice – minimum buy-in £2,500.
- New packs to be provided on request (no one was going to even the odds by marking the cards in Jake's home!).

As usual, the game ebbed and flowed dramatically, but, unsurprisingly, Ruthless Ricky was a clear leader. He was not the curious sort and knew when to stack and leave his gun nestling in its holster. The table conversation ranged from the best new restaurant in town to the best new hooker in town. In twenty years, no woman had ever graced the table. The very thought of losing to the female sex was more than any of them was prepared to stomach.

'So, Jake, what do you think of that plucky guy on trial at the Bailey for sorting out Bob the Merc? He's going to be eating a fair amount of porridge for about thirty years and that's a safe bet.' The trial was hot news in all the dailies, and Rolex Ron was keen to hear Jake's slant on the subject.

Jake's ears pricked up. He hadn't breathed a word to any of them of his inside knowledge of the case.

'A safe bet, eh, Ron?'

'Of course it's a safe bet. From what I've read, he hasn't got a prayer. There's more chance of your dating Cindy Crawford than his getting off.' Ron was talking a big game, but had he picked on the wrong opponent? 'Yep, he needs a miracle, Jake.'

'He's not looking for a miracle – he's looking for justice,' quipped back Jake.

'Your sort of justice, Jake?' teased Ron.

'Exactly.'

'*Jake's Justice*, that could be the title of your memoirs.'

'Yes, me and Halfpint could write a great one together – eh, Halfpint?'

Halfpint started turning pale at the thought.

'Anyway, Mr Cocksure, what odds are you offering?' ventured Jake.

'What – you want to bet on it, Jake?' replied Ron, his eyes lighting up.

'At the right odds, I'll take my chances – why not?'

Ron gave it some serious consideration, and sought the advice of a whisky sour before answering. 'OK, Jake, I'll offer you 2:1 against him walking.'

'2:1 against! Bravely spoken, Ron, bravely spoken – you're a real hero. Now, come on, you've just said he hasn't got a prayer. 2:1's an insult. I would say 10:1 is more like it.'

Ron sought some more liquid advice and started puffing and shifting uncomfortably in his seat.

'How much are you thinking of, Jake?'

'Well, at the right odds, let's say ten grand – or is that a bit out of your league, Ron?'

Ron started puffing a bit harder. 'Ten large! At 10:1! No, no, you never know what crackpots might be on the jury. But, if you're serious, Jake, I'll give you 5:1 on £5,000. It'll be like taking Mars bars from minors. You're throwing horseshoes at the moon.'

Before Ron could chicken out, Jake stretched his right paw across the table. 'Done, you're on, Ron. Payment in full, and in cash, the day after the verdict, which should be next week – agreed?'

'It'll be my pleasure, Jake.' The two of them shook hands. 'My missus has got her heart set on a really cool mink-lined raincoat for Christmas.' Ron was crowing already.

'Has she now, Ron? Well, you can take it from me, and I should know, it's always a mistake to share the spoils before you rob the bank. You never can tell – she may have to settle for a hot-water bottle this Christmas.'

Too late, Rolex Ron was starting to get suspicious. Was Jake holding an ace in the hole? 'Is there something you know about this trial that you're not telling us, Jake?'

Twelve inquisitive eyes stared straight at Jake, but a nervous Halfpint, head down, started shuffling the cards for the next deal.

'Not a thing, Ron, cross my heart, not a thing. Now, let's play some cards.'

Chapter 40

Mental Gymnastics

'Well, that takes the cake. Just as we're getting back into the ball game, we get kicked in the goolies. This is all we needed.'

Thursday morning. Patrick Gorman QC was sitting in his shirt and braces at the kitchen table, a bowl of Alpen topped with a sliced banana acting as a paperweight for *The Times* on the table underneath, a large piece of kitchen paper tucked deep in at his neck – an essential precaution.

'What's the matter now? You can't expect to win every case.' Roberta, his wife, was busy percolating his morning coffee before he took off for court to suffer Percival's closing speech.

'Well, if it wasn't a certain loser before, it is now. There's a better prospect of Martha cooking up a decent dinner than my client getting off. Listen to this.'

Gorman started reading aloud.

'RAPE WITNESS ARRESTED FOR ASSAULT ON DEFENCE BARRISTER'

An alleged rape victim, who cannot be named for legal

reasons, was herself arrested outside the entrance to the Old Bailey late yesterday afternoon on suspicion of assaulting the defence barrister who had cross-examined her at length on the previous day.

The jury had just returned a not guilty verdict after a fifteen-minute retirement against Mr Donald Peabody, fifty-three, a City stockbroker, who had claimed that the witness had consented to a four-hour sexual encounter in a bedroom at the Savoy Hotel, where he admitted he regularly took women for sex.

On leaving the building, the barrister, Mr Frederick Fairbrother, was approached by the witness, who is alleged to have taken a pair of scissors from her handbag and stabbed him twice in the left arm. A police source confirmed that a 27-year-old woman had been arrested at the scene.

A spokesman at the Old Bailey said that the court was taking the matter extremely seriously and reconsidering all security arrangements outside the building, bearing in mind that this is the second attack to have taken place in a seven-month period.

At present, David Dennis is on trial for the murder of Robert Maynard in May this year. Mr Maynard was shot dead on leaving court. His trial continues.

Roberta tried her hand at consoling him. 'Well, I'm sure your judge will tell the jury that they must put it out of their heads, so what's the problem?'

'The problem, my dear, is what we lawyers refer to as "mental gymnastics".'

'What's mental gymnastics?'

'Who can take out of a juror's head what's already deeply ingrained in it?'

'You can, darling, you're doing it all the time, you're very good at it. It's what you do for a living.'

Gorman looked up in feigned astonishment at his one-member fan club. 'That coffee ready yet? Better make it black.'

Chapter 41

Percival's Last Stand

'Court rise.'
    'My Lord, there is a short matter I wish to raise in the absence of the jury before Mr Percival begins his closing speech, which I have no doubt will enthral us for most of the day.'

'Oh, surely not that long, Mr Gorman. I was hoping he'd finish it by the mid-morning break.'

'Well, if, by some miracle, he does, I won't be going outside for a quiet smoke – it's simply too dangerous these days. I'm sure your Lordship has read about the unfortunate incident that occurred late yesterday afternoon.'

'Yes, I have. And I intend to direct the jury in my summing up to put it completely out of their heads – just after I direct them to put out of their heads the remark, "I'd feel safer in a Siberian labour camp", which you so ingenuously slipped into play in your cross-examination of Mrs Maynard before anyone could stop you, Mr Gorman.'

That took the wind out of Gorman's sails, but he still had some more fish to fry. 'Might I ask your Lordship to deal with it now, so we can clear the air straight away?'

'You certainly can ask, Mr Gorman, but, in my experience, the more I mention something like this, the more likely it will remain in their minds. I'll deal with it in my own time, Mr Gorman – don't worry.'

The judge then turned his head towards the prosecutor. 'I'm not putting any pressure on you, Mr Percival, but how long's your speech likely to be?'

'With a fair wind, I hope to finish it before the lunch break, my Lord.'

'Let's all pray for a fair wind then,' said McIntyre.

Gorman felt like kneeling and praying for a tempest. Three hours of purgatory in its purest form – what a prospect. Just look at that pile of notes he was holding on Garrick Club-headed paper.

Percival's speech dragged on and on. Would it never end? 'Now, members of the jury, what did you make of the evidence of Mr Samson, Dennis's cellmate? A cunning fraudster? Agreed. A con artist? Agreed. But is it conceivable that he would sink so low as to come to this court and swear under oath in a murder trial that Dennis had confessed to him that the whole Russian roulette episode was pure fiction, if it was not the truth?

'More importantly, what does it mean if you take the view that Dennis had invented that whole episode to provide himself with a stronger defence? It means, does it not, that Dennis real-ised well before the killing that he would be left with a woefully weak case without it. His defence needed bolstering up, and the Russian roulette incident fitted the bill perfectly. I put it to you that he trusted Samson – what with the two of them locked up in a cell together, week after week. Putting it simply, Dennis showed poor judgement in trusting Samson and now, of course, he is left with no option but to call Samson a liar.

'And let us not pretend for one moment that Dennis is anything other than a cunning man himself. Did he not visit Ede & Ravenscroft, lie to the sales manager and spend a considerable sum buying a wig and gown to use for his crime? A cool customer in the extreme, you might think. And what do you make of Dennis removing his wig before he fired the second shot? That can only mean that he wanted Maynard to know who had killed him before he died. A cruel gesture in the extreme, which the prosecution submit must have been planned.

'Now, we've all been treated to a fascinating insight by the defence into the life and times of Mr Sherlock Holmes and the dog that failed to bark in the night. What about Dennis not taking the stand – is that not a dog that failed to bark? All very well, members of the jury, for Mr Dennis to read out a prepared statement in his police interview, but does he let anyone test it? No, he does not; not the police, not me and most importantly not you, by listening to his answers under cross-examination and judging them for yourselves.

'So, now you'll never know how or when he obtained the gun or what happened to the missing bullets or why he fired two shots and not simply one. Nor will you have the benefit of hearing his explanation as to why he felt it necessary to study the law of self-defence on no fewer than three occasions in the week before the Russian roulette incident. But do you really need to hear it anyway, members of the jury? Can it be anything other than he was trying to find out what his prospects were of getting off if he killed Maynard in cold blood? What other reason could there possibly be? He obviously didn't think much of his prospects, and so I put it to you he decided to invent the whole incident to strengthen his hand.

'Oh, yes, he's told us what he wants to tell us in his statement, but he won't go any further. Just compare him to a boxer who lands a punch in the ring and then jumps out before his opponent has a chance to land one in reply. Not a fair fight, you might think.

'Now, it may well be you didn't find Mrs Maynard an attractive witness. She wasn't called by the prosecution to be an attractive witness. She was called because she was an eyewitness when her husband was shot dead in cold blood. Was she asked one single question about it by Mr Gorman? Not one. Another dog declining to bark, you might think.

'And did the defendant call one single witness or scrap of evidence to support his story? His wife, you might think, has been conspicuous by her absence. Could she not have confirmed a great deal of what the defendant said in his second interview – if it were true?

'Other than Dennis's say-so, there is no hard evidence before you as to how the deceased earned his living. For all we know, he might have been a drug dealer or a fraudster or, dare I say it, a pimp. Or maybe he was merely earning a good living from honest employment and not paying his taxes. His nickname, Bob the Merc, doesn't make him a loan shark. Yes, it's a possibility, but it's not a certainty just because Mr Gorman so eloquently says so. Keep your eyes on the known facts and not on conjecture. And the known established facts are—'

'Please, please, I beg of you,' mumbled Gorman, 'not again.'

228

His prayers fell on deaf ears. Percival was in full flow and time had no meaning. Mack the Knife, though, must have heard Gorman's prayers. 'I'm sorry to interrupt you, Mr Percival, but it's now 1 p.m.' (It felt like late evening to Gorman.)

'I'm happy to break for lunch now, should your Lordship wish. It will give me an opportunity to consider my peroration.'

'Yes, that's what I'm afraid of,' replied the judge cynically after giving the matter but a moment's thought. 'No, on reflection, let's bat on, it might prove to be quicker in the long run.'

Percival batted on, hitting fours and sixes all around the court. The very walls appeared to be sagging from the onslaught. 'And finally, was Mr Dennis's plight so terrible that he was justified in taking the law into his own hands – not on the spur of the moment, members of the jury, but with cold-blooded planning, and this the defence cannot dispute – to justify the slaughter of a fellow man outside this very building, the bastion of justice in this country? I said to you in my opening speech, there is only one verdict for you to return and, I submit, it is your duty to return on the facts that you have heard in this very troubling trial.' Finally, Percival's ramblings had run their course.

Stokes, at the back of the court, wanted to applaud. Halfpint, in the public gallery, did not. Rough Hands, in the jury box, still had two pens in his shirt pocket from before Percival had begun his speech. Halfpint wouldn't have been surprised if Rough Hands returned that afternoon in a fresh shirt with no pocket at all.

'Will you finish your speech this afternoon, Mr Gorman?' enquired the judge hopefully, just before the late lunch recess.

Gorman's reply was emphatic: 'Oh, yes, indeed I will, my Lord – with or without a fair wind.'

Chapter 42

Cannibalism at the Bailey

After suffering hours listening to Percival gabbling on and on that morning, Gorman and his junior, Jacobsen, were seeking refuge and having some lunch in the Bar Mess together with other ardent defenders of the innocent. Percival was sitting at the next long table together with the angelic Angelina and a large number of his old prosecuting cronies, there to gaze into Angelina's eyes and dream rather than be bored stiff listening to his assessment as to the prospects of a conviction. Percival was treating them to a soporific version of his morning's tour de force, salivating at the prospect of a conviction.

'Yes,' Gorman could hear Percival saying, 'believe me, I held the jury in the palm of my hand. They were sitting there nodding and winking at me and hanging on my every word. I think I've got him. It'll be interesting to see what Pat's going to do about it this afternoon. Mack the Knife's going to dish out a recommended twenty-five years minimum – possibly thirty. Quite right too, in my view. Where does Dennis think he is, running around with a loaded gun, the Alamo?'

Gorman, for his part, was telling his assembled audience an

anecdote that he'd penned during the latter part of Percival's mammoth peroration that morning. He had plagiarised the theme from a joke he'd heard years earlier but changed the participants. It was a moveable feast.

'So, Mack the Knife, Percival and I are on a cruise together, but our boat is shipwrecked. We end up on a remote island which turns out to be inhabited by cannibals. We're all captured and the cannibals are boiling up three huge pots to cook us in for dinner. Mack the Knife pleads with the Chief for a dying wish before he's cooked.

"What is it?" enquires the Chief.

"Before I'm boiled, I'd like to make one last speech – on the rise and fall of the Roman Empire."

The Chief's getting hungry. "How long will it take?"

"Well," says Mack the Knife, "I've been practising it for years now – I think I can cut it down to under four hours."

The Chief sighs. "OK," he agrees reluctantly, "I grant you your last wish."

"What about me?" pipes up Percival, "I've also got a last wish. I'd like to make a speech summarising all the notorious cases I've successfully prosecuted."

The Chief is getting impatient. "How long?" he asks.

"Well, with a fair wind, I'm pretty confident I can do it in five hours at most."

"Alright," says the Chief wearily, "I'm a fair man; I grant you your last wish."

Finally, the Chief turns towards me and says, "I suppose you too have a last wish."

"Indeed I do," I answer.

"What is it?" enquires the Chief, sizing me up whilst licking his lips.

"Cook me first!"'

They all laughed, Gorman the loudest. Percival, who happened to have first-rate hearing, remained unamused.

'Right, Daniel,' said Gorman, whilst polishing off a stale Danish pastry. 'It's 2 o'clock, fifteen minutes before we sit again. Plenty of time to write out a few headings for my speech.' His junior looked deeply concerned.

'Daniel,' continued Gorman in a fatherly tone, 'you've got to keep a sense of humour in this game, or you'll be a spent force before your time. Actually, I prepared my speech during Percival's opening three days ago and, frankly, as his closing speech was a thinly disguised replica, I haven't had to add that much. But I can tell you what you won't be hearing me talking about, and that's our client looking up the law of self-defence on his iPad. I can't deal with it and I don't intend to try. I am just going to pretend that that crippling piece of evidence doesn't exist. Otherwise, it'll be like struggling in quicksand – the more you struggle, the quicker you sink. Now, let's go and set out our simple stall and see if we can attract a few customers to buy our wares.'

They both stood to leave. 'What are all those sheets of paper you're holding in your hand, Daniel?' Gorman recognised the spidery writing and feared the worst.

'Oh, yes, I nearly forgot. Our client gave them to me just before the lunch break for you to have a look at before your speech.'

Gorman gave a deep sigh. 'Daniel, here's another lesson for you. Never let your client call the shots. Chuck them in the dustbin over there, there's a good fellow. Anyway, what's he know about this case? He's only the defendant!'

Chapter 43

Bury Me Not at the Bailey

'Ladies and gentlemen of the jury,' began Gorman to a packed house as he stood to begin his final address, 'there's an ever-increasing tendency in cinema these days to begin a film at the end and work backwards. Personally, I'm not a fan of it. You know the end of the story before the beginning. It's never a whodunnit, and Agatha Christie, for one, wouldn't have approved, nor would Inspector Poirot.

'So, in this case, if you were to see on-screen a man dressed as a barrister, standing outside the Old Bailey and pulling a gun from his brief and firing two shots at virtually point-blank range at an unarmed man, it's murder in cold blood. That's the prosecution case, after all. And were the film to end there, and the jury asked to return its verdict, they would be back in no time at all – crying guilty. Even in one's wildest imagination, it would be difficult to conjure up an explanation which could possibly justify such a blatant killing. But, as we all know, and experience in our private lives, fact is often stranger than fiction. So, let's rewind the video a little and consider whether the

killing was a cold-blooded one, or the act of a basically good
man in a lose–lose situation.

'There's an old Native American expression with a good deal
of truth in it: "Never judge a man until you have walked ten
days in his moccasins." Now, let's put on Mr Dennis's moccasins and take a stroll. Let's rewind the video to the beginning
for this walk. You have in your hands Dennis's life story and
indeed, in effect, his very life. You have seen on the monitors
Mr Dennis reading out his statement, his feeling helpless, deciding that there was only one route to survival and taking the
law into his own hands. What would you have done, members
of the jury, in his moccasins? It may well be that not one of us
would have had the guts to get a gun and kill, but, in your heart
of hearts, can you blame him for doing so?

'Other than the preservation of life, what other motive could
he possibly have for killing Maynard? Revenge? If it was revenge, why stay to be arrested? Why leave the bullets on the
kitchen table for the police to find?

'Does Dennis have to wait for Maynard to strike first before
he defends himself and his family? Had he not tried every other
avenue open to him and repeatedly sought the assistance of the
police? But what could they do? They had no hard evidence
against Maynard.

'Had he not told Maynard he couldn't pay? Did it help him?
No, it did not. The threats merely got worse and worse, ending
in the frightening and haunting episode on the A12 with perhaps the cruellest of games known to mankind – Russian roulette! Imagine a gun planted to your head on a deserted road in

the dead of night. What sort of an animal is it we are dealing with who could think up such a threat, which would undoubtedly haunt you for the rest of your life – a life which might have been very short?

'Agreed, Mr Dennis could have gone back to the police again for help, but with what result? Maynard arrested perhaps, but what sort of a case would they have had? Was it not more likely that Mr Dennis would receive yet another apologetic call from the police saying, "Sorry, we had to release him. There's no direct evidence, but don't worry, we'll keep a lookout on your home and let's hope Maynard calls it a day." Mr Dennis knew only too well that Maynard was never going to call it a day. He wasn't that sort.

'Should Mr Dennis sit at home waiting for the inevitable to happen, or wait for his wife and two boys to be tracked down at his sister-in-law's home? In Dennis's mind it was Maynard's life or his. If you were in his shoes, would you not have thought the very same? His family were his life and only Maynard's death could guarantee their survival. So he did it.

'Ah, yes, Mr Dennis was cunning in the extreme in the way he disguised himself as a barrister – but, frankly, so what? Having taken the decision to kill Maynard, can you blame him for being cunning in his planning to ensure it succeeded?

'Much play has been made by the prosecution that he fired two bullets and not one. Is this not, in an odd way, a point in his favour? Does it not clearly illustrate to you that Dennis believed his plight to be so serious and hopeless that only Maynard's certain death could save him?

'And was he not right in that belief? Maynard: a heartless,

ruthless loan shark who took no prisoners and was not put off continuing with his appalling threats, even after his own arrest for threats to kill. Dennis had tried to reason with Maynard – useless. The police had intervened – useless. The threats continued.

'Maynard, you may think, considered himself to be above the law. Money was his god, and woe betide anyone who failed to pay up.

'Let's suppose for one moment that Dennis had done nothing and that he had been murdered by Maynard's thugs, and that we are comfortably seated in front of our fires at home, reading the whole account of Dennis's history with Maynard in one of the newspapers. Is it not possible, or indeed likely, that we would have said to ourselves, "Mr Dennis was a fool! The police had tried but they could not help. If I'd have been in Dennis's shoes I'd have killed Maynard myself and to hell with it." There was no other way out, not with a powerful, lawless thug of a loan shark like Maynard.

'When one thinks of the law of self-defence, the type of facts that appear in this case do not readily spring to mind; this is true. But take the Second World War, for example: a man doesn't have to wait to be attacked before he can make a pre-emptive strike, as long as the attack is imminent. We knew Hitler was coming, we knew it was imminent, so that's the explanation for the Expeditionary Force being sent to France. A pre-emptive strike when nothing else would do.

'Was Mr Dennis not in exactly the same position? I put it to you that he was left with no other realistic form of defence. If this is true, can you blame him?

'Now, members of the jury, we have all heard the expression many times in our lives that attack is the best form of defence. It's true in chess, football and even in war, to name but a few examples. So, where you know as a certainty you're about to be attacked, you cannot be blamed for defending yourself by a pre-emptive strike. Can you blame Mr Dennis for fighting fire with fire rather than awaiting certain disaster?

'Ask any member of the public to explain what they understand by self-defence and they are likely to reply with words to the effect, "Well, when someone attacks you or is about to attack you or your family or a friend, you are entitled to defend them or yourself, even if your attacker comes off worse. You don't have to stand there and do nothing. After all, you didn't start the fight." No one has a problem with that – it's common sense. But not all cases of self-defence are as simple as that.

'If you're sure you are about to be attacked, you're entitled to strike first. You can't kill someone who is just going to kick you once or punch you, but what if you have good reason to believe your days are truly numbered, and something quite terrible is going to happen to you or your family, or both, and very soon indeed because the police, willing as they are to help, simply can't?

'Mr Percival, in his opening speech to you, said words to the effect that Dennis should have stopped at the traffic lights when they were red. Easy to say, but the traffic lights weren't working for Mr Dennis. The police, unfortunately, had failed him. He drove through the faulty lights to save himself and his family from a ten-ton lorry about to kill or maim him and his family – with Maynard as the gloating driver.

'And finally, what about Mr Samson? I'm not going to spend

much time on his evidence – he doesn't deserve it. I put it to you, you cannot trust a word he says and he has made all this up to secure a lower sentence for himself, to set his wife free and to save the £5 million family home. Just remember, please, my cross-examination of him. Did his evidence not leave you with a deep sense of unease? The sort of unease that gets you shifting restlessly in your chair as you hear it. The evidence of a man who takes an unhealthy advantage of any situation he finds himself in. "Pull the ladder up, boys – I'm in" might be his personal motto.

'Let me put it another way. If you feel it unsafe to convict my client without Samson's evidence, then how can you convict him with it? It's not as if you'd heard independent evidence from, say, a prison doctor that he made this admission. A prison doctor would have nothing to gain by lying – Samson undoubtedly has.

'And let me make this clear. If, when you retire, you consider that Mr Dennis's acts were completely over the top and grossly unnecessary and there were other steps he could reasonably have taken, and should have taken, then go ahead and convict him of murder.

'I close my speech with the words spoken by Mr Dennis in his interview and I make no apology for repeating them again: "What would you have done if you were me? – I really had no other choice."

'In all justice, members of the jury, on the facts of this most worrying case – did he?'

Chapter 44

Threats and Promises
at the Artesian

1975

The bank cashier's eyes wandered in the direction of the cherry-red alarm button protruding from just under the counter.

'Don't even think about it or you'll be just another dead hero pushing up daisies,' the robber whispered through his balaclava whilst a sawn-off shotgun tickled the cashier's temple. 'Load us up and then we'll be out of here and you'll live to tell the tale.' The shotgun prodded the cashier's head a little harder.

The cashier needed no such encouragement – it wasn't his money anyway. He couldn't load the large holdall fast enough. 'OK, OK, don't look so keen,' said the man behind the mask, 'or they'll think you're in on it.' Then the robber strolled out of the bank, careful to raise his balaclava above his eyes with his back to the bank's cameras, and with his sawn-off shotgun safely hidden inside the holdall, before crossing the road and jumping into the waiting Cortina GT, which sped off into the late afternoon sunshine – heading south.

A nice little earner, thought the robber – about forty grand. My half will be just the ticket for that bungalow in Greenwich the missus has been after, leaving a bit over to cover the exes for next week's trip 'across the pavement' – and back, hopefully!

He'd been the bank's last customer of the day. Always a good time to draw out a few quid from somebody else's account.

* * *

'We're doing OK, Jake, I've got good vibes, I can see him walking,' was Halfpint's opening remark as he sat down at the Artesian after day four of play.

'So now you're a clairvoyant as well, Halfpint? Next you'll be getting out the tarot cards.'

'Well, I think your money's been well spent, Jake. Our man on the jury's giving me all the right signals with those biros I bought for him.'

'Easy for you to say, Halfpint. Someone else's money being spent doesn't make you lose any sleep at night. And, as you know, I stand to lose another £5,000 to Rolex Ron if our man's potted. The shame of it; I'll be a laughing stock. Now, how was our brief's closing speech – any good?'

'Excellent, if I say so myself. He's ditched Sherlock Holmes and moved on to Agatha Christie and Inspector Poirot. We've got the judge's summing up tomorrow and then out go the jury. That's when our man will have to get down to work and earn his pay.'

'What about the prosecution speech?'

'Long, very long. I could hardly keep my eyes open – nor

could half the jury. The judge seemed miles away and our brief was visibly yawning by midday. I've worked out why this pros never gets any defence work. If he was paid by the day, no one could afford him.'

But Jake wasn't listening. 'Well, as you say, we've got the judge's summing up to come yet. He's a real hard man who hands out plenty of bird. He's been hand-picked for this trial to get our man down, so I'll want a full report tomorrow night. And another thing, tomorrow's Friday so we'll meet at Luca's before the boys arrive. If you turn up at, say, 6.30, I might stand you a pizza – or if the case is looking good, possibly a spaghetti Bolognese and a small glass of the house red before I send you on your way. Yes, as I've said many times before, Halfpint, I look after my own.'

'What if the news is bad, Jake?'

'Take to the hills, Halfpint,' ordered Jake sternly, 'and take that old crock of a Honda with you – new tyres and all. It's been cluttering up our streets for far too long. You chose that juror, Halfpint, not me. So, if it all goes belly-up, I'll be looking your way – rest assured.'

'And will you be looking my way if it all goes well, Jake?' Halfpint was starting to get cocky.

Jake pretended to look shocked at Halfpint's lack of faith. He put an ample arm around Halfpint's timid shoulders and squeezed hard. 'Of course I will, Halfpint. Naturally, I'll take all the credit, but you and I will have our own little secret. If our hero walks, I'll see you right. I might even treat you to a decent second-hand watch or a package holiday with your missus in Tenerife as a bonus.'

'And for present purposes, Jake?'

'A drink of course, Halfpint, what else? Call it a payment on account. Waiter!' barked out Jake, waving an imperious hand in the air. 'Two Old Cubans – on the double, please – and while you're at it, order us a couple of large plates of smoked salmon from the restaurant. My guest's looking for a show of commitment.'

'That's really generous of you, Jake, thanks very much.'

But Jake was not to be outdone. 'Generous, eh? Don't worry, if our man doesn't smell the fresh country air next week, I'll be taking the salmon off your pay.'

'I bet you would an' all, Jake.' Halfpint was now plainly rising above his station in life.

'That's one bet you'd win, Halfpint, you can count on it. Do you have any idea what a plate of smoked salmon costs around these parts?'

'Not a clue, Jake.'

'Well, let's hope it remains that way, Halfpint – cheers.'

Chapter 45

Strictly X-Rated

———————————

Poor old Magnus couldn't wait to race home after Gorman had finished his closing speech in good time, as promised. When he arrived, Frances was already out at her weekly cookery course.

First, he checked the whisky bottle level. Magnus reckoned someone had helped themselves to a nice double shot. The writing was already on the wall – in bold print! He poured himself a glass of Madeira to steady his nerves and went upstairs to their bedroom, heart pumping. The iPhone charger was winking at him from the table by the window, eager to disclose its secrets. He took it with him to his study and connected it to the computer. He half hoped he had set it up incorrectly, but no, sadly, it was working to perfection and the film show started.

'Darling, I've got a little present for you – guess what it is?' Charles's unmistakable voice had begun proceedings, together with the sound of the bedroom door being opened, then closed and locked.

'I'm in the shower, sweetie. I'll be out in just a minute.' Frances – his wife.

Charles's frame came into view by the bed. He was naked save for a towel wrapped around his waist. He placed a glass of whisky down on the bedside table.

He's in good shape for his age, admitted Magnus to himself ruefully. *No loose flesh hanging around his stomach. He always did look after himself.*

Next, Magnus saw Charles pull back the white duvet and place an ivory-coloured gift bag on the bed. It had the words La Perla printed in large black lettering across the side.

Magnus had no inkling what La Perla actually sold – chocolates, perfume, cheese?

Frances then made her entrance from the en-suite bathroom with a cream bathrobe tightly clinging to her slim figure, revealing a provocative cleavage.

'Wow,' sighed Charles, 'you look breathtaking. And wait till you see what's in this little package.'

'Calm down, darling, we've got plenty of time – hours. Magnus is going to be stuck at the Old Bailey all day in that dreadful murder case. What do you have for me there, Charles? You do spoil me – but I love it. I'm lucky if Magnus buys me a coffee percolator – he's such a meanie.'

'You don't have to tell me, I've had to put up with his stinginess for over forty years. Do you know that at boarding school he used to keep his tuck hidden under his mattress?' *A sneak as well*, thought Magnus, his temperature rising by the second.

'Doesn't surprise me in the least,' said Frances as she started delicately unwrapping the package, removing a black, silk, see-through negligee from the box inside and holding it up.

'Oh, it's absolutely beautiful, Charles.'

'Well, put it on – put it on and then we can both admire it and particularly what's in it. It's your size, I should know.' *Good Lord! How many times has this happened before?* thought Magnus.

'Oh, darling, don't speak like that, you're embarrassing me.' Magnus could see Frances's cheeks reddening.

'You know you love it, really.'

'I'll be back in a jiffy,' whispered the mischievous Frances, pecking Charles on the cheek before leaving for the bathroom. Then Charles reached for his glass of whisky and took a sip. Magnus joined him with his glass of Madeira. Charles closed the curtains and switched on the bedside light. Finally, Frances emerged.

'Dah-de-le-dah,' she sang, swishing her hips to and fro like a flirtatious teenager. 'It's a little bit tight, but I bet you knew what you were doing, you naughty boy.'

'I certainly did. I like to see every single curve. Come over here, my pet.'

'No, you come over here,' teased Frances in a husky voice. She raised a beckoning finger – reminiscent of Marlene Dietrich in her prime.

'Alright, I will, you don't have to ask me twice.'

Magnus was watching on, helpless. His glass of Madeira empty and his mouth wide open.

'My, my, what do we have here?' murmured Charles as the two of them embraced.

'And what do we have here?' whispered Frances, releasing the towel around Charles's waist.

'Dear me, what a big boy you are today,' she moaned shamelessly, as Charles eased her body onto the bed.

'That's your fault,' said Charles pretending to be embarrassed. 'Nobody but yours. Now let's see what's hidden under here.'

'Enough, enough! How much of this can a man stand!' cried Magnus as he jabbed the off button on the computer and went in search of another glass of Madeira – or two.

Chapter 46

Egregious Treachery

———————————

'Fancy a sherry before dinner, Charles?' called out Magnus, as Charles let himself into their home after work that evening.

'I'd prefer a whisky, if you don't mind,' replied Charles.

Don't I just know it, thought Magnus. 'I see Frances has left us a cold supper,' continued Magnus as he poured their drinks. 'She's out at her cookery course tonight, so it's just the two of us – cheers. Charles, I've got a little problem that's been bothering me lately. I'd like to ask your opinion, if you don't mind.'

'No, I'd be only too pleased to help, if I can.'

Will he indeed! thought Magnus. He had his ambush all ready. He had brought down the iPhone charger from his bedroom and planted it on the mantelpiece in the lounge, ready to be sprung on Charles at a suitable moment.

'Let's go and sit in the lounge,' suggested Magnus. The two old friends took their seats either side of the coffee table. 'I'm very worried about Frances. To cut to the chase, I think she may be having an affair.'

Charles looked amazed, or rather tried his best to. 'Surely not,

Magnus, I can't believe it – Frances having an affair? Impossible – not Frances – absurd.' *He's good*, thought Magnus. *Very good.*

'Well, I agree it's hard to believe, but I'm sorry to say the evidence is very strong, some might say conclusive.'

Charles appeared astounded. 'You'll never persuade me she's got another man. You couldn't ask for a better wife, Magnus, I should know, I'm on my third.'

Yes, and you're on my first as well, mused Magnus.

'OK, OK, I respect your opinion, Charles, so just hear me out. Here are the plain facts. About a week or so ago, when I came home from court, I found an empty glass in my bedroom.'

Charles began to perspire and redden. 'So?'

'Well, this empty glass, Charles, smelt of whisky.'

'Well?' responded Charles as casually as he could.

'Well, Frances doesn't drink whisky and neither do I, so naturally I was suspicious.'

'Might it not be the cleaning lady? God knows what they get up to when we're not at home,' offered Charles feebly.

'It's a bit worse than that, Charles, because the same day as discovering the glass smelling of whisky, I checked the Johnnie Walker bottle I'd just brought back from France. The very one you're drinking from now, Charles,' said Magnus, pointing at it sitting on the table between them next to the sherry decanter. 'Someone had opened it and helped themselves to a glass. Now, frankly, I can't see Gladys, our cleaning lady, opening a new bottle and helping herself.'

'Did you ask Frances about it?' queried Charles nonchalantly.

'No, I decided not to in case my suspicions were ill-founded.'

'So, what sort of a case is that, Magnus? You're becoming

paranoid. I'd just forget about it if I were you. Believe me, there's nothing in it,' Charles reassured his old school friend. 'To put it in your legal language, there's no case. Now let's go and have some supper and talk about old times.'

'Let's stick with the present for the moment, if you don't mind, Charles. Now, of course with the whisky glass alone I had no case; only suspicion. But unfortunately, these were deep suspicions, and so I decided to take it further.'

'So, what did you do, Magnus, hire a private detective?'

'Yes, in a funny way I did. Tell me, Charles, what would you do in my position if you suspected someone you had known for years and years was having an affair with your wife under your own roof?'

'I'd confront the bounder and banish him from my home and life for ever.'

'Egregious treachery, Charles, don't you agree? The behaviour of vermin – worse than the lowest criminal.'

Charles was no doubt wishing Frances would return early from her cookery course and put an end to this unnerving doubletalk. He looked as though he could bear it no longer but felt he ought to say something. 'So, what did your private detective report to you, Magnus? Did he find out who it was?' Magnus took his time in answering, salivating over Charles's obvious unease. He rose from his chair and walked to the mantelpiece and picked up the iPhone charger – his personal private detective.

'See this, Charles?'

'Yes, what of it? It's a phone charger,' replied a mystified Charles.

'Really?' said Magnus. 'Never judge a book by its cover, Charles. It may look like a simple phone charger but in fact it's much more – oh, yes, a good deal more.'

Charles looked terrified.

'This innocent-looking phone charger leads a double life, Charles.'

'I really don't understand what you're getting at, Magnus. What's all this gobbledygook? I'm afraid you've lost me.'

'Have I? Ever been to the spy shop in Baker Street, Charles?' Magnus was not going to put Charles out of his misery just yet.

'No, can't say I have. Why on earth would I want to?'

'Interesting stuff they've got there, Charles. Every sort of bugging device you could imagine. I bought this iPhone charger there – not cheap, but it certainly does the trick.'

'And what sort of trick might that be, Magnus?'

'It's an amazing box of tricks. It records video, sound and can charge your phone all at the same time.'

Charles seemed paralysed; he was lost for words.

'Yes, you can plant it anywhere you like – and hey presto.' Magnus knew how to milk the moment.

'So, what did you do with it, Magnus? Where did you place it?'

Now Magnus let it rip. 'In my bedroom, Charles. Yes, in my bedroom, before I left for court this morning. I also marked the whisky bottle with a line, so I could see if someone had helped themselves whilst I was out. Didn't you see the phone charger sitting quietly by the window minding my business for me?'

Charles froze but couldn't divert his eyes from Magnus's searing gaze.

An eerie silence followed. 'Do I have to play it for you, Charles? Do I really have to? Does the name La Perla mean anything to you, Charles? Paid the shop a visit recently, have you?'

Now Charles knew the game was most certainly up. Finally, he found what was left of his voice. 'That won't be necessary, Magnus – I'm truly sorry, I really am. Forgive me, if you can, I beg of you.'

Magnus was not in the forgiving mood. He walked up to Charles, dragged him to his feet and then, grabbing his old school friend by the shoulders, started violently shaking him to and fro.

'Sorry, are you?' he raged. 'Oh, yes, you're sorry alright – sorry you've been caught; that's your only regret. You're nothing but a filthy traitor. No better than some of the detritus who pass through my court. If I wasn't a judge, I would kill you here and now without feeling an ounce of remorse.'

Magnus looked around the room for a weapon and picked up a heavy Lalique cut-glass ashtray from the coffee table, lifting it high above his head, ready to smash it into Charles's face. He swung his arm back and then, at the last moment, slung the ashtray against the wall, splintering it into thousands of pieces.

Magnus was now out of control. 'Get out! Get out of my house. I never want to set eyes on you again as long as I live! May you rot in hell! Don't ever contact me again. You can tell Frances that Janet suspects you. Write her a sad letter if you like, but if you ever so much as whisper a word to her of what's happened here tonight, I'll tell Janet the truth. So help me, I'll send her a video of what's on this iPhone charger as well.'

Magnus collapsed exhausted into his armchair, urgently pouring himself a much-needed refill as Charles rushed upstairs, packed his case in a hurry and fled for his very life.

As soon as he heard the front door slam, Magnus rose from his chair, walked into the kitchen and buried the phone charger deep inside the dustbin. It had proved a fine investment, but it had had its day, just as Charles had had his.

Chapter 47

Late for Court

———————

'Right, lads – all in!'

8 a.m., a freezing Friday in December – snow lightly falling in Angel, north London. Rough Hands's premises were being raided by six police officers on a hot tip-off that the tyre shop was being used as a safe house for a consignment of high-purity cocaine, fresh in from the Netherlands.

Rough Hands had rolled up early before court to get an hour or so of work in. He'd just opened the shutters when six officers piled in, flashing a search warrant. Detective Sergeant Fleming was in charge and straight off asked Rough Hands:

'Got any weapons here?'

'No.'

'Any drugs?'

'No.'

'Any large amounts of cash?'

'No.'

'Well, then you won't mind if we have a look around, will you?'

What could Rough Hands say? Anyway, they had a warrant.

Rough Hands was asked, or rather ordered, to stay in his tiny office, which was the first place to be searched, with him watching on. It drew a blank.

Next, the two vehicles left overnight by customers. The first, a Volvo estate – a flat tyre and no road tax! Who cared? The second, an old Triumph Stag with four new tyres propped up against it, ready to be changed – a dead loss. Not an auspicious start.

'Right, lads,' called out DS Fleming, 'get every tyre off the shelves and have a good look behind, and don't worry about getting your pretty little hands dirty.'

Rough Hands was now outside his office watching on silently in disbelief. He'd learnt from Dennis's trial that it was best to keep your mouth shut.

'Nothing there, guv, except a few old copies of *Playboy*,' called out one of his officers. Fleming was not best pleased. It was meant to be his day off and a round of golf with his local publican had to be put on ice, whilst he busied himself in what was beginning to take the shape of a wild goose chase in deepest Angel. *Oh well*, he sighed to himself, *at least I can clock off early*.

'That's a nice vintage MGB you've got on the wall there, Mr Lomax – yours?' said Fleming glancing at the picture in Rough Hands's office.

'Was mine,' answered Rough Hands. 'Had to sell it the other week to pay off the bank.'

Christ almighty, thought Fleming, *some drug dealer we've got here. Next he'll be asking me if I can lend him a few quid*.

'Right, lads, let's get the hell out of here,' said Fleming, now totally deflated. 'It's bloody freezing and I've had no breakfast.

Put those tyres back on the shelves and we'll be off.' Fleming turned towards Rough Hands to apologise for the inconvenience the raid had caused. But twenty years in the force had taught him that Mr Peter Lomax was looking a little too relieved. Had he missed something?

'Just a minute, lads. Get those tyres back down, let's have a look inside them.' Groans all around from his officers. Rough Hands started to stare down at his dirty boots.

'Hello, hello, what have we got here?' shouted out one of the search party, pulling out a firm brown package from a Pirelli tyre. Rough Hands looked mystified.

'Open it up,' ordered Fleming. Two plastic-wrapped packages emerged with white powder inside them. Fleming examined the packages gingerly. 'Keep your mitts off them, lads; we'll need to have them tested for fingerprints.'

Rough Hands was now cautioned, as the police had good reason to believe the packages contained cocaine. 'I can't believe this,' he moaned. 'I've never seen them before in my life. You'd better ask my scallywag of an employee. Jesus, what's he done to me now?'

'Where is he, Mr Lomax?' asked Fleming. Rough Hands looked at his watch – 8.20 a.m.

'He's late.' And then, glancing towards the door, he called out, 'There he is.' Joey, the scallywag, had just arrived. He stared in, but as soon as he saw what was going on, he was up and running with two officers in hot pursuit. Joey's daily McDonald's and roll-up diet did not serve him well in the chase. He was flattened in under thirty yards, handcuffed and dragged back to the tyre shop, screaming ignorance and innocence.

Rough Hands was himself now arrested and handcuffed as the search continued. 'Guv, what've we got here? A second package!' cried out a jubilant officer. A fat white envelope had been discovered in a Goodyear tyre bearing a large cross mark in pink chalk.

Rough Hands was taken back into his office, where Fleming, now showing his worth, had just located a used piece of pink chalk on Rough Hands's office desk.

'Before we open this up, Mr Lomax, do you want to tell us what's inside? More coke?' Rough Hands looked terrified. The right to silence, which he'd learnt from the Dennis trial, flew out the window.

'No, that's not drugs,' he replied defiantly, 'that's my savings.'

'How much is in there, Mr Lomax?' enquired Fleming before opening it.

'Five grand in fifties. I've been saving them up for years for a rainy day.'

Then, delicately, Fleming opened the package. 'Saving it for years have you, Mr Lomax?' repeated Fleming, as he flicked through the notes with a satisfied grin spread across his face. 'These notes are all brand new with running numbers. Now, of course, I'm just a dumb police officer, so I'd be grateful if you could explain to me how you've saved £5,000 in brand-new £50 notes "for years".'

Rough Hands couldn't. 'There's something you boys ought to know,' he mumbled as if about to make a confession.

Fleming's eyes lit up. *What's this?* he thought. *Is Lomax going to grass up Mr Big? This could give me a real leg up for promotion.*

'I've got to be at the Old Bailey by 10.30 this morning,' Rough Hands announced.

'10.30 at the Old Bailey?' repeated Fleming, his hopes in tatters. 'What for? Are you on trial?'

'No, actually I'm on jury service in Court 1.'

'Jury service in Court 1?' Fleming, now dumbfounded, was in parrot mode. 'Are you trying the Maynard killing?'

'Actually, I am.'

Fleming reached for his mobile phone and walked a few paces away so as not to be overheard. 'Bloody hell, that's all I need on my plate,' he mumbled. Eventually, someone picked up on the other end. 'Get me Chief Superintendent Simpson. Tell him I need to speak to him now. I need his personal authority. Something very unusual has just happened – unique in fact, in my experience. Yes, I'm sure he's very busy, but this can't wait. Tell him I've just arrested a juror in the Maynard murder trial with two kilos of cocaine and I think he's going to be a little bit late for court today. How late? About seven years late – if he's lucky!'

* * *

Whilst Rough Hands's tyre shop was being spun, Mr Justice McIntyre was cooling his fevered brow, taking an early morning stroll in the snow in Green Park on his way in from Kensington to the Old Bailey. He was doing some serious soul searching. What a night it had been. He looked back on it with both horror and sadness.

Frances had returned after 9 p.m. Magnus had just finished

cleaning up the mess from all the broken glass. She was carrying a tray of mushroom vol-au-vents from her cookery class. Magnus put on a brave face and tried one. Worse still, he had to explain to her Charles's absence. The truth wasn't an option: that would mean the end of their marriage. So, he told her that Charles had received a frantic call from Janet, who was sounding very upset, and he'd rushed home straight away, before dinner. But who could blame her for taking a lover? You reap what you sow, and he had taken her for granted for far too long – what with his bridge and ancient history and righteousness. Now he had to pay. He would start afresh, he concluded. A long holiday far away in the sun or perhaps a cruise in Alaska. No one's perfect.

What a quality liar he'd become. He had lied to the assistant at the spy shop as to why he needed the secret camera. Then to his wife that he'd forgotten that Charles was coming to stay for a couple of days and again to his wife as to why Charles had to leave on the hurry-up.

And what low cunning he'd sunk to. Drawing cash to buy the phone charger – refusing the receipt at the shop – marking up the whisky bottle – and then using the gadget as a peeping Tom.

And what violence as well – grabbing Charles and shaking him like a madman before smashing the ashtray for all it was worth against the wall. And he was supposed to be a High Court judge preaching perfection to all around. So, for the first time since the murder trial had started, during this peaceful early morning walk in the park, Mack the Knife started thinking what he would have done in Dennis's shoes. *Never judge*

your fellow man until you walk ten days in his moccasins was ring-
ing in his head from Gorman's closing speech the previous day.
And here he was about to sum up in a murder trial and subtly
chuck in his own views.

Suppose he hadn't been to Oxford and earned a fine living
at the Bar before becoming a judge. Suppose he'd been forced
to borrow money in an emergency from a loan shark and then
continually and mercilessly been threatened and blackmailed
the way Dennis claimed he had. What would he have done?
Dennis had brought his misfortune on himself, but had he not
done the very same in the way he'd been treating his wife?

By the time he'd returned to his car, he'd reached his verdict.
I'm going to show Percival and Gorman what I'm really made of. Per-
cival may have a heart attack, but Gorman will want to kiss me. 'Alea
iacta est!' he exclaimed to himself. Yes, the die was cast. He would
cross the Rubicon that very day. His summing up would be his
sword and, by the bones of Julius Caesar, would he wield it!

*   *   *

'Morning Pat, morning Daniel, can I have a quiet word with
you both?' Percival had entered the Bar Mess at the Bailey
before the court was due to sit. The three of them wandered into
the library for some privacy.

'So, what's up, George?' enquired a curious Gorman.

'Plenty. One of the jurors has just been arrested with two
kilos of cocaine. The police interview is later this morning.'

'Which one is it?' asked Daniel, who already had his strong

suspicions. In fact, he would have happily bet his entire fee that he knew who it was. Who else could it be? One of the five women? Not a chance. The two jurors in suit and tie? Very unlikely. The man who lived a long way from London with his *Daily Telegraph* crossword puzzle? Highly improbable. The two youngsters? Children. Mr Polo Neck? Didn't have the guts and wouldn't need the money. That left one juror: the man in the grubby jeans with the unused pens in his pocket.

'Well, I don't know what he looks like or where he's sitting,' answered Percival, 'but his name's Peter Lomax. I've discussed our position with old Stokes and we're going to apply for the trial to crack on without him. What's your view, Pat? Speaking for myself, I've never had this situation in over thirty years of prosecuting. Mack the Knife isn't going to be best pleased about this – he'll have a fit.'

Gorman appeared unconcerned. 'Strange as it might seem to you, George, I'm not here to best please Mack the Knife. I'm here to get my client off. And when we've heard his summing up, I think you'll agree he's here to get my client down. Give us half an hour. Dennis is no bit-part player in this case, so I'm going to ask him his views first – for what they're worth.'

Chapter 48

Deaf Ears

'So, Pete, what are you doing with two kilos of cocaine hidden in one of your tyres?' asked DS Fleming in the interview room at Islington Police Station.

Peter Lomax knew all about police interviews. He'd been hearing about little else for four days in court. But now he was experiencing one for himself and, worse, he didn't have an expensive brief like Stanford sitting next to him, but the local legal-aid duty solicitor, whose shoes were dirtier than his own boots. He'd been advised to remain silent, so Lomax did just the opposite. Who could blame him? He had a fair bit of explaining to do – two kilos of cocaine and £5,000 cash.

'I know nothing about the drugs, I swear on my kids' lives. It's that scallywag Joey who works for me. You saw him scarper for yourself the minute he looked in the door this morning.'

'Well, strangely enough, Pete, he's telling us the very opposite,' said Fleming.

'I didn't run – he did.'

'But, Pete, the difference is that you've admitted the five grand was yours, and I'm still puzzled by your reply at the scene that you've been saving it for years. The notes are all in consecutive numbers, so that can't possibly be the truth. And then there's the fresh chalk marks on the tyre and the matching chalk in your office. So, where did you get that £5,000 from?'

'I can't tell you. I just can't, but I repeat, it's nothing to do with drugs, that's for sure.'

'You also told me at your shop that you had to sell your MGB recently, so the evidence is starting to stack up, isn't it? You were hard up?'

'It's looking bad, I agree, but I swear to you I had no idea the drugs were there. It's got to be down to Joey. He's been selling tyres for cash behind my back.'

'Has he got a set of keys for your shop, Pete?'

'No, he hasn't, I'm not that crazy.'

'We searched your home after your arrest, Pete. Plenty of unpaid bills knocking about, but also plenty of kitchen brochures in the front room. Is your wife ordering a new kitchen?'

'Well, I've been promising her one for a long time,' replied Lomax, sadly.

'So, how were you going to pay for it, Pete? With that five grand we found? Or was that just going to be a deposit? I ask you, once again, where did that five grand come from, and why, if you didn't trust your employee, did you hide the money at work, and not at home?'

'I can't tell you, I simply can't, but I repeat, I've got nothing to do with the drugs. You won't find my prints on that package – that's a cert.'

'Maybe not, maybe not. Time will tell, but that doesn't clear you. Perhaps you're just a careful man.'

'I'm no drug dealer, I'm a simple hard-working man with a small tyre business,' pleaded Lomax.

Fleming had heard it all before. 'So, if that's the case, why don't you just tell us who gave you the money?'

Lomax just sat there, lost for an answer.

'You can't, Pete, can you?' pressed Fleming. 'You and I both know it's drug money, that's the truth, isn't it?'

Rough Hands had heard enough. 'That's it, put me back in the cell. I'm not answering any more questions – I'm an innocent man – do your worst,' he cried out, as it dawned on him that his next view of a courtroom at the Bailey was likely to offer a rather different perspective to the one that he had been used to from the comfort of the jury box.

Chapter 49

An Interesting Coffee Break

'So, what's the reason for this coffee invitation, Daniel?' enquired Gorman, as the two of them, together with Stanford, sat down in the restaurant on the second floor of the Bailey. 'Speaking for myself, I'd prefer to have a whisky before Mack the Knife's summing up.' The defence trio, together with the prosecution team, had just come out of the judge's private room. He'd called all the barristers in to decide what to do after hearing that a juror had been unavoidably delayed, courtesy of a couple of unfortunate packages.

The judge had said that he wouldn't be surprised if both sides had wanted to crack on with the trial, but for different reasons. The prosecution because they could do without having a drug dealer on the jury; and the defence because they feared that if he returned to jury service, he might repent and vote for a conviction. He was spot on. He ruled that he was going to delay a decision until 2 p.m. If the juror was charged by then, the trial would proceed with eleven jurors; if not, he'd reconsider.

'I'll tell you why I've asked you for a coffee,' answered Daniel. 'It's to do with the missing juror. I've been studying him carefully and he keeps changing the number of pens in his shirt pocket. But he never uses any of them, nor the one the court provides free.'

Gorman failed to see the point. 'Well, that's a very interesting observation, Daniel, but, unless I've got behind on the law, it's not a criminal offence to change the number of pens you're carrying around during a trial.'

'It's more than that,' continued Daniel. 'I think it's a code.'

'Code?' repeated Gorman. 'Why would a juror want a code?'

'Well, I think he's signalling to someone in the public gallery how the trial's going. When it's going badly – no pens. Mediocre – one pen. All good – two pens. And when the jury came back after a break yesterday afternoon, halfway through your speech, Pat, he had three pens for the first time.'

'Well, that's music to my ears, Daniel. Let's hope you're the real deal. So, to whom is he signalling? I suppose you've worked that one out as well?'

'Actually, I think I have. There's a small, dapper fellow who's been at the back of the public gallery every day without fail. I'm pretty sure it's him, and I intend to put it to the test this afternoon.'

'So, why does he bother to signal to somebody in the public gallery? Why doesn't he just meet him after court each day to find out what the jury are thinking?'

'My guess is that whoever's organising this won't allow anyone to meet with the juror after or before court. They're protecting themselves, and so they've arranged this system between them.'

Both Gorman and Stanford gave Jacobsen a look as if his unexpected elevation had gone to his head.

'Angelina's perfume making you a trifle dizzy, Daniel?' Gorman well knew how to mock.

Daniel blushed.

'Oh, yes, I've seen you staring at her all day,' continued Gorman. 'Can't say I blame you either. In any event, put me out of my misery, Daniel, and tell me how you're going to test your theory this afternoon? Are you going to ask this fellow in the public gallery for a coffee as well?'

'Nothing so vulgar; he's going to tell us.'

'Is he? What are you going to do – put a gun to his head?' said Gorman.

'No, I intend to watch his reaction if he discovers at 2 o'clock that his inside man's no longer on the jury.'

Gorman and Stanford just stared at each other. 'This boy will go far, Pat, I told you he's no mere pen-pusher,' said Stanford.

'That's what I'm worried about, Adrian. Let's hope he's wrong, and then I can tease him about it for ever more.'

'And what if I'm right, Pat?' interrupted Daniel jovially.

'Then for the rest of this case I'll sit behind you, and you can lead me. That's bound to impress Angelina. And who knows, if your luck's in, she might even condescend to have a coffee with you – but I wouldn't bet my fee on it!'

Chapter 50

A Medical Vignette

L ate on Friday morning, on the fifth day of trial, Jake was in Harley Street to receive his annual medical check-up results.

'You can go in now, Mr Davenport. Professor Lawson's ready for you.'

Jake wasn't ready for Professor Lawson, nor his gruelling questioning. But if Jake had to fly, he always flew first class. And if Gorman was the *man to see* when in murky illegal waters, then the Prof was his medical counterpart.

The Prof had a sharp sense of humour. He also had a pretty shrewd idea of how Jake made ends meet. He had taken his wife to Il Consigliere for a Friday night dinner a couple of years earlier and seen Jake and his boys seated at the other end of the room – it was no Oxford dons' reunion.

'Well, at least you've made it here, Mr Davenport, which in itself is rather a feat looking at your test results,' said the Prof as Jake entered. Jake didn't care much for the cut of the Prof's jib. 'You'd better sit down while we go over them.' Jake needed a drink or, more accurately, another one. He had already downed two Scotches before leaving home.

'Weight: up for the fifth year running – increase of twelve pounds since last year.

'Body mass index: thirty-six. That comes under the heading of severely obese.

'Cholesterol: eight. That's 60 per cent higher than what is considered the safe upper limit.

'Blood pressure: 160/100 – critical.

'Sugar levels: borderline diabetes.

'In short, Mr Davenport, as we say in the trade, you've booked yourself in for a heart attack, and you're making a determined effort not to be late!'

Jake asked for a glass of water; he didn't much care for the Prof's directness either.

'You're looking very strained, Mr Davenport. Are you worried about something? Business problems?'

'Well, err, I've got something on my mind. Hopefully it will sort itself out next week. I've thrown a lot of money at it.'

'Yes? What is it, if you don't mind my asking?'

'Let's just put it this way: I've invested heavily in someone's future, and all I need to hear are two words. I can't say more than that.'

The Prof sat back in his chair and studied Jake's face. He couldn't quite work the riddle out but was going to have a crack at it anyway.

'Deal done?'

'No, nothing like that.'

'Eagle landed?'

'Wrong again. But not a bad try.'

The Prof gave up. Obviously, the two of them were not on the same wavelength.

Finally, Jake asked a question to which he well knew the answer. 'What do you think is the cause of all this, Prof?'

The Prof removed his glasses and leaned forward from behind his desk. 'Your diet – or more accurately, your lack of one. Life is not a Bavarian beer festival, Mr Davenport. You've got to know where to draw the line.'

Jake knew where to draw the line with some precision in his business affairs, but the Prof was not talking about avoiding loan sharking or drug deals.

'What exercise do you take each week, Mr Davenport?'

'Ah, well, once a week, on Friday afternoons, I always take a long walk in Kenwood. And I've got this fancy jogging machine at home – bloody useless, I've had it for three months now and I haven't lost a pound.'

'How often have you been on the machine, Mr Davenport?'

'Twice!'

The Prof just sighed. 'Just tell me your daily diet then, Mr Davenport. I'll double whatever you say anyway, so you might as well come clean. Breakfast?'

'Two or three fried eggs and a couple of slices of bacon or a plate of kippers and some toast.'

'May I suggest just Weetabix in future? Low-fat milk, of course. Lunch? Oh, I'm sorry, anything between breakfast and lunch?'

'Well, I might have a few biscuits here and there, if there's a packet open, or maybe a doughnut.'

'Nothing in future, please. Lunch?'

'Well, if I'm at Harry Morgan's I might have a plate of chopped liver and a salt-beef sandwich.'

'And to drink?'

'Well, I never have more than two glasses of wine with my lunch.'

'May I recommend a fresh tuna salad at the most, and no alcohol. Tea?'

'Well, I have to admit, I do like the occasional plate of smoked salmon sandwiches or a millefeuille from Valerie's, but only one – they're bloody enormous anyway.'

'Two sugar-free digestive biscuits from now on, Mr Davenport, if you're feeling a bit peckish – nothing else. Dinner?'

'Well, you know by 8 o'clock I'm usually starving. I do a lot of entertaining in restaurants.'

'Typical dinner, please, Mr Davenport.' The Prof wasn't interested in Jake's prebuttal.

'Well, I might start with a lasagne and then perhaps a fried veal chop with a few zucchini to cheer up the plate, maybe a macaroni cheese on the side. But I rarely have a dessert.'

'Rarely, Mr Davenport?'

'Well, not unless there's a nice homemade tiramisu on offer, or a crêpes Suzette.'

'No desserts from now on, Mr Davenport – and nothing fried. Grilled fish for you, or roast chicken – skin removed. So, what do you drink with your evening meal? And don't tell me Diet Coke.'

'Well, if I'm out with the boys we knock back a few bottles of Tignanello and finish off the meal with a grappa. You know, grappa's really good for indigestion – far better than Gaviscon.'

'Smoke?'

'A couple of Havanas here and there, to cut the tension.'

'So, Mr Davenport, you tell me, having heard yourself just now, are you surprised at your constant indigestion?'

'Actually, to be honest, Prof, I'm a bit surprised I'm still alive.'

The Prof passed judgement and he didn't hold back. 'Your problem, Mr Davenport, is that for the way you eat, you need at least two digestive systems, and the good Lord only gave you one. But you knew all that before you came to see me – didn't you, Mr Davenport?'

Jake just nodded, like a naughty schoolboy being caught stealing from the tuck shop.

'So, why did you bother coming then?'

'Prof, I've been asking myself that exact same question.' Jake rose to his feet. He'd heard quite enough. 'See you again next year as always – if I'm still kicking, which, according to you, Prof, is by no means an evens bet.' *Weetabix and grilled fish*, thought Jake. *Sod that for a game of soldiers!*

Two minutes later, Jake was out in Harley Street, hailing a taxi. The Prof was watching out of his open window on the first floor. He could hear every word.

'Cabby – Harry Morgan's, St John's Wood – doctor's orders – and make it sharpish – I'm bloody starving. I haven't eaten a thing since breakfast!'

The Prof shook his head ruefully and smiled. *A typical lovable rogue*, he thought. Then it hit him what the two words were that Jake was hoping to hear and be worthy of an investment – *not guilty, of course!* Well, in Jake's particular case, what else could the two words possibly be?

*   *   *

At around the same time as Jake sat down at Harry Morgan's for a light lunch of chopped liver and a couple of salt-beef sandwiches on rye, Peter Lomax was brought in front of the station sergeant to be charged with possession of class-A drugs with intent to supply and being in possession of criminal property, namely £5,000 cash. Joey the scallywag had been released on police bail without charge, awaiting the results of fingerprint tests on the drug packaging.

On being charged, and being asked if he had any reply to make, Lomax, now a forlorn figure, turned towards DS Fleming and said, 'Well, I suppose bail's out of the question, then?'

It was.

Chapter 51

Mack the Knife
Wields His Sword

'**M**embers of the jury, as you will have observed, one of your number is missing,' began Mack the Knife, as the court finally resumed on the Friday afternoon, the fifth day of the trial. 'We're going to continue without him and I don't want you to speculate as to the reason. It's absolutely nothing to do with this case – do you understand?' Several jurors nodded.

Halfpint, high up in the public gallery, did not. He sat there gobsmacked, with six staring eyes watching him from the lawyers' rows below. Then Daniel Jacobsen rose from his seat and ambled, as innocently as possible, to behind the dock for a better view.

Halfpint was staring down into the court, his features show-ing a mixture of disbelief and horror. Daniel could almost read Halfpint's thoughts: *What the hell's going on here? What's happened to him? Have I been spotted? Has our cover been blown? What should I do now? Do I stay or leave quietly?* After no more than two minutes, the little fellow had apparently made his mind up and slipped out quietly.

A faint smile of satisfaction crossed Daniel's features. On returning to his seat behind his leader, he cheekily wrote out a short note and handed it to him. It read:

Pat, when do you want to swap seats with me – now or just before the verdict?
Regards,
Your new leader, Daniel

Gorman scribbled just five words in reply:

Get back in your pram!

A sore loser – but then, he lacked practice.

*   *   *

'Mr Percival and Mr Gorman,' said Mr Justice McIntyre, just before he was about to begin his summing up. 'As you've just seen, I've sent the remaining eleven members of the jury back to their room for a few minutes before I start my summing up. I've been giving the case some serious thought overnight, in fact I've been clearing my head with a refreshing stroll in Green Park early this morning.

'I've come to the firm view that there is little purpose in cluttering up the indictment with more than one count. The first charge is murder – Dennis's case is he acted in self-defence. The second and third counts relate to the gun and the bullets – Dennis's defence is duress. Putting it simply, if the jury conclude Mr Dennis was acting in self-defence, are they not also bound to conclude he was acting under duress when obtaining the gun and the bullets?

'On the other hand, if they find him guilty of murder, then of course the use of a firearm would be an aggravating feature when I come to sentence him. Assuming my logic to be correct, I needn't burden the jury with the intricacies of the law of duress.' McIntyre was already wielding his sword.

'I know, normally, I should have raised this before your closing speeches, but quite frankly, I cannot see how either of you are disadvantaged by my raising it now. So, unless you are able to persuade me otherwise, I intend to sum up the law on self-defence only, leaving the jury to decide whether Dennis murdered the deceased or was acting in self-defence.'

Neither Percival nor Gorman could believe what they were hearing. Nonetheless, they couldn't fault the judge's logic. But Percival had to stick his oar in. 'My Lord, I would specifically draw your attention to the case of *Fisher* before you make your final decision.'

'Yes, I've read it and I intend *specifically* to ignore it!' was the judge's immediate rebuff. 'Usher, call in the jury.' The jury returned to court and Mack the Knife began his summing up, going through the facts without expressing any particular opinion. But then, nearing the end, he let loose.

'Members of the jury, you must place yourself in the defendant's shoes. If you decide that the defendant really had no other alternative after all those terrifying experiences at the hands of a ruthless loan shark, and his very life and that of his beloved ones were in imminent real danger, then you will find him not guilty. Remember his desperate plight and how he had sought the help of the police time and time again – unsuccessfully, despite their best efforts.

'Now, the prosecution have quite properly made a good deal of play of the defendant's use of his iPad, and you may agree it could only mean he wanted to know where he stood if he took the law into his own hands. But it does not mean that the Russian roulette incident has been fabricated. Far from it. Any man in his predicament might have checked the law themselves.

'More importantly, remember his account of the Russian roulette incident on the A12 that dark rainy night and remember how he told it in his interview. You may feel he was at his wits' end. Is it not hard to imagine a nastier threat or a more traumatic experience?

'And last, but by no means least, members of the jury, you must put out of your minds completely the incident you may have read about in your newspapers of an assault outside this very building, yesterday. It has absolutely no bearing on this case. You must not hold it in any way whatsoever as a point against the defendant, even if you believe in some ways yesterday's incident was a copycat event. Do I make myself clear?'

Gorman nodded vigorously his approval of the judge's remarks and hid his surprise. Percival was so distraught by what he'd heard that he completely forgot to remind the judge to tell the jury to put out of their minds Gorman getting into play the words 'I'd feel safer in a Siberian labour camp'. Angelina, sitting next to him, reminded him of this, but Percival just closed his eyes and nodded, as if to say, 'What does it matter now?' Stokes rushed out of court. He could take no more. His calming tablets had met their Waterloo. Percival stared at Gorman in utter disbelief. Was this really happening? Mack the Knife, the hard man of the Bailey, making a second closing speech for the defence? Unreal, unthinkable, preposterous.

Gorman couldn't resist scribbling a note to Percival:

'Someone's bribed him!'

He received a one-word response:

'You?'

Jacobsen passed his leader a note, which read:

'Mack the Merc (Merciful) – the Great Defender.'

Finally, Merciful Mack finished his summing up, and his metaphoric, razor-sharp sword was replaced in its sheath, dripping with blood – Percival's!

Chapter 52

When Drink Goes in...

'Is that you, Ernie?' Halfpint sounded desperate.

'Of course it's me, you idiot. Who else could it be when you ring this number – Scotland Yard? You sound terrible, what's happened?' Halfpint *was* feeling terrible. He was seriously thinking of heeding Jake's advice at their daily briefing the night before. *Take to the hills and don't look back.* 'I've got to see Jake straight away, otherwise I'd never be calling this number,' stuttered a distraught Halfpint.

'Can you tell me what's wrong on the phone?'

'No, I can't, but it's not good news. I might never see the morning sun.' Halfpint remembered only too well that it was he who had chosen Rough Hands as a suitable case for treatment.

'OK, I'll see if I can find him. I think he's out with his missus or his bird doing some Christmas shopping at Harrods.' *Jake paying retail? No chance*, thought Halfpint. 'Aren't you supposed to be meeting him at Luca's at 6.30? Right, get there at 5.30 and I'll try and dig him out and have him there by then. And calm down, Halfpint, calm down. Remember, where there's a problem there's always a solution. See you then.' Ernie hung up.

Ernie's advice did little to comfort Halfpint. He knew only too well that Jake's *solution* was unlikely to be a consoling arm around his shoulder.

*　　*　　*

'If you want to live your life like Big Jake, here's what you have to do, Ernie – it's a cinch.'

It was 5.30 that Friday night and Halfpint and Ernie had already been at Luca's for a good half-hour, waiting to break the news to Jake about the missing juror. Both were in need of some Dutch courage, and neither could wait for Jake's arrival to cut the tar out of their dry throats. They were propped up at the bar downing whisky sours – Luca made a pretty good one. The restaurant was deserted and didn't officially open until 6 p.m., but any friend of Jake's was a friend of Luca's and would not be refused early entry.

Halfpint was already half-blasted. His diminutive frame did not take well to alcohol. Now on his third round, he was saying the first thing that entered his giddy head. 'When drink goes in, secrets come out' was a saying that had obviously passed him by at a rate of knots. 'Yes, Ernie, my boy,' continued Halfpint. 'Here's what you do, and you become a Jake look-a-like in a flash. First, you buy yourself a large house in Primrose Hill, well away from us scumbags in south London, but not too far so that you can't remind us all that you still remember your roots – and what a pie and mash looks like.'

Little did Halfpint or Ernie appreciate that Jake had just entered the establishment, and was standing about five yards

WHEN DRINK GOES IN...

behind them, pulling hard on his cigar and glaring at their backs as they sat there on the high bar stools, bending each other's ears.

'Then you order the *Telegraph* every day at home, and *Private Eye* once a fortnight, and sit down to a plate of kippers and scrambled eggs while your missus scratches her way through the *Mirror*. You get the History Channel running on the TV so you can chuck in a few Napoleon and Churchill quotes in your conversation, to show everyone you're not empty-headed like the rest of us, nor were you hiding behind the door when the Lord handed out brains. And you keep an old book of famous sayings next to your bed and practise a few every night before lights out instead of saying your prayers – so you've got a clever remark ready for every situation and can feed a few to us brain-dead morons, like "casting pearls to swine" and "if they haven't got cigars and bourbon in heaven, I ain't going". And you don't swear every second word like the regular gangsters. No, you keep your swearing for special occasions, so that people know you mean it and start quivering.'

'Yes, and I think one of those occasions might be today when he hears what you have to say,' interrupted Ernie, rubbing salt into the wound.

'Then you ponce around town in your vintage Bentley,' continued Halfpint, as if Ernie had never spoken, 'with your size thirteen Berluti boots – stolen to order by the hoisters – and with Tchaikovsky's 1812 blasting from your speakers in case anyone doubts that you're a regular *Telegraph* reader. And you have a thick Cohiba at £30 a shot dangling from your lips with the yellow band left on, so that at the traffic lights everyone knows you're the business.

'The next thing you do is get yourself a high-class restaurant to visit regularly, and take your team there once a week, flashing fifties – so everyone knows you're caked up. And you make sure your sleeves are rolled up so no one misses your swanky platinum Rolex. And you order high-priced vintage wines which you never get decanted, so that no one makes the mistake of thinking you're drinking the house plonk like the rest of them.

'And, of course, you get someone else's wife as your bit on the side so she doesn't pester you all the time. Or, better still, a long-haul air-hostess, so that she has three days off and then three days on – for you to rest up. Then you bribe one of the staff in the food department of Harrods so everything's half-price. And, just to keep things kosher, you buy yourself a rundown mini-market for a pittance, where cash is king, and you can pay in some of your dirty money and draw out enough to keep the taxman away from your door.

'Then, before Christmas, you parade up and down in your manor chucking turkey and whisky at every pauper in sight, so when your missus drags you screaming to church on Christmas Eve you can clear your slate, before doing exactly the same the next year. And when Christmas arrives, you fly your whole family up to Scotland to stay at Gleneagles, and start handing out goodies to all the kids in the hotel, so that you make Father Christmas look like a real scrooge, in the hope that you get yourself a ticket to heaven.'

'Well, he certainly won't have either of us for company up there,' cut in Ernie.

'Speak for yourself,' retorted Halfpint, now on full throttle. 'And then, when you see some poor bastard's been nicked for blasting Bob the Merc straight to hell, you get busy – calling me off the bench to do your dirty work, whilst you waltz around town with your bit on the side. Meanwhile, I'm risking life and limb trying to suss out what twelve of our fellow men and women are thinking – or should I now say eleven. And when it all goes pear-shaped, who's to blame? Me, of course!

'Yeah, and finally,' concluded Halfpint, 'it doesn't do any harm if you happen to be the size of a sumo wrestler, so that no one takes any liberties with you.'

'That counts you out, Halfpint, doesn't it?' Ernie had been tickled pink by the accuracy of Halfpint's monologue. Jake had not. Nor had he been amused when Ernie had called him while his bit on the side was slipping a pair of overpriced Chanel crocodile shoes onto her delicate feet to match the black lace, semi-see-through dress and the perfume he'd already bought for her. She would surely be paying him for this in kind in his cosy little flat off Sloane Square.

But then Halfpint and Ernie started sniffing. They smelt expensive cigar smoke wafting in their direction. Turning around, their worst fears were realised.

'What are you two gossiping about?' enquired Jake, pretending he had caught only the fag end of their conversation.

Halfpint and Ernie both just stared at Jake – their mouths open. They were petrified that Jake might have picked up more than the tail end of Halfpint's soliloquy.

'Oh, hello, Jake. Didn't see you arrive. How long have you been here?' Halfpint stuttered.

'Long enough to hear every word, Halfpint.'

At least he's not swearing, Halfpint consoled himself.

'Yes, every fucking word, Halfpint. You and I will be having a little chat about that, and it won't be at the Artesian either. I might be the size of a sumo wrestler, but you forgot to mention that I've the memory of an elephant. Now, instead of being flat on my back listening to sweet nothings, I find myself vertical, and it's not what I had in mind for this time of the afternoon. This had better be good news.' It wasn't, as both Halfpint and Ernie's expressions plainly revealed. 'Pour me a large Averna, Luca – I feel some serious indigestion coming on,' said Jake.

Luca obliged.

'The trial's taken a turn for the worse, Jake,' trotted out Halfpint, trying his best to break the news gently.

'Yeah? What's happened?'

Let's get this over with, thought Halfpint. 'Our man's not on the jury any more, Jake, and I don't think he's gone AWOL, I think he must have been nicked by the Old Bill. It can't be anything else. The trial's going on without him.'

Jake started scratching the eczema on his left forearm. 'Oh, that's great news, Halfpint – really great news. I lay out five large and now he's been arrested. What for?'

'I don't know for sure, Jake, but it must be that he's been sussed. What else could it be? I suppose it's also possible he's ill or he's just disappeared, or something like that.'

Jake was unconvinced and drank the Averna in two gulps. 'Or his conscience has got the better of him and he's talked. What about that, Halfpint? You tell me. You chose him, remember?'

Halfpint remembered only too well.

'I thought you were a good judge of character, Halfpint, I really did,' said Jake, as he held out his empty Averna glass at full stretch for Luca to refill. 'You told me you were holding an ace in the hole, but it turns out to be nothing but a busted flush. You're no brighter than Luca's dumb waiter. Not only is my five grand down the tube, but another five large on that bet with Rolex Ron. And, worse still, the way things are going, you and I could be sharing a cell with Dennis come Christmas, instead of me and my family sitting pretty in a suite at Gleneagles. We're in muddy waters alright – and I want to see some dry land.'

'Right, Ernie,' Jake decided after a moment of tense silence. 'Ring our man at the Yard and find out if he's been nicked. In the meantime, tell the boys that dinner's off tonight. You can take them to McDonald's for all I care. I'm taking to the hills, and not with you, Halfpint. And I won't be returning 'til the smoke's cleared.'

Jake pulled out his Dupont lighter and relit his cigar, which had itself suffered a relapse on hearing the bad news. He took two deep puffs, sized Halfpint up with his head at a slant and then, charitable as always, gave him some fatherly advice: 'If I were you, Halfpint, I'd get onto lastminute.com and get yourself a cheap ticket to the Himalayas. And do us all a favour, make sure it's one-way!'

Chapter 53

Mama

—

When Angelina had left school, her father had wanted her to study law in Rome and then come into his legal practice. But she hated commercial law, and anyway she had wanted to escape the family yolk. So, a compromise was reached and she went to King's College London to study law there. She then did a master's in international law – much to the joy of her parents, who hoped that it would lead to her return and joining up with her father.

She tried it for two years but missed dear old London. She was also desperate to flee the constant pestering of young, horny Italians, who, understandably, didn't give her a moment's peace in her hometown.

Her university being near the Old Bailey, she had often wandered in and sat in the public gallery, fascinated by the murder trials permanently taking place. And so it was that she ended up as a barrister in a foreign land – and without a shadow of doubt, the prettiest one around.

Three days before Dennis's murder trial was about to start, she had been on the train home, having just lost a death by dangerous driving prosecution at Harrow Crown Court, when her senior clerk telephoned and asked her to come straight back to chambers. Percival wanted to see her most urgently. The omens were not good. Had a client complained – or, even worse, a solicitor? Or perhaps Percival was going to tell her, as sympathetically as possible, that unfortunately she was not up to the mark and should consider returning to Italy.

After a nerve-racking journey, she finally arrived and, with her heart in her mouth, tapped lightly on Percival's door, hand-kerchief at the ready. It had to be bad news – what else could it be so late on a Friday afternoon? Percival was busy on the phone and gestured to her to sit down. The suspense was unbearable.

'Well, you'll have to have dinner without me, darling – Nick Denning's got laryngitis – can't put two words together. I haven't even got a junior to replace him yet. Don't wait up. I'll be home late.'

Finally, he put the phone down and stared across at the pet-rified Angelina.

'Well, Angelina, what do you say?'

Not a sound from Angelina. *What was he talking about?* she thought.

'Are you up for it?'

'Up for what, George?' she asked timidly.

'Being my junior on Monday, of course, in the Maynard murder case at the Bailey.'

Her relief was manifest, and she showed it by bursting into tears. 'Dear me, Angelina. Being led by me is not that bad, is it? Patrick Gorman's defending, so don't worry about my falling ill and your having to take over. He's bound to be nicer to you than he is to me. I'm sorry to put this pressure on you, but no more senior member of chambers is available at such short notice. You'll sit behind me, take notes and smile at Mack the Knife – the old misery guts. Don't worry. You'll do just fine. Are you in?'

More inexplicable tears.

*　*　*

'There's a very nice young man in my case, Mama.'

'What did you say, Angelina? I can't hear you – I'm in the kitchen.'

A week later, Angelina was having Friday night supper with her mother in her flat in Maida Vale. Her father had remained at home in Italy, whilst Mama had come to London to spend the weekend Christmas shopping with her daughter.

'I said, there's a very nice young man in my case,' repeated Angeline as her mother brought out a piping-hot lasagne. Mama had heard her the first time. She was just taken aback by what her daughter was saying. Angelina rarely confided in her when it came to men.

'What's his name?' Mama was already getting excited.

'Daniel – I quite like him.'

'What's he like?' Mama was more than curious.

'He's not like the other barristers. He's so quiet and reserved, but I can't help thinking he notices everything.'

'But has he noticed you, Angelina? Is he going to ask you out?' Mama was getting down to business.

'Never in a million years. And if he did, it would probably be by email and for lunch at one of the Inns of Court. But his solicitor and leader seem to respect him a lot. They're always asking his opinion, as far as I can tell.'

'Will you accept if he does?' Mama knew how to cross-examine.

'Oh, I don't know, Mama. I'd have to think about it. I doubt that we've much in common. God knows what we'd talk about.'

'Is he good-looking?' Mama remembered her youth.

'In an odd sort of way, I suppose he is, Mama. He looks a bit like George Segal in those old films we used to watch together, but with an English accent. He's very unassuming, but he's got a lot of class. He stares at me a lot in court – I think his leader's noticed it. He's much more flamboyant than Daniel, and makes jokes the whole time – even in a murder case. Actually, he's very good. The police officers in the case loathe him, but I can tell the jury love him. Daniel and I were alone in the lift yesterday, and I had a sixth sense that he was about to ask me out. Then the court usher got in, and that was that. He seems very shy really – not like Pietro.'

'Oh, I don't know why you turned Pietro down, Angelina. Good Roman family, successful business, handsome – what else do you want? He was heartbroken when you said no.' Mama was feeling nostalgic.

'Oh, Mama, let's not go over that again. He just wasn't for me. He's such a terrible flirt, so full of himself and so vain. I simply couldn't bear how long he took in the morning, standing in front of the mirror with the hair dryer and when choosing a shirt. It just wouldn't have worked.'

'Well, why don't you ask Daniel to Papa's sixtieth birthday in January? Do you think he'd come?' Mama was getting desperate.

'It's in Rome, Mama! How can I do that? It would look pathetic.'

'Yes, I suppose you're right. So, will you go out with him if he asks you?' Mama was unrelenting.

'Not if he asks me by email, I won't. He'll have to do better than that, Mama – a lot better!'

Mama just smiled.

*   *   *

Whilst Angelina and Mama tucked into their lasagne, Daniel and his old school mate Harry had been slogging it out on a squash court in Swiss Cottage. Daniel had been taking out his pent-up emotions on the hapless ball. Usually it was a close game, but tonight he murdered Harry 3–0.

'Well, you certainly upped your game tonight, Danny boy. What the hell's going on? Who's been upsetting you in court?' The two of them had just sat down to a well-earned supper at Côte in Hampstead.

'Believe it or not, it's my leader. He thinks I've got the hots for the prosecuting junior in our case and keeps taking the mickey.'

'Have you?'

'Yep.'

'Who is she?'

'She's an Italian beauty – makes Marilyn Monroe look like one of the three witches in *Macbeth* – and she's no airhead either.'

'Married?'

'Nope.'

'Engaged?'

'Don't think so.'

'Steady boyfriend?'

'Well, she doesn't secretly text in court, and she's rarely on the phone out of it, but how should I know?'

'Well, if you can't tell, nobody can. Have you asked her out?'

'Not yet.'

'So what are you waiting for, you old ditherer, an Act of Parliament?'

'Probably!'

Chapter 54

No Hills in Sloane Square

'False alarm, false alarm! You can go home,' announced Ernie over the phone to a prostrate, stark-naked Jake.

Like Halfpint, Jake himself had taken to the hills, but his *hills* were the pied-à-terre he had bought off Sloane Square, with the magnificent Carol as his trusted thoroughbred for company. Sunday afternoon found him lying belly up on the queen-sized bed, receiving lipstick lies in his left ear, whilst his mobile phone was at his right one. On his expansive stomach rested a plate of meatballs, which Carol had been sent to pick up from Luca's. By the side of the bed rested a bottle of virtually empty Bollinger. It's truly an ill wind that blows no good.

'Yes, the coast's clear,' continued Ernie as Jake finally managed to persuade Carol to restrain herself. 'Our man's been nicked for two kilos of cocaine in his tyre shop. Great news, Jake, don't you think?'

'I'm not so sure it is, Ernie, I'm not so sure at all,' replied Jake, glancing over at Carol's curvaceous lines, whilst stroking her waist-length silky blonde hair with a surprising tenderness for a man of his bulk. 'Where's Halfpint?' he added, almost as an afterthought.

'He's been holed up in Bolton at a B&B run by his aunt. He went off pronto as soon as he left Luca's last Friday night. I've spoken to him and he's taking the first train back to London.'

'The train?' queried Jake. 'What's happened to his old banger?'

'You won't believe this, Jake, but his tyres got nicked overnight as he lay sleeping.'

'Couldn't happen to a nicer fella – another £400 down the Swanee,' Jake added, before switching off his phone and turning his undivided attention once again to one of his more gratifying investments.

Chapter 55

It's Dark in the Dungeon...

On Monday morning, the sixth day of trial, with the jury just sent out to consider their verdict, Gorman, Jacobsen and Stanford were gathered deep in the cells below Court 1 of the Bailey.

'Get Dennis out, he's got three important visitors and Mr Gorman doesn't like being kept waiting,' shouted the jailer down the corridor, as Dennis's defence team took their seats in a room that in its time had witnessed hundreds of scenes of both jubilation and despair – mostly the latter.

'He's just being given his breakfast, Mr Gorman. He'll be about ten minutes,' called the jailer through the door.

'Where are you going for Christmas, Adrian – anywhere special?' asked Gorman.

'Yes, actually I'm off to Courchevel for some skiing with my family, so I can get nicely ripped off.'

'What about you, Daniel? I suppose you'll be too busy filling out your application for Silk to get away,' joked Gorman.

'No, actually I'm off to the Reichenbach Falls in Switzerland, where Holmes had his final problem with the Napoleon of crime – Moriarty. I've always wanted to go there, and now, finally, I can afford to.'

'How romantic. Angelina going with you?'

'Not at present,' answered Daniel, deeply wounded. Would he never let the subject go?

'Where are you going, Pat?' enquired Stanford, trying to ease Daniel's embarrassment.

'I'll give you a clue. It's a four-letter word and it's the same place as our client may be going.'

'The Ritz?' chanced Jacobsen.

'Jail?' joked Stanford.

'No – home! I've a boring fraud case starting in January, and to my shame I've hardly glanced at the brief. I take one look at the papers and doze off. Thousands of pages of bank statements. I had my first conference with the client last week. I thought I'd come clean from the outset. "Mr Gregory," I said, "I've got a confession to make to you. I've hardly read a single word of your case, but I will do before the case starts." I was hoping he might fire me there and then. Instead, he jumped up and shook me by the hand. "You're the first honest lawyer I've ever met, Mr Gorman," he said, "and I should know – I've had a few." I think he meant it. He then went on to say, "If you're good enough for that poor bugger on trial for murdering that no-good loan shark, you're good enough for me." I told him it's a pity he wasn't on the jury.'

'Here's your client now, Mr Gorman,' called out the jailer as a sombre Dennis entered the room.

'How's it looking, Mr Gorman?' asked Dennis.

'Well, I don't know what's happened to our judge, but he's definitely suffered some sort of epiphany before his summing up. I simply couldn't believe my ears; he couldn't have been fairer. I wouldn't have been surprised if Percival had jumped to his feet and shouted out, "Wait a minute, judge – which side are you on?"'

'How long do you think they'll be out, Mr Gorman?'

'Oh, quite a while. I'd be surprised if they're back before tomorrow at least. They look well split to me. But you'd better ask Daniel – he's the one with X-ray vision.'

'I've got a little thank-you note I've written out,' said Dennis, fishing out a folded piece of paper from his back pocket. 'I thought I might as well give it to you before the verdict. Please don't read it in front of me, I'd be too embarrassed.' He handed the note to Gorman.

The three lawyers were deeply moved. Stanford tried to lighten the uncomfortable moment with a story. 'This reminds me of my first armed robbery case in this very building. By some miracle, Victor Drummond QC had agreed to do the case, and after my client had been acquitted, I went up to him outside Court 7 and said, as respectfully as I could, "You made a great closing speech, Mr Drummond – if you don't mind me saying so." He looked down at me as if he was the headmaster and I an ignorant pupil and said in that deep, velvety voice of his, "You never told me that while the jury were out!"'

'So, what are you waiting for, Adrian? I made my speech, the jury's out, and no one's told me how great it was,' said Gorman. 'What do you think, Daniel?'

'Like Adrian in his story all those years ago, I'll give you my opinion as soon as I hear the verdict.'

'Well, I'm no results merchant, Mr Stanford,' said Dennis, 'and that's why I've written this note out before the jury returns.'

'Good on you, Mr Dennis. I look forward to reading it, and if it says something nice, I might even show it to my clerk. That'll give him an excuse to put my fees up in the future.'

Stanford had been waiting for a lull in the conversation. 'David,' he said, 'you promised to tell me after the trial who it was that recommended my firm to you. I'm still really curious to know.'

'And I intend to keep my word, Mr Stanford. After the trial – whichever way it goes.'

Chapter 56

Back from the Hills

'Good to have you safely back from the hills, Halfpint. I hear you're looking for a set of wheels for your old crock. You'd better give Wally a ring, I'm sure he'll find a fine set for you overnight.'

'I already have, Jake. He's scouring London as we speak.'

'Great, let's hope he gets nicked. He could do with a short stretch inside to get his mind straight after he ripped me off six months ago with that van load of cashmere jumpers.'

Jake, Ernie and Halfpint were cooling their heels at Sweetings fish restaurant, about a mile from the Bailey, gulping down two large plates of oysters at the bar and easing their passage with a bottle or two of Meursault. The jury had gone out a couple of hours earlier, and Jake had decided to locate himself in the vicinity of the Bailey in case there was a verdict.

Sweetings was one of the oldest fish restaurants in London and Jake's favourite one. You could smell the sea in the air from twenty yards away. It had a good deal in common with the Old Bailey: shared tables, only open Monday to Friday, closed at nights. But it had three major differences as well: better food, no handcuffs allowed on the premises and, most importantly, you could come and go as you pleased.

'So, Ernie, give us the lowdown about the missing juror,' demanded Jake. 'What's our man at the Yard told you?'

'Well, apparently, the Old Bill raided his tyre shop early Friday morning. They found £5,000 cash in one tyre and two kilos of coke in another, which he swears is nothing to do with him. But more importantly, he claimed the £5,000 are his savings. They're in consecutive numbers, so he's shot himself in the foot. Now he's banged up in the Scrubs looking seven years or so straight in the face.'

'Thank God for that, at least it leaves us in the clear,' said Jake, before turning towards Halfpint. 'Halfpint, in all the panic on Friday with the missing juror, I forgot to ask you – how was the judge's summing up?'

Halfpint was dreading this question. 'Err – I didn't stay for it, Jake. As soon as I saw our man was missing from the jury box, I was out the blocks faster than Usain Bolt.'

'I can't say I'm surprised. Ever heard the expression "when the going gets tough, the tough get going"?'

'Of course I have,' replied Halfpint indignantly. 'What do you think I am, a registered moron – like you call Wally?'

Jake was more than happy to answer. 'You had twelve customers to choose from, Halfpint. You studied them the whole first day of the trial. So, who, in your wisdom, do you pick? A drug-dealing tyre man who hasn't the savvy to keep our five grand under a different roof to the cocaine he's peddling. Has that answered your question?'

Halfpint was lost for a suitable response. But now Jake had him on the ropes and couldn't resist pummelling him a little more.

'Cat got your tongue, Halfpint?'

Chapter 57

A Real Softie

———————

'It's a mighty fine letter,' declared Gorman. 'I'm really moved. A bit more sympathetic than the one I received from a client the other month after he'd gone down for eighteen years, telling me I'm a *has-been*. I felt like writing back saying, *better than a never-was!*

'The problem with this barrister game is that slaving away on a case doesn't guarantee your success. It's not like an exam, where you work hard and feel that you've earned the right to pass. You never know where you stand with the jury. They can smile and nod at you for days on end, scribble down every word you say in your closing speech – but it counts for nothing.'

Gorman, Stanford and Jacobsen were seated in armchairs in the Bar Mess – it was Monday lunchtime, and they were killing time after returning from visiting their client in the cells. Gorman handed Dennis's letter to them to read for themselves.

Dear Mr Gorman, Adrian and Daniel,

Anyone who has sat in court watching my case could only be deeply impressed with the dedication you have given it.

No one could have asked more. If I'm convicted, you will never hear me complain. In fact, it will be my pleasure to recommend all of you to any inmate in need of a top team (assuming they can afford you!).

Adrian, I still don't have a clue who paid for my defence but, whoever it is, whatever the verdict, I would ask you to thank them from the bottom of my heart, although I doubt whether my thanks will be much comfort if it all goes wrong for me here.

If I walk free, it would be an honour for me to take you all out for dinner (maybe not at the Ritz – but not at McDonald's either!).

Mr Gorman, if I am convicted, please tell old Percival that I'm sorry he didn't have the chance to cross-examine me. If I'm acquitted, tell him I'm pleased (I might even tell him myself!).

May God bless all three of you – I am for ever in your debt.

Yours most sincerely,

David Dennis

PS Adrian, one final favour please. If I go down, please can you call my wife on the number I gave you and break the news to her gently. I would hate for her to find out on TV. And who knows – if I get off, perhaps you would wait for me outside the Bailey and lend me your phone for one short call. DD.

When they had both finished reading it, the letter was handed back to Gorman, who folded it neatly and placed it carefully in his wallet. At heart, he was a real softie. The other two just sat there staring at him in silence. But he could read their minds. He knew exactly what they were thinking.

'OK, OK, I admit it,' Gorman finally confessed. 'I'm going to show this letter to my wife at home tonight. If Dennis goes down, I'll be in need of a little tender loving care – nothing wrong with that, is there?'

Chapter 58

Stand Aside, Sherlock!

'Lunch is on me today,' announced Jim, senior clerk of Everest Chambers, as he, together with Gorman, Stanford and Jacobsen, sat down at table 15 at Ciao Bella, about a mile from the Old Bailey. It was Tuesday – the jury had been out for over a day, not a murmur from them.

'Quite right too – I paid last time, remember, Jim?' replied Stanford jovially.

'Yes, I do – when you slaughtered me over the fees for this case.'

As always, the restaurant was packed, and why shouldn't it be? Great Italian food, sensible prices, the best Wiener schnitzel and tiramisu in town, not to mention Felice, the kindest proprietor you could ask for, who had built up the establishment's name from nothing. 'Drill a hole in any wall here and blood comes pouring out – my blood!' he would say proudly.

Felice had laid on a minicab that was waiting outside the front door to rush them all back to court should there be a verdict. Jeremy, Stanford's office manager, had drawn the short straw and been left in charge at the court. He was keeping

Dennis company in the cells and had strict orders to telephone the moment there was any news.

Table 15 sat right in the corner of the restaurant, almost in its own cubicle. Jim always reserved it. It brought him good luck, as it was from this very table that, in his time, he had persuaded many a solicitor, with the invaluable assistance of a couple of bottles of Brunello, as to the obvious advantages to be derived from instructing one of his barristers, for what he always referred to as 'a most reasonable fee'.

'I went down to the cells to see our client this morning,' announced Gorman once they were all seated and tucking in to chunks of bruschetta and Parmesan. 'Understandably, he's nervous as hell. He thinks the longer they are out, the worse it looks for him. I told him that it's meaningless and he can't draw any inference from that at all. They could be out for days. Anyway, the good news is that I spent the rest of the morning reading up on this turgid fraud case I'm starting in January, so hopefully I'll be able to show my client that I'm not entirely hot air at our second conference later this week.'

'How was Mack the Knife in your bail application this morning, Mr Jacobsen?' asked Jim. 'Was he in good form?'

'Unbelievable – truly unbelievable. My man's an accountant, charged with breaking his wife's arm when she rolled home blind-drunk late one night with her blouse buttons done up in the wrong order and carrying her shoes in the hope that he was already asleep. He wasn't! He was waiting in the kitchen and accused her of having it off with his partner at the office, to which she replied, "Wouldn't mind if I did." Well, that was it. He lost it and down came the broom with the words, "I'm going to kill you here and now – you old whore." Their son had to pull him off, otherwise he would have finished her off there and then. The prosecution objected to bail, saying that if he was set free he might kill her. But Mack the Knife wasn't having it.

'I can still remember his very words: "It's clear this man may have been severely provoked, and we are all capable of saying things we do not mean. We are all but human. I see no reason why he should remain in custody for six months or so until his trial, when he can stay at his brother's home." Even his own court clerk was amazed. If I was a betting man, I'd lay a fair wage that he's got a problem at home with his wife. I was watching our judge carefully during the trial. He looked very pent up, and you could see his mind wandering.'

'Not as much as your mind was, Daniel,' cut in Gorman.

'What's that supposed to mean?' Jacobsen was getting irate. He could see where this was going.

'You haven't told us the whole story, have you, Daniel? You've left something out.' Gorman almost sang the words like a soothing lullaby.

'OK, OK. Angelina was prosecuting me. How did you know that, Pat?'

'I took a break from working on those fraud papers, slipped into your court and sat quietly at the back to watch you perform. I had my pen at the ready to make a list of all the legal clichés you used.'

'Use any ink?'

'No, it saddens me to report that I did not. And, as for Angelina, I thought she was rather good. "How nice to hear your voice for the first time, Miss Russo," said Mack. "What a pleasant change from Mr Percival's." And I couldn't help noticing that, when you were on your feet, Daniel, she was staring at you. You've got some chemistry going there – you lucky blighter.'

Daniel blushed and moved on. 'You were in court with him, weren't you, Adrian?'

'Yes, I was. How did you work that one out?'

'Your body language – or rather, lack of it, when Pat was just speaking.'

'Who's this Angelina?' Jim felt left out.

Gorman answered for all of them. 'Angelina, my dear boy, is a solo cabaret act, at present performing in Court 1 at the Bailey. And if you could summon up the energy to lift your backside out of your leather chair at chambers and pop down to court, you'd see her for yourself. Who knows, you might even poach her. We could do with a touch of class in chambers.'

'Anyway, Pat, back to the case…' interrupted Jacobsen, keen to change the subject.

'OK, so, the judge has now got a problem with his wife at home, has he? Here we go again. The problem you've got, Daniel, is that you see a conspiracy in every cloud. By the way, does this accountant of yours have any money? I'm looking for a brief after Easter.'

'Actually, Pat, I was hoping you'd allow me to climb out of my pram and do the case myself.'

'Touché, touché,' replied Gorman. 'I've been asking for it. Let's move on,' he said, turning towards his instructing solicitor. 'Adrian, who is actually paying for this case, and more importantly, why? Like our client, I'm aching to know.'

'I'm afraid I can't tell you, I'm sworn to silence.'

'Well, tell us why then,' probed Gorman.

'The donor insists on remaining anonymous, but he told me he was no friend of Bob the Merc. More than that I can't say – under pain of certain death, I wouldn't wonder.'

'OK, Sherlock,' said Gorman, turning his head towards Jacobsen, 'work that one out for us.'

'Well, OK, if you insist, I'll try, but I might be a long way off the mark. There are certain indicators. First, do you remember in Dennis's police interview, he said that before he approached Bob the Merc for a loan, he asked somebody else but was turned down because he couldn't provide any security?'

'Yes, I certainly do,' replied Gorman, 'but where does that get you?'

'By itself, nowhere. But, of course, we also know that Dennis won't tell anybody how he got hold of the gun.'

'True,' said Stanford.

'Nor will Dennis tell us at the moment who put him on to you, Adrian, in the first place. Yet, on his arrest, he had your details written out on a scrap of paper.'

'So?' interrupted Gorman. 'I'm still not with you.'

'Nor will you, Adrian, under pain of death, apparently, tell Dennis who's paying for his defence,' continued Jacobsen.

'I certainly won't.'

'We can also assume, can we not, that whoever's paying for his case is comfortably off. After all, he's not going to spend his last penny on Dennis's defence. Can we not also add, with some confidence, that he feels it's his moral duty to pay?'

'Agreed,' said Gorman, still at a loss as to where Jacobsen's analysis was going.

'And can we also not take for granted that whoever Dennis first approached for a loan and by whom he was refused is also comfortably off?'

The penny was beginning to drop for all three listeners, who sat in silence, awaiting Jacobsen's denouement.

'Well, as I said earlier, it's really a long shot, but I wouldn't be at all surprised if the man who refused Dennis the loan, and the man who got him the gun, and the man who recommended him to use Adrian as his solicitor, and the man who is now paying for his trial are all one and the same person. And I would venture it is that very same person who sent the little fella to watch the proceedings from the public gallery each day during the trial, and who had some sort of hanky-panky going on with the juror.'

There was silence all around. A highly impressive piece of deduction had just been performed before their very eyes.

Eventually, Gorman found his voice.

'Can't fault your logic, Daniel, and if you're right, there's only one person at this table who knows his identity,' and then, tilting his head towards Adrian, he added, 'not looking at anyone in particular.'

'And there's something else,' continued Jacobsen, now appreciating that he was the centre of attention. 'Something much more interesting for us as his lawyers.'

'Go on, Daniel,' said Gorman, 'what other revelation have you got for us?'

Daniel needed no encouragement. 'Well, you know all the DVDs the police found on Bob the Merc's shelves in his study? Hundreds of them, virtually every gangster and war film one could imagine.'

'Yes, of course I remember them. I cross-examined Stokes half to death all about them – so what?'

'Well, there was one missing – I should know. I had all the prosecution photographs of his study blown up. Yes,' continued Daniel to his rapt audience, 'there was definitely a dog that should have been barking in the night but wasn't.'

'Tell us, Daniel. What film was missing?' Gorman was now completely hooked by Daniel's account.

'The one with the Russian roulette scenes in it – the one which, apparently, according to Dennis, was the favourite of his two passengers on that terrifying journey down the A12 towards Chelmsford.'

'*The Deer Hunter*,' exclaimed Stanford.

'Yes, *The Deer Hunter*,' confirmed Daniel.

'No case – no case at all,' said Gorman. 'Pure conjecture.'

'I haven't quite finished yet, Pat. At the same time as I had the police photos of Bob the Merc's study enlarged, I also had the photos of Dennis's kitchen blown up. The ones showing the kitchen table with the bullets on it and the rack of DVDs on the shelf in the background.' Daniel removed a large, folded colour photograph from his jacket pocket, and with a dramatic thud banged it down on the table for all to see. Six eyes gazed at it spellbound.

'The police missed it, but I didn't,' declared Daniel. 'Third DVD from the left – if I'm not mistaken.'

'*The Deer Hunter*! Magnificent. Well, stand aside, Sherlock – absolutely magnificent,' declared Gorman.

Daniel gave his audience a little breathing space before continuing and poured them all a welcome grappa from the bottle on the table. 'Of course, I had never met Bob the Merc. But I simply couldn't quite convince myself that he had the imagination or the cunning to get his enforcers to play Russian roulette with Dennis as a last warning on the A12. I wouldn't be surprised if Dennis bought himself a pay-as-you-go phone earlier on the very day he travelled to Chelmsford and used it for one call to the minicab office, giving a false name as the customer and booking the journey himself before disposing of the phone. Now, I don't know whether he told his cellmate that the Russian roulette business was a pack of lies or not. And I have no doubt that he did drive his minicab to Chelmsford that night as he claimed. But I believe he travelled alone. Frankly, I think he's had us over – he's cleverer than all of us. I think he made up the whole Russian roulette episode.'

Gorman could only admire what he'd just heard. He sipped his grappa, smiled and nodded approvingly at his junior. Daniel's analytical thinking was in a different league to his own.

Finally, he gave judgement. 'You know what, Daniel? It irks me to say it – but I think you're right!'

Chapter 59

Lurking

———

'Two and a half days and they're still bloody out. What's there to talk about that takes so long? Bob the Merc gets his comeuppance, the jury see the whole show on CCTV and our man says he had no choice. Now, how long can that take to decide, Ernie? I ask you, how long? How much are they paying jurors these days? Make them do jury service for nothing, I say, and they'd have been back with their verdict by lunch on Monday – latest.'

It was now 4 p.m. on Wednesday afternoon. Jake was becoming decidedly impatient. He had installed himself at El Vino's wine bar in Fleet Street, about half a mile down the road from the Old Bailey. There he and Ernie sat with a bottle of port, with Jake doing most of the talking. Halfpint had been left on duty at the court, ready to summons them as soon as there was any news. For decades, El Vino's had been a haven for scandal-mongering journalists and barristers. Its decor was unique. The mustard paint on the walls had the patina of a vintage Patek, and in their time the cracking leather armchairs had accommodated many a famous (and infamous) *bohunkus*.

'You know, Ernie,' Jake continued, 'there was a documentary on TV last night called *DIY Defence*. This retired QC was saying it didn't matter a toss which barrister defended you. He claimed the jury sees straight through all this play-acting, and you might just as well defend yourself and save your money. He was so convincing that I started to believe him. If this programme had been on six months ago, I could have saved a cool 300 grand. Yes, if ever I get nicked again, I think I might just defend myself, or go on legal aid.' Jake reconsidered. 'No, on second thoughts, from what I've heard, I'm probably better off defending myself.'

'What's it they say, Jake? A defendant who acts for himself has a fool for a client?' said Ernie, showing off.

'Very good, Ernie, very good. You were watching that programme last night, weren't you? I can see you're getting yourself an education.'

'I learn from you, Jake,' replied Ernie. 'I'm dreaming of becoming a Big Jake lookalike – that's my ambition in life.'

'Good,' answered Jake, 'I'm pleased to hear it. And when you dream again tonight, treat yourself to a Bentley and take plenty of pills, so you never have to wake up to reality. There's only one Big Jake and you happen to be looking at him.'

Just then, Ernie's mobile rang to the theme tune from *Bonanza*. It was Halfpint. 'They're coming back, Ernie, they're coming back,' were the only words he uttered.

'Right, let's get down there and wait outside, nearby,' said Jake, slapping down two £50 notes in a hurry on the table and not waiting for the change. 'And let's pray we see Dennis leaving the Bailey on his own two feet – and not in a prison van.

Vámonos!' They both rushed out and hailed a taxi for the short journey down the road.

'Cabby,' shouted Jake brusquely as they jumped in, 'do you know the fastest way to the Bailey?'

'Sure, I do,' replied the cabby, before adding with a typical cockney sense of humour, 'you commit a murder and you get there double-quick.'

*   *   *

'Put up David Dennis,' called out the court clerk, sombrely, to the dock officer. It was now just gone 4.15 p.m. Court 1 at the Old Bailey was packed to overflowing with the press, three rows of lawyers and all the police involved in the inquiry, Stokes pumped up with his mouth full of his calming tablets and, of course, the guest of dishonour – Halfpint, in the front row of the public gallery, now having thrown caution to the wind. At the back of the large court there was standing room only by the doors. It was a moment not to be missed. High up on his throne sat Mr Justice McIntyre, now looking truly interested in proceedings for the first time since the trial had begun.

Gorman was the last to arrive in court. It was an affectation of his to make a grand entrance at the very last moment before a verdict – like the Queen taking her seat at the Royal Variety Performance. It gave the distinct impression to all around that this was just another case for him, and that the great man had seen it all before.

The court fell silent and the only sound that could be heard were the footfalls as Dennis trudged up the twenty steps from the cells into the dock. Everyone present was there to hear whether one word or two were to be uttered from the lips of the jury foreman. What a difference one three-letter word could make.

The judge nodded to his clerk to call in the jury. None of them looked at the defendant as they entered and took their seats. *Meaningless*, thought Gorman, who had seen a fair few jurors in his time.

'Will the foreman please stand,' called out the clerk. Mr Polo Neck rose to his feet.

'God help us all,' muttered Halfpint to himself, 'a yes-man for a foreman, that's all we need.'

'Mr Foreman, please confine yourself to answering my first question, yes or no,' continued the clerk. 'On count 1 of the indictment, have you reached a verdict on which you are all agreed?' There was a momentary pause. 'Yes,' came the reply in a quivering voice.

'On the charge of murder – do you find the defendant guilty or not guilty?'

* * *

'Not outside the door, cabby, not outside the bloody door – I'm too well known around these parts – here will do nicely,' growled Jake as the taxi pulled up, tyres squealing, about fifty yards from the Old Bailey entrance. Jake and Ernie jumped out at speed to watch proceedings from afar.

It was now 4.45 p.m. and all nineteen courts had risen for the day. Police, lawyers, jurors all through with their day's work and exiting the revered building. But the verdict was still a complete mystery to Jake, until he saw seven or eight crime reporters and cameramen setting up their equipment and jockeying for position outside the main entrance.

Jake was no Sherlock Holmes, nor even a modest Daniel Jacobsen, but neither did he need a weatherman to know which way the wind was blowing. When he saw the excited crowds gathering, it was surely a good omen.

'Hello, what's going on here, Ernie my boy?' whispered Jake in high excitement. 'We may be in business – I think our boy's going to walk.'

Next, when they witnessed four burly uniformed police officers emerge from the building, standing guard outside and clearing a passage, was it not determinative of the issue? Jake thought it was, and his voice reached fever pitch. 'He's walked,' he cried out jubilantly, no longer caring who might overhear him, whilst crushing Ernie in a bear hug. 'Our boy's bloody walked!'

But hold your horses, could that possibly be a tiny tear Ernie detected, lurking in the corner of Big Bad Jake's left eye?

Surely not!

Chapter 60

If You Go Down to the Woods Today...

———————————

Dennis was getting some quality early morning fresh air in Broomfield Park near his home, a somewhat less depressing pasture than the prison yard at Belmarsh.

It was Friday, two days after he was acquitted upon hearing the two magic words, 'not guilty', ring out from the jury benches. The snow was fresh from an overnight fall and a couple of inches deep, and the air was crisp. He had felt like singing and the old *Oklahoma* tune 'Oh, what a beautiful mornin'' just sprang out of him from nowhere.

He had been there waiting for them the day before at Euston Station, his heart pumping in just the same way as when he climbed the twenty steps into court for the verdict. The joy as his two sons raced along the platform, calling out 'Daddy! Daddy!' was like none other. The family huddle – Linda's tears mingling with his own. What a great reunion. And then back to a warm flat, which Linda's generous ex-boss had left empty – at least until the verdict.

He had risen early. He was far too excited to waste time lying in bed. To make the most of his liberty, he had crept out for a walk, leaving the three of them asleep at home. They had all sat up late the previous night, snuggled together on the settee watching *Spartacus* on TV. He never did like the ending. What was he going to do for the rest of his life? He had no idea. His acquittal for murder was not exactly going to give him the edge in any job interview. But still, he was free and nothing else much mattered. All in good time.

'*Guajira Guantanamera*.' Dennis's singing had gone off on a tangent in a rich baritone voice usually reserved for the bath. He had passed the deserted children's playground and, turning left into a secluded area, had sat down on a bench under an old snow-covered yew tree that resembled an enormous white cartoon mushroom.

'Good morning, Mr Dennis. What a beautiful day for a walk.' Dennis glanced round. Two men were fast approaching. They were no more than fifteen feet away. They looked vaguely familiar.

'We've got a message for you.'

Then he recognised them and stopped singing.

Chapter 61

Jake's Justice

'Waiter, bring me a bottle of the Marchese Antinori and a plate of macaroni cheese to go with my T-bone. No chips, mind, doctor's orders, I'm on a strict diet. I've had a bit too much excitement lately – my blood pressure's right up.'

The gravelly voice was unique. Stanford had wandered into Goodman steakhouse off Regent Street at lunchtime, two days after Dennis's acquittal, in search of a quiet meal alone. It was the last Friday before Christmas and snow was settling all around. He'd been out with his wife doing some last-minute shopping, and a steak and a beer held no attraction for her. She had gone off to have her hair curled. The restaurant was packed, and all that was on offer to Stanford was a seat at the bar. There he sat at peace, eyes deep in the latest issue of *Classic Cars* magazine reading about the comparative virtues of his beloved Jensen C-V8 against a 1962 Alfa Romeo SS coupé. What could be better? On hearing the voice he assuredly recognised, he peered round from his high seat at the bar, praying he was mistaken. He wasn't.

'Well, if it isn't Mr Stanford,' boomed Jake as their eyes met.

'And both of us here alone. What a stroke of luck. Come and join me.' It was a command not an invitation. 'Waiter,' called Jake, 'cancel the Marchese and bring me a bottle of the Sass-icaia. Now there's two of us we can have a proper celebration. And make sure it's got some age on it – we don't want to be drinking grape juice.'

Jake was in fine form. Just the previous day, the day after the verdict, he'd arrived in his Bentley in Hatton Garden at 9 a.m. sharp to collect his winnings from Rolex Ron. He couldn't resist turning up carrying a Boots hot-water bottle, with a fake fur covering, as a Christmas present for Ron's wife. 'Not quite a mink-lined raincoat, Ron – but, then again, cheaper to replace.' Jake loved a good gloat. He had taken his leave with a beaming smile and a cool £25,000 cash.

'I was coming to see you on Monday morning to thank you personally,' said Jake in a lower tone, as Stanford joined Jake at his table. 'I've got those other two magnums of Petrus I promised you and a nice little present. I'll give you a clue, it comes in a thick brown envelope, and it's not drugs.'

'That's very kind of you, Jake, but quite unnecessary. You paid me handsomely for my labours and, anyway, I got more than my fair share of kicks out of the verdict.'

'Didn't we all,' agreed Jake.

'You should have been up there in the public gallery when the jury came back,' continued Stanford. 'It was a great moment. Our QC was quite overcome by it all. He could hardly rise to his feet to ask for Dennis to be set free from the dock. Even the prosecutor walked up to Dennis, shook him by the hand, asked how his kids were getting on and wished him well. And before that there was a greater surprise when the judge thanked the jury for their obvious care in reaching their verdict, which in the circumstances he could well understand.

'And then afterwards, outside the court, six of the jurors came up to Dennis and asked if they could shake his hand. He bummed a cigarette from one of them, claiming it was only the third he'd smoked in twenty-one years. Three of the female jurors had been to Hamleys over the weekend and had bought his two boys some Christmas presents. That did it for him – he started blubbering like a kid. It was really very touching and made the whole job worthwhile. Then he borrowed my mobile to phone his wife to tell her the news. "It's all over, darling, I'm coming home" were the only words he could get out. She didn't believe him and was crying hysterically. She even insisted on hearing it from me. I had trouble getting any words out myself, I'm ashamed to say.'

'No need to be ashamed, Mr Stanford,' said Jake comfortingly, or as near as he could ever get to it. 'We're all proud of you. I won't forget what you've done. You know, it was the second-best three hundred large I've invested in my entire life.'

'Really?' enquired Stanford. 'What was the first?'

'Let's not even go there, Mr Stanford, you won't be impressed,' replied Jake with a shudder.

'Tell me, Jake, did you know Bob the Merc well?'

'I met him at university.'

Stanford found this hard to believe. 'Yes, which one? And what were you studying?'

'Borstal – and we were both studying crime, if you must know. Even then, he had his own protection racket running, threatening anyone he thought might have a few quid. If it wasn't for my size, I'd have had a serious problem myself.

'About five years later he was deep in the drugs game and putting his weight about town. He tried it on with my crew, putting the word about that he wanted a cut from one of our more successful visits to a bank, threatening to tip off the police if we didn't pay up. Me and a couple of the lads cornered him outside his home one night and put him straight, with a loaded sawn-off tickling his two quarter-pounders. He got the message loud and clear alright.

'I last saw him about four years ago. He walked into Luca's on the Old Brompton Road for dinner on a Friday night with his boy and a couple of his henchmen. Our eyes locked and he was off quicker than a getaway from a blagging. Bullies are always cowards. Yes, I'm well pleased that Dennis instructed your firm. Somebody *in the know* must have pointed him in the right direction.'

Boldly, Stanford grabbed his moment. 'Wasn't you, Jake, by any chance?'

Jake looked surprised at the very suggestion. 'Me, Mr Stanford? What makes you think it might have been me? I didn't even know you.'

'True, but as you yourself admitted when we first met, you knew *of* me, and you had, as you put it, *put out a few feelers*. Tell me, honestly, Jake, had you ever met Dennis before his arrest?'

'Don't press me, Mr Stanford. Let's just have a nice Christmas drink and then we can both go our separate ways. Besides, whatever makes you think I might have?'

'Well, Jake, you see, it's like this. We've had a bit of a whiz kid as our junior barrister in this case – a real modern-day

Sherlock Holmes. He's heard me refusing to tell Dennis who's paying for his case, and Dennis refusing to tell me who recommended him. He thinks it may be one and the same person.'

Jake started shifting in his seat. 'Well, suppose it was me – so what? That's not a crime, is it?'

'No, certainly not, but it means you must have met Dennis before his arrest, doesn't it? Tell me, Jake, I give you my word, it's just between you and me – did Dennis approach you for a loan before he approached Bob the Merc?'

'I never lent him a penny,' replied an irate Jake. 'Not a brass farthing.'

'Jake, there's something else I've got to ask you. I just can't get it out of my mind and, of course, you don't have to answer.'

'Go on.'

'What was the real reason you paid for his case? I'm sure you're a generous man, but paying for the defence of someone who meant nothing to you – it's simply too much to swallow.'

Jake hesitated. 'I'd tell you, Mr Stanford, but I've got to look after *numero uno*, and you're not my brief, so you're not sworn to silence, are you?'

'True,' agreed Stanford, 'very true. Well, there it is, you can't blame me for trying.'

'No, I don't blame you at all, but what I tell you might amount to a crime and I really don't fancy a nicking – not at my age.' Jake started scratching his chin as if he was desperate to find a way around the problem. Finally, he did. 'But, of course, if you were my brief, I'd be safe, wouldn't I?'

'Well, this is a first. I've never signed up a new client over a T-bone steak before.'

Now Jake felt safe. 'Right – well, you've signed one up now. God knows I'll probably regret what I'm about to tell you, but what the hell. I wouldn't mind getting it off my chest and, anyway, there's bugger all you can do about it now you're my official brief – right?'

'Right.'

'OK, but before I grass myself up let's celebrate your appointment with a little sweetener. Waiter!' called out Jake. 'Two large glasses of the d'Yquem, please!'

On the arrival of the amber nectar, Jake took a healthy swig, leaned forward and started to whisper. 'Now, it's like this. Dennis had serious money problems. He was put on to me by a businessman in the fur trade to whom I'd lent money years ago, when he needed a few quid to pay for his daughter's wedding. But I'm no loan shark. I only lend on security, and not at crazy rates of interest like Bob the Merc either. If the money is never repaid, I just keep the security and that's that. I draw the line firmly in the sand and I don't cross over it.'

'Never?'

'Never,' Jake replied firmly before speedily moving on. 'Well, this fella Dennis owed money from gambling debts, as well as to friends. But he had no security to offer me – so I couldn't help. I never put him onto Bob the Merc either. Why should I? I hated Mercenary Bob's style of business and, anyway, I liked Dennis. Basically he was a decent man drowning in debts.

'Sometime later he asked to see me again. I remember we met in Harry Morgan's salt-beef bar in St John's Wood. I used to do a bit of business from there and treated it like my office. He told me that after I'd turned him down he'd been to see a man called Bob Maynard. I almost choked on my borscht. "You couldn't have made a worse choice if you tried," I told him. I remember his very words. "It's any port in a storm." So, I asked him why he'd come back to see me. He said he owed Maynard a lot of money and couldn't pay. He told me that he and his family had been threatened more than once, and he was in real danger. He'd been to the police, but it hadn't helped – there was not enough evidence to charge Bob. I felt sorry for him, but I told him there was nothing I could do and that was that. He just sat there helpless. Finally, he broke down like a little girl. "I'm not even safe in my own home," he cried. "I've got to protect my wife and kids. I don't care what happens to me – I've got to have a gun and so help me, if he sends his boys at night, I'll use it."

'Now, hard as it may be to believe, Mr Stanford, I haven't owned a gun in years – not since the old days, when me and the boys used to *cross the pavement*. I thought I had a nutcase on my hands and laughed at him, but I could see he was deadly serious. Frankly, I wouldn't have shed a tear if he'd blasted Mercenary Bob to hell, and actually, when I heard that Maynard had taken his last ride, I had a champagne celebration. But I swear to you I had no idea that it was Dennis who had gunned down that no-good son of a bitch.

'Anyway, when I made it clear to him I didn't deal in guns and I couldn't help, he looked a broken man. "Just give me the name of someone – with your connections, you must know someone, Mr Davenport. On the life of my wife and kids, I'll never breathe your name whatever happens." It was pitiful listening to him.

'I said to Dennis, "Look, go round to Maynard's home and face him out. Give him a few quid and tell him that's that and he can do his worst – he may well call it quits."

'"But I haven't got a few quid," he pleaded. "All I've got left is a pocket watch which my old boss gave me as a leaving present, and I'm on my way into Hatton Garden to flog it for whatever I can get." He pulled the watch out and showed it to me – I didn't have a clue what it was worth, but it looked the business.

'"How much do you want for it?" I asked him. "I don't know, but I think it's quite valuable," he said.

'I rang my old mate Rolex Ron from the restaurant and sent him a picture of the watch on my phone. He was really excited about it. "Do you know what you've got there? It's a Breguet, and it's worth a mint – minimum £25,000. Napoleon and Wellington both wore one at the Battle of Waterloo – and Phileas Fogg an' all."'

'And you stole it for £8,000, didn't you, Jake?' chimed in Stanford.

'OK, OK, I did. I'm not proud of it, but business is business. As the Greeks say, "There's no man born who can stick his finger in a jar of honey without licking it." Anyway, Dennis thought that going round to Maynard's was a pretty good idea. Then he went into one, saying what if it didn't work and the threats continued and worse if Bob's men came to his home at night.

'Eventually, he wore me down, and like the soft touch that I am, I gave him the name of an old timer who might supply him with a gun. But I made him promise me he would go and see Maynard at his home first, to reason with him just one last time, before he would try and get a gun. I even left the restaurant to make a call from the street to find out Maynard's home address for him. I never saw him again.

'And there's another thing, Mr Stanford. Just before he left, he asked me if I knew a top brief in case he was arrested protecting his family at home with a gun. I used to use old-man Sydney from the East End as my brief, but frankly, I didn't know if he was still kicking, and anyway, I certainly wasn't going to give him the name of my own brief. True, I never knew you, but I knew your reputation – so I gave him your name.

'When I heard that Maynard had been murdered – eh, sorry – killed, it never crossed my mind it might be Dennis's doing. God knows, Maynard had hundreds of enemies who might have wanted him out of the way. Dennis has had me over and that's for sure. It doesn't happen very often.'

'No, that I can believe.'

'Well, after I recovered from the shock that Dennis had been nicked, my conscience started prickling me – my eczema as well. If I hadn't given him the name of a gun dealer, it would never have happened. I should have put pressure on Maynard to call it a day, but I was weak – I didn't need the grief. Yes, I'm sorry to say I turned my back on him and I could have helped.'

'Well, you did a very noble deed, Jake – there's no denying it. But I still don't really understand why. All that money on a comparative stranger; there must be something else you haven't told me.'

Jake sized Stanford up – could he be trusted? He started tapping his hand lightly on the table, before replying. 'I'm going to tell you something now, Mr Stanford. I've never spoken about it to anyone before, not even my wife.' Jake hesitated, as if in two minds about whether he was doing the right thing. Then on he went. 'In 1956, I was still just a toddler. My father was a scrap-metal merchant over London Bridge way. My mother used to wash and iron shirts at home to help out. I was an only child. My old man was out on a Friday night, having a good drink at the pub across the road from our home with a few mates. A couple of young drunk punks from our patch were taking the piss out of him, saying that they wouldn't mind going around to his home and giving my mum a seeing-to. And what a pretty little thing she was and she must be aching for it. The two of them came right up to my dad and carried on ribbing him. My father was a big man and fit as well from his work – not like me. He roughly pushed them away and told them to get the hell out or else he'd knock seven shades of shit out of them. But they were cocky and reckoned that, together, they could handle him. They challenged him to come outside for a fist fight to sort it out. He agreed. I suppose, by then, he was too proud to back down and the drink didn't help either.

'A crowd gathered to watch, egging him on. The noise had woken me up and I saw the end of the fight from my bedroom window. I will never forget it for as long as I live. The insults were still flying and my old man laid into them with no mercy. One of them had a broken jaw, a bust ribcage and had lost three teeth. The bigger and more leery of the two was smashed to pieces and given a really good kicking once he was down and out. He died five days later in hospital.

'My old man was nicked and three months later stood trial at the Bailey. On the first day, he was offered a deal. Plead guilty to manslaughter on the grounds of provocation, and to grievous bodily harm on the other kid, and the prosecution would drop the murder charge. His brief said he'd be looking at ten to twelve years' clink if he took the deal. Of course, I was very young then and didn't hear this whole story until years later. He wanted to take the deal, but his young, cocksure, legal-aid QC, trying to make a name for himself, said, "Don't – we'll run self-defence – you're bound to be acquitted. You'll have the sympathy of the jury on your side. Take it from me, the prosecution think you're going to get off, otherwise they wouldn't be offering you this deal."

'There was still hanging in those days for murder, but his barrister told him that no British jury would convict him knowing he would swing if they did. He was given overnight to think about it. But his barrister's fancy words had gone to his head. He turned the deal down.'

'So, what happened?' asked Stanford.

Jake started swaying in his seat before he could find his voice to answer. 'He swung! Then they abolished hanging the next year – a year too late.'

Stanford looked down, gripping the arms of his chair. He simply couldn't think of anything to say.

'I did it for my father – and my mother,' continued Jake. 'I just had to make sure Dennis had a proper brief. I said to myself, "God knows I've done enough villainy in my life, and if I do one good deed, let this be it." I had as good as put the gun in his hands. To be quite honest, when I look back on it now, had it been anybody else but that scumbag Maynard, I never would have given him the name of the gun dealer at all. I had helped Dennis get into this mess, so I just had to get him out. Anyway, I could well afford it. I wasn't going to end up on the breadline.'

'Is your mother still alive, Jake?'

Jake shook his head. 'No, she killed herself with an overdose, three years later. I can't blame her. She was crazy about my old man and had nothing to live for. She always had my breakfast neatly laid out when I was a kid, but one morning there was nothing there, so I went into her bedroom. I found her dead in her bed. I thought she was asleep – she looked so peaceful – but I couldn't wake her up. She left me a letter on the kitchen table. I still have it in my bedside drawer, but I can't bring myself to read it any more. There were about 500 people at her funeral, you know. She was a really kind and soft lady, and never had a bad word to say about anybody. I think of her a lot. I still see her in my dreams.

'My two uncles were the ones who told me about what had happened to my father. After my mother died, they weren't allowed to bring me up, as they had both served time, and so I was put into an orphanage and then farmed out to foster parents. To tell you the truth, I preferred it in the orphanage.

'I ran away from my foster parents' home at fifteen and never returned. I think they were glad to see the back of me. For two years after that, I laid my head at night wherever I could, all over south London. I cleaned cars, painted houses, unloaded lorries – mostly without permission – and even worked as a porter in the old Covent Garden fruit market, before ending up in Borstal for being caught robbing a chemist with a fake gun.'

Jake looked exhausted and sat back in his chair with his hands stretched out on the table between the two of them. He'd opened up his heart to Stanford. 'Well,' he concluded, 'now that you've heard my story – the good, the bad and the ugly – I suppose I've gone down even lower in your estimation, if that's possible.'

'Actually, Jake, you've risen considerably. One last point, and then, as you put it, we'll go our separate ways. There's been a little dapper fellow in the public gallery throughout the trial – right there in the back row. Anything to do with you and your own sense of justice?'

The delicacy was not lost on Jake. 'That's a bridge too far, Mr Stanford. Yes, definitely a bridge too far – and I don't intend to cross it.'

The lawyer and his unexpected new client stood to leave. Jake paid the bill from a wad of £50 notes and they strolled out into the afternoon snow together. They walked to the corner of Regent Street, about to go their separate ways. Stanford picked up an *Evening Standard* and glanced at the headlines.

'ACQUITTED MAN SHOT DEAD IN PARK'

He stopped in his tracks and prodded the paper in front of Jake. He had an enormous lump forming in his throat. They both stared at the article below:

A man acquitted at the Old Bailey of murder on Wednesday this week was himself gunned down in a park near his home in Southgate, north London. David Dennis had apparently been taking an early morning walk in the winter snow after spending months in custody awaiting trial.

Mr Tom Trivett, a local greengrocer, who found the body near a large yew tree, immediately called for an ambulance and the police, but Mr Dennis was declared dead on arrival at hospital.

A distressed Mr Trivett said to the press at the scene, 'He was lying on his back with a folded piece of paper half in his mouth. While we waited for the police and ambulance, I took the paper out to try and help his breathing. It had some writing on it and I handed it to the police when they arrived.'

When pressed as to the written words, Mr Trivett replied, 'It just said, "Better to pay your debts."'

Jake was boiling over. 'I should have known it. Again, I'm at fault – I should have threatened Bob Jr to let him be. I've said it before, I'm losing my edge. I should have seen this coming. Now it's too bloody late.' He paused for a second before adding grimly, 'Or is it?'

Stanford knew exactly what he meant. 'Let it pass, Jake, let it pass. It's all over – what good can it do?'

Jake didn't reply; his mind was elsewhere.

'I need a drink,' muttered Jake finally.

'Me too,' agreed Stanford.

'Let's walk down to a quiet bar,' suggested Jake, pointing in the general direction of the Artesian, about a half a mile away. 'We could both do with some fresh air.'

The odd couple ambled in silence up Regent Street at a snail's pace, as if they were in a funeral procession. On the crossing at Oxford Street there were two old buskers, one playing a battered accordion and the other a beaten-up violin. Their hands were gloved to keep out the freezing snow, but the fingers of the gloves had been cut out to allow them to play. They were well past their prime. The sonorous refrain of 'Torna a Surriento' filled the air, but few shoppers paid them any notice. Propped up in their old instrument cases at their feet were two large pieces of paper smeared by the snow but still with vaguely decipherable writing on them. One read: 'I once too was a respected man.' The other: 'Friend for life – 50p.'

Jake and Stanford stopped, both looking into their heavily lined faces. *There but for fortune go I*, thought Stanford.

'I bet they've got a few sad stories to tell,' said Jake, glancing at the miserly collection of coins in the two caps on the ground. 'Come on, let's give these two miserable bastards a Christmas to remember. God knows they need it.' Placing his hand in his back pocket, he pulled out two £50 notes. Stanford was happy to follow suit. They both bent down and carefully dropped one in each of the old men's caps, their eyes catching those of the musicians. Each gave them a heartfelt nod of thanks.

It was the sternest of reminders of what the Romans knew only too well, and what Dennis could only have appreciated for the briefest of moments, as the bullets rained into his defenceless back that very morning. That life is short – all glory but fleeting – and that everything passes.

The unlikely couple walked on together, both deep in their own thoughts. Eventually, they were in sight of the Artesian Bar.

'Want to hear the rest of my life story?' said Jake, trying to ease the painful silence.

'Not particularly, Jake, I think I've heard quite enough of it for one day.'

'You do?' replied Jake, enthusiastically, as if Stanford couldn't wait to be given chapter and verse. 'Well, then, I'll be glad to tell you. Now, let me see – where shall I begin?'

'Try the end for size, Jake – it's usually best.' Stanford was in no mood for Jake's nostalgic reminiscences.

'Well now, let me see,' repeated Jake. He was not going to be denied. 'I suppose it all started to go really pear-shaped when I came out of Borstal. As you've just heard, I came from a pretty poor background and enough was enough – so I turned to some serious crime. I wasn't educated like you, Mr Stanford. No real schooling and no legal training like you either.'

'No – distinctly illegal, from what you've told me today.'

Jake continued, undeterred. 'I started drifting even further from the shore. Yes, too far for comfort when I look back on it now. I needed a quick fix. I wanted to be rich and respected overnight – I was looking for a profitable career.'

'Well, you appear to have found one.'

But Jake simply wasn't listening. 'So, what else could I do? You tell me, Mr Stanford – what else could I do? You see, I really had no choice.'

Now, where had Stanford heard those very same words before?

Chapter 62

Aftermath

George Percival

George Percival gave up his membership of the Garrick Club within a week of the trial finishing. He had felt like an outcast there. He'd been lunching on his own at the long communal table when his unusually fine antennae overheard two judges at the other end, mocking him.

'See old Percival over there – calls himself a top prosecutor. He gets a case where the defendant shoots an unarmed man dead on CCTV right outside the front doors of the Bailey, confesses and gets off. Perhaps he should try defending.'

'Or retiring,' added the other judge cruelly.

Percival heeded the first judge's advice. He resigned that very day from the club and rang his clerk at chambers telling him to get him some defence work – he would prosecute no longer.

Mrs Linda Dennis

The funeral of David Dennis took place four weeks after his

335

brutal murder. Some forty motley types attended the cemetery in East Finchley where his parents were also buried. A few old school friends turned up and some other acquaintances, who had sadly, over the years, passed out of his life. The most touching moment was near the end of the service, when his two young sons recited the poem 'Vitaï Lampada' in honour of their departed father's bravery.

> *There's a breathless hush in the close tonight*
> *Ten to make and the match to win*
> *A bumping pitch and a blinding light*
> *An hour to play and the last man in...*

Gorman, Stanford and Jacobsen were all there to pay their respects, standing right next to the now retired Iron-Rod Stokes. After all was said and done, he'd always held a sneaking admiration for Dennis.

But then, just before the poem was recited, two uninvited guests arrived and stood way at the back. One was very large, broad and overweight, keeping the winter chill at bay with a luxuriant camel-coloured overcoat. The other was diminutive and looked as though he would have comfortably fitted in the larger man's coat pocket.

After the service, a moving incident occurred which only Stanford really understood. The man in the camel coat pulled out of his pocket a shiny gold pocket watch and, whilst comforting Dennis's widow with a few words, eased the watch into the palm of her hand – the return of the family heirloom.

Stokes gave the man in the camel coat a curious glance. 'I

know this man,' he muttered to himself. 'I definitely know this man – but from where?' No, he couldn't place him. Their eyes met and the man in the camel coat simply nodded at Stokes, who found himself nodding back.

Finally, it came to Stokes as he was driving home from the service. *Big Jake Davenport.* What the hell was he doing there? Davenport – the very man whom he'd arrested years and years earlier, when he was in the Flying Squad, after he had caught him and his mates spraying a stolen van in the middle of the night in preparation for a robbery. Davenport – who had *walked* far too often for his liking.

Stokes started to piece the puzzle together, figuring it out as if he were still a serving detective. *Dennis's defence paid for privately; top defence lawyer in place before arrest; supplied with a gun and bullets; Dennis finding out Bob the Merc's home address; first man Dennis approached for a loan turned him down; Big Jake personally attending the funeral.*

Stokes started laughing hysterically, tickled by his fine deduction. 'So, what do you know,' he said smugly to himself. 'Old Big Jake's finally found himself a conscience. Boy, is he going to be lonely when he passes on. He's going to be the only gangster in heaven!'

Bob the Merc Jr

Two months after the trial, Bob the Merc Jr was gunned down in Soho leaving a dive at two in the morning – a brass on each hand and a curse on his lips.

A volley of bullets from an Uzi, fired from a black Range Rover with darkened windows, laid him low. A debt had finally been repaid – with interest.

As Bob Jr lay dying on the pavement, a brick wrapped in brown paper was slung out of the half-open window of the vehicle, landing next to the prostrate body. Across the brown paper in large black print, seven words were written:

When you seek revenge – dig two graves.

Surprisingly, underneath was also written the name of the author, but the first senior officer at the scene, having checked that the Police National Computer showed *no trace*, speedily concluded that his arrest was highly unlikely: Confucius!

By a strange quirk of fate, around the very time that Bob Jr was taking his last ride straight to hell, Big Jake was at his local police station, reporting vandalism to the windscreen of his Bentley, and making a lot of noise about it as well so no one could ever forget his presence. Jake was there alone, his trusted lieutenant, Ernie, being engaged on important business *elsewhere*.

Daniel Jacobsen

Daniel wasn't very good with women – better than Holmes, but not a patch on Warren Beatty. Certainly, he'd had a few girlfriends here and there, but they'd all found him a touch too intellectual. Not his fault that he'd rather discuss why he preferred Steinbeck to Hemingway or Dylan to Cohen, as opposed to what his favourite Beatles tunes might be. The fact was that women made him nervous, and this was never an auspicious start.

Sure, he had been to clubs and parties, but if he saw a girl he liked, he spent so long thinking about what his opening line would be that by the time he decided to mosey over and make his move she had been whisked away by some more courageous foe.

But fate, in the form of Percival's junior's laryngitis, had thrown his way an opportunity not to be missed. He had to make his move. It was now or never.

Finally, the very evening of the verdict, ably assisted by a bottle of rosé, Daniel plucked up the courage to ask Angelina out. He sent her an email and got straight to the point:

Hi Angelina,

I've been wondering whether you'd go out for dinner with me – tomorrow night? Or any night at all?

Best,

Daniel

Two miserable days and restless nights passed by without a reply. He'd given up all hope. Well, who could blame her? She was, after all, in a very different league.

But then, just as he was consoling himself with a few lonely lagers in Daly's Wine Bar off the Strand, he received a reply – also straight to the point:

Hi Daniel,

Tomorrow night, 9 p.m. Il Consigliere – Old Brompton Road. My father's booked for us – the owner's dad used to be his client – don't be late!

Angelina

Daniel felt dizzy. He swore he could detect the lemony scent of her tantalising perfume rising from his phone. But why the slight abruptness in her reply? And why the two-day delay? The nuance of her being peeved by being asked out by email, and not by a telephone call, flew right over his head.

A cosy tent for two at the Reichenbach Falls over Christmas? dreamt Daniel.

Dream on!

* * *

Egged on by his virtuoso performance as a private detective in Dennis's trial, young Daniel penned a monograph entitled *The Difference Between Seeing and Observing – and Its Use in Criminal Trials.* Jake, having seen them on show in Stanford's waiting room, bought two copies at full retail. One he kept on his bedside table, next to his well-thumbed book of quotes. The other he gave as a present to Halfpint. Jake himself scribbled some esoteric words inside, as a permanent reminder to Halfpint of his poor choice of which juror to bribe: 'This book should teach you the difference between an ace in the hole and a busted flush!'

It was, of course, unsigned.

Halfpint

Despite his, at best, variable performance at the Bailey, Halfpint was elevated to Jake's inner sanctum on a *better the devil you know* basis. Jake had whispered to Ernie behind Halfpint's back, 'There's work in this mule yet.' He had told Halfpint that the deciding factor was the way he had kept a straight poker face when Jake was lying his head off to Rolex Ron that he had no inside information on the Dennis trial.

So, Halfpint became a regular at Jake's Friday night extravaganza at Luca's, where, in his honour, a couple of extra cushions would be placed on the seat reserved for him, on Jake's immediate left. Now he could sit high amongst his peers – albeit not quite so high as Jake.

Jake had made it clear that he was only being promoted on the understanding that he was never to drink alcohol at their table – a life sentence for a loose tongue after Jake had overheard him telling Ernie how to become a Big Jake lookalike.

Halfpint had also become the proud owner of a five-year-old Golf, a generous treat from Jake for services rendered, as well as a brand-new Omega wristwatch (of dubious parentage), with three words deeply engraved on the back: *Guard your tongue!*

Ex-Detective Chief Superintendent Rodney 'Iron-Rod' Stokes

Having finally retired from the police, Iron-Rod Stokes did exactly what every other self-respecting ex-chief superintendent does – he took a job as a private investigator, watching wives let handymen and such in during the day, and husbands letting lovers out of their offices at night.

He had radically reduced his consumption of calming tablets to two a week, and those only on Sundays when en route to visit his mother-in-law for lunch. In his new job, other people's problems rarely gave him high blood pressure.

Stokes bumped into Stanford again about a year later in Holborn, where the old Iron-Rod was keeping watch on an errant solicitor's second-floor window. The two of them went for a drink at El Vino's and prattled on about old times – neither any longer holding a grudge.

When Stanford asked Stokes if he believed the Russian roulette incident in Dennis's case, Stokes replied, 'Actually, I did. Bob the Merc was capable of anything.'

When Stokes then asked Stanford the same question, he replied, unhelpfully (and untruthfully), whilst averting his eyes, 'What do I know? I wasn't there. I was only the solicitor in the case – remember?'

Rough Hands

Rough Hands stood trial in Court 4 at the Old Bailey for drug and money-laundering offences, the very next court to where he had sat as a juror in the Dennis case some six months earlier. He took the gamble of getting off altogether by blaming Scallywag for the cocaine (which, after all, was the truth) and not introducing at his trial that the £5,000 found inside a tyre was a bribe. *Faites vos jeux!*

Joey the scallywag never faced a jury. His fingerprints were not found on the packet of drugs hidden in the tyres, which left no real case against him, despite his fleeing from the scene.

Rough Hands had the grave misfortune to be represented on legal aid by Miles Hartford-Jones, the self-same barrister whom Stanford had declined to take as the junior in the Dennis trial – despite being referred to by his clerk as a 'safe pair of hands'.

But this was one snick to the slips that Hartford-Jones dropped. Rough Hands went roaring down.

'Stand up, Mr Lomax,' said the judge when passing sentence. 'You've been found guilty on the unanimous verdict of the jury of a very serious crime indeed. It is not suggested that you were the owner of the drugs, but rather a trusted servant, allowing your tyre shop to be used as a safe house and being paid very well for your services. I take into account your previous good character and work record, and the fact that you appear to have been hard up when this crime was committed. I also take into account that you have a wife and three teenage daughters. But, sadly, it is always the family who suffer in such cases.

'I do not add to the sentence the fact that you contested this case, against what some might consider to be overwhelming evidence, nor the fact that there has been no assistance what-soever from you as to the source of the drugs. But, of course, I can give you no discount either. In all these circumstances, the least sentence I can pass on you is one of seven years. Take him down.'

Rough justice for Rough Hands – yet another victim to the tomb.

And what did he have to show for all his labours?

Nothing but three cheap biros!

Adrian Stanford

Adrian had little difficulty in persuading himself to celebrate Dennis's acquittal by using some of his lawful ill-gotten gains to visit Bonhams classic car auctions, where he successfully bid for a red Alfa Romeo SS coupé, so his beloved Jensen C-V8 would no longer have to sleep alone at home at night. Boys' toys.

Having witnessed for himself Daniel's superior powers of observation, Adrian decided to join the Sherlock Holmes Society in the hope he would soon be able to practise a little detective work in court himself. So embroiled had he become that he was foolhardy enough to suggest to his wife that they might consider spending the Easter break in *Baskerville* territory on Dartmoor instead of the Danieli in Venice. The idea was immediately put to bed when, in reply, his wife asked him if he knew the name of a good divorce lawyer. No tagliolini al tartufo on Dartmoor!

Having Big Jake as a new client had its positives and negatives. Occasionally, Jake would turn up unannounced, plonk himself down in an armchair in the waiting room and order a cup of tea from Joanne, saying he was just passing by. He would then sit there studying the glossy magazines, claiming it was the most peaceful place in London – before dozing off. On awakening, he would rush off to an urgent business meeting at the Artesian Bar. But he never arrived at Adrian's office without some chocolates for Joanne.

The upside was that Jake announced all over town that Stanford was now his brief, before adding, 'If he's good enough for me – he's certainly bad enough for you!' New work flocked in.

Mr Justice Magnus McIntyre

The very day after the verdict, Mack the Knife booked a month's cruise for his wife and himself on the *Queen Elizabeth* – and not in any cheapo berth either. His having heard Frances refer to him as a 'meanie', whilst entertaining Charles in their bedroom but a few days earlier, had hit home. No, nothing less than a Grills Suite with a balcony was good enough for *su sueño* on their Cunard cruise, and damn the cost.

The news soon spread onboard that old Magnus had presided over the infamous Maynard murder trial, and he became somewhat of a celebrity. He was asked if he would care to give a lecture on the law of self-defence and how it impacted on Dennis's case. It was particularly well-attended. When asked by one of the audience if he agreed with the verdict, he produced a copy of his summing up, saying, 'Read this and you'll soon see which side I was on – you'll find it on every page!'

And so it was that he concluded that Dennis's acquittal was entirely down to his favourable summing up, which itself came about as a result of witnessing his wife's adultery – in technicolour – the very night before. Wisely, this conclusion did not form a central plank in his lecture.

The link between Charles's sudden disappearance and Magnus's newfound generosity was not lost on Frances, but she kept her peace and their marriage. Perhaps her husband had been born and not hatched after all. Anyway, dear Magnus had now become human – almost!

Patrick Gorman QC

A month after the trial, Gorman was back at the Bailey, down in the cells. 'Come and look at our scoreboard, Mr Gorman,' said the jailer. 'You'll like what you see – you're top of the pops.'

On the wall above the reception desk was chalked out a recommended list of barristers, drawn up like a league table by those *in the know*. Before the Dennis trial, Gorman had been sitting in third position, unable to shift two elderly statesmen. But now he was at the very top. He was well chuffed, although he remembered clearly what a client had once told him some twenty years earlier: 'Criminal lawyers are like dentists, Mr Gorman – pull out the wrong tooth and you're out of fashion in a flash.'

'You'll get plenty of work now, Mr Gorman, you can count on it,' said the jailer, watching Gorman staring up at the board.

'Great,' replied Gorman, 'but for how long? Anyway, if that's the case at present, you won't mind my adding a little addendum. Where's the chalk?'

The jailer was mystified, but a wide grin crossed his face when he saw the words Gorman had chalked in brackets next to his name: 'No Legal Aid.'

Naturally, his wife, Roberta, was thrilled with her husband's famous victory ('against all the odds', as he put it) and insisted on giving him a present.

'Your wish is my command,' she declared. She lived to regret it.

'Six months, no dinner parties?'

'Granted.'

The months flew by all too quickly. But in the meantime, his evenings were well spent. He decided to write his memoirs. The longest chapter was reserved for the Dennis trial, highlighting his devastating and humorous cross-examination of Mrs Maynard. The chapter was suitably entitled, 'A Murder Most Fair'.

As all novice authors tend to do, he spent many an hour ruminating over a suitable title for the book. He had considered a good number.

Lonely at the Top – no, too arrogant.

As Far as My Client Is Concerned – no, too clichéd.

Only a Pawn in the Game – no, too modest.

Defending for Fun – no, too flippant.

Tiger Defence – no, too vain.

The Science of Defending – no, too intellectual.

Evening the Odds – no, too mathematical.

But then it came to him in the middle of the night. He dreamt his book had been launched and he was signing copies at Waterstones, seeing hundreds of them stacked in front of him. The title was etched in his mind when he awoke. Fearful he might forget it by dawn, he rose from his bed and crept to his study downstairs. Pouring himself a cognac to celebrate, he wrote down across the top of the front page of his draft the title of his dreams:

Famous Cases I Was Almost Involved In

He stared at the words whilst sipping the brandy, imagining his offering crowding the shelves in all respectable bookshops. But something was not quite right. The title needed a minor amendment – a mere twitch. Putting a line through the words he had just written, he penned in large print underneath his final effort:

Infamous Cases I Was Almost Involved In

'Yes,' he whispered, whilst nodding approvingly to himself. 'That's much better!'

Big Jake

Big Jake was well out of pocket over the Dennis caper: £300,000 on legal fees; £5,000 bribe to juror; £8,000 handed out for a pocket watch; £400 for Halfpint's new tyres; not to mention Halfpint's commission paid in advance at the Artesian in the form of a fat brown envelope. And what could he show in return? The acquittal of a man since shot dead, a £25,000 bonus on a winning bet with Rolex Ron and maybe – just maybe – a ticket to heaven for a good deed or two, when he passed on (which might not be all that far away, according to the Prof), if the good Lord had a selective memory. But his job was not quite over. *Never ruin the ship for a ha'pworth of tar* was another of Jake's favourite expressions, and before he could close this bloody chapter in his life, there was still some snagging to do. One more *beau geste*. Linda Dennis and her two boys had no home.

And so, Jake, Ernie and Halfpint found themselves up in Southport, scouring the estate agents for a little cottage near Linda's sister's home. Nothing too extravagant, mind, but with a garden for the boys to play in.

The gift was supposed to remain anonymous, but the name of the benefactor was no mystery amongst Jake's circle. 'Nasty rumours, nothing but nasty rumours,' he would say when it was suggested he was getting soft and had actually forked out himself. But the twinkle in his eye left no room for doubt.

A few months after the Dennis trial, once all the gun smoke had settled, Big Jake finally decided to hang up his criminal boots. They were layered in dirt and mud and not without specks of blood. They were way past cleaning. But, alas, he couldn't persuade himself to hang them quite so high as to be out of arm's reach, ready to be brought back into action should a suitable occasion arise when the pickings were rich. The loving of the game and the pull of the current were too strong for Jake. He was itching for a comeback, keen for a return to the fray. A trifle too keen for his own good, a few might have been bold enough to whisper. But then, as they say, *if it's in the blood – it's in the blood!*

Acknowledgements

My heartfelt thanks to my son, Jonas, and my good friend Tony, both of whom have made significant contributions to this novel as well as restraining me from *drifting too far from the shore*.

To my daughter, Sophie, for her most excellent design for the book's cover. To my wife, Maggie, for her patience in listening to endless late-night chapter read-outs and to my PA, Olivia, for her endurance in countless retypes of virtually each and every chapter.

Finally, for the invaluable input (unconsciously given!) of all those who have crossed my path over the years, be they clients, judges, barristers, police officers or restaurateurs. Without their rich tapestry this novel would have been a slim volume indeed.

To those of you who doubt that the type of characters depicted in this book exist in real life, I can only say this: believe me, they do – I have met them all.

About the Author

Henry Milner has been one of the UK's top criminal defence solicitors for more than forty years, during which time he has defended some of the most infamous names in recent criminal history. He founded Henry Milner & Company, which is described by Chambers and Partners as a 'Rolls-Royce outfit'. His autobiography, *No Lawyers in Heaven: A Life Defending Serious Crime*, was published in 2020.

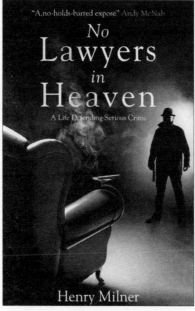